The shelter of the balcony

*could not still the
yearning of her heart.*

THE BALCONY

THE
BALCONY

LYNN MORRIS

BETHANY HOUSE PUBLISHERS
MINNEAPOLIS, MINNESOTA 55438

Published by Bethany House Publishers
A Ministry of Bethany Fellowship, Inc.
11300 Hampshire Avenue South
Minneapolis, Minnesota 55438

Printed in the United States of America.

Library of Congress Cataloging-in-Publication Data

Morris, Lynn.
    The balcony / by Lynn Morris.
       p.   cm. — (Portraits)
    ISBN 1–55661–981–2 (pbk.)
    I. Title. II. Series: Portraits (Minneapolis, Minn.)
PS3563.O874439B35   1997
813'.54—dc21   97–21008
                                                      CIP

Just for Johnnie

Portraits

Balcony

Blind Faith

Endangered

Entangled

Gentle Touch

Heaven's Song

Impasse

Masquerade

Montclair

Stillpoint

Walker's Point

LYNN MORRIS is half of the dynamic father-daughter team who created the bestselling CHENEY DUVALL, M.D. series. This is her debut solo novel. Lynn and her daughter, Dixie, live in Texas.

Poetry has always started here,
In some misunderstanding
Of someone's will or wish or voice.

—From *Haunting the Winerunner*
by John Wink

One

When she first glimpsed Taíno Castle, she thought of a pearl, surrounded by emeralds, surrounded by sapphires. The island was a swatch of jewel green against the Caribbean, and at the highest eastern point the sheer walls of the castle were a creamy white against a flawless blue sky.

"*Señorita?* A drink, please?" asked Mateo with exquisite politeness. He was only ten or eleven years old, but he was quite an efficient and polished steward. Shyly he bowed his head as he offered her the tray with the single ruby red juice drink. The ice was crushed to fine shards, and a *mavi* blossom floated across the top.

"Thank you kindly, Mateo," she said politely, and he set the drink on the glass-topped table with only a single glance at her face.

What he saw was an unmistakably American woman, thirty-ish, with thick ash-blond hair and unusually light brown eyes. She was finely, though severely, dressed in a tailored gray double-breasted suit with a straight skirt. Nervously she smoothed the sides of her hair—it was drawn back into an elegant French roll—and squinted a little as she watched the growing outline of Taíno Island in the blinding Puerto Rican sun. As Mateo withdrew to the stairs, he saw her reach into the somber black briefcase at her feet and pull out a long red scarf and sunglasses with red rims to match.

As he went into the tiny hallway, he heard his brother Pablo call down from the pilot's cabin, "Is she all right, Mateo?"

"Sure, brudder," he answered softly, nimbly maneuvering down the narrow stairway into the galley.

Johnnie James was better than just all right; she was almost euphoric. She loved Puerto Rico. Mostly she loved the southern Caribbean beaches, and as Taíno Island grew nearer in her sight, she thought that it looked like paradise. But none of these emotions reflected on her calm features. After tying the scarlet scarf tightly over her wildly blowing hair, she sat quietly, not fidgeting, merely sipping at the refreshing fruit drink held in her hand.

Though Johnnie's client, Esteban Ventura, had not deigned to meet her plane in Ponce, he had sent Pablo and Mateo to escort her on his sumptuous yacht to the island. Methodically Johnnie wondered if he provided the yacht to transport all guests to the island. If so, it was an expensive ferry. A forty-footer, sleek and elegant, it had quarters and a galley below the main deck and a sun deck above. Her name was *Flamenco*.

Johnnie sat forward and removed her stylish sunglasses as her new client's home came into view.

Taíno Castle had been built in the sixteenth century—in 1582, to be exact—by Esteban Ventura's ancestor, Roberto Diego Ventura. He was a pirate whose hunger for loot eventually extended even to the ships of his own countrymen as they transported the valuable sugar, ginger, and tobacco from Puerto Rico to Spain. Landing on Taíno Island strictly by accident one lucrative night, he found plenty of Taíno (pronounced TAH-ee-no, also called Arawak) Indians to enslave, and eight years later his island fortress was completed.

The two great towers that faced the sea were round with walls ten feet thick. From the outer rampart, guns had once pointed toward the Caribbean, ensuring that no sea assault would ever threaten Taíno Castle. The only openings in the towers had been tiny keyhole-shaped gunports, although some of them had recently been converted to long, slender windows with leaded panes.

Suddenly alert, Johnnie narrowed her eyes and shaded them against the afternoon sun. Now she could see some detail of the island, and for the first time she noticed the balcony.

It was true; Esteban Ventura had widened one gunport opening in the tower and had installed a small wrought iron balcony that seemed to hang defiantly over the rocky 160-foot-high promontory of the island's west end. Johnnie could even see smudges of green and tiny spots of wild color blossoming in defiance of the salt spray and sea wind.

As the jewel-like island grew closer, Johnnie roused herself to perfunctorily check her nose and lipstick in her compact, smooth her gray linen skirt, and look carefully at her shoes. She hated to have dusty shoes. Impatiently she pulled a tissue out of her briefcase to swipe them. They were black leather pumps with three-inch heels, which she also checked carefully, then rubbed them, too.

The yacht nosed into a small boathouse at the far end of a creamy swath of deserted beach. Without waiting for Mateo or Pablo, Johnnie negotiated the ladderlike stairs back down to deck level—thankful for the kick pleat in the back of her slim skirt—and waited by the swinging door on the side of the boat. Expertly Pablo eased the sleek yacht only inches from the walkway built inside the boathouse, and Johnnie heard Mateo thump onto it at the bow to tie off. Pablo killed the motor, then called down, "Please, Señorita James, wait for me to help you!"

"All right." Johnnie wasn't too eager to sample the Caribbean Sea at this particular moment anyway.

Soon Pablo scrambled down to the deck. "Excuse me, please," he murmured as he brushed past her to stand on the walkway and offer his hand. Johnnie gave him her briefcase first, then grasped his hand and struggled only a little to take the tricky step off the boat up six inches onto the dock. He smiled at her, so she smiled back briefly. He was only seventeen, with the dark, brooding eyes and rich features so common to Latinos.

Unlike Mateo, Pablo was old enough to be shy around women such as Johnnie, and he quickly dropped his eyes.

As no motor vehicles of any kind were allowed on Taíno Island, a cart drawn by two horses stood at the end of the dock to carry Johnnie and her luggage to the castle. It was a rather crude wooden buggy, with only bench seats. But baskets of hibiscus were set behind the passenger's seat, and she felt enveloped in the extravagant yellow-orange blooms and lush foliage. Pablo and Mateo carefully loaded her three suitcases, then sat down on the back edge of the cart, their feet dangling. The driver, who had only tugged at the brim of his flat cap when Johnnie climbed into the cart, now snapped the reins, and the horses started their slow, careful ascent to Taíno Castle.

The track wound in a lazy curve up from the beach to the highest point of the island. This easternmost end was a green plain, broken occasionally by huge boulders squatting on the carpet of lush green grass. To the west the forest began abruptly on the lower stretch of the island, the huge trees cutting almost in a straight line from north to south. Johnnie knew that about half a mile through the forest was a steep cliff, with waterfalls tumbling deep into a valley rain forest. It was only about a mile square, but it was a real rain forest nonetheless.

Ahead of her Taíno Castle loomed up, a severe and foreboding structure that only looked benevolent from a distance. It was, after all, a fortress, not a fairy-tale castle, and Johnnie noted with approval that Esteban Ventura had merely whitewashed the outside walls rather than painting them a solid stark white. It softened the sternness of the fortress somewhat, but the cunning masonry work could still be seen, for Taíno Castle was built of native rock, ingeniously mortised by slaves' hands.

The cart clattered through the gatehouse, which had thirty-foot-tall guard towers on either side. The double doors of the gate opened to the outside, and Johnnie noted with interest that they were fifteen feet high and two feet thick, built of sturdy oak, and studded with massive black iron hinges and nails. On impulse she looked up. Sure enough, just behind the arched gate she could see the spikes of a portcullis in the ceiling of the gate-house, ready after over four hundred years to be dropped on an invader. Also in the ceiling of the gatehouse were symmetrical rows of holes about six inches in diameter, enabling the defenders to drop burning tar and pitch on intruders who made it past the gate and the portcullis. Johnnie felt a slight thrill; this place was not only of another time but of another world.

To the left and right were expanses of green grass, and Johnnie noted many arched entrances in the stone walls. Straight ahead loomed the monolithic keep, with the great sea towers on either side and the smaller north and south towers to her left and right. The castle enclosed about two acres, she judged, with roughly one-half consisting of the yard, or bailey, as it was properly called. At the far eastern half of the castle enclosure, in front of the keep, were lush gardens. The cart pulled up to a brick footpath, and Pablo and Mateo hurried to assist Johnnie down from the cart.

"Straight ahead to the keep, señorita. I am sure that *Señor* Ventura will be in the office on the left side of the great hall," Pablo told her. "Mateo and I will bring up your luggage."

Johnnie nodded, arranged her heavy briefcase by the shoulder strap, and walked confidently into the shade of Taíno Castle's gardens.

The air temperature dropped several degrees under the canopy of lush greenery. She saw chinaberry trees everywhere, laden with the small native oranges. Huge rhododendron shrubs, some eight feet high, nodded gently in the cool drafts of air. Laser rods of yellow light occasionally broke through to blaze onto the black squares of *adoquines*—blocks of slag from the lowland smelting mills of Spain's sixteenth-century empire—that formed the pathways. She was studying them—to tell the truth, they were tricky to navigate in heels—when she caught movement out of the corner of her eye. She looked up and saw the gardener.

He had his back to her. Standing in a narrow clearing to her left, the sun blazed down on him as he reached into a square wheelbarrow piled high with fifty-pound bags of soil. He easily lifted one up, then tossed it carelessly into a rock-lined flower bed still bare of plantings. Johnnie blinked, then stumbled a bit as she stared.

He turned. He was a big man, tall and bulky, with legs like tree trunks and muscled arms glistening with sweat. Wearing a sleeveless white T-shirt and faded blue jeans, his skin was burnished bronze and his short hair glossy blue-black. He wore a red bandanna as a headband and wraparound sunglasses, so she couldn't see his eyes.

"Señorita—" he began, putting out a hand as if to assist her, though she was fully twelve feet away.

Johnnie swallowed hard and felt her cheeks burning. *The gardener!* she told herself angrily. *As if I haven't learned to put away such childish things!*

Stiffly she nodded, then hurried on.

"But, señorita—" he tried again, his voice soothing, with a pleading note.

"No," she said coldly. She'd been down that road and heard that song before. For years when she was younger she'd been drawn to such men, and somehow they always knew it. Weight lifters, football players, exercise instructors. They could still spot her a mile away, and after years of sadly empty relationships, Johnnie had put such men away forever. *Or so I thought*, she taunted herself. *Stopping in my tracks to gape openmouthed at a man is hardly the way to tell him I'm not interested. . . .*

Johnnie was not a snob; she didn't believe that all football players and weight lifters were worthless. It was just that she'd always had a strong physical attraction to such men, and regardless of what kind of man they were, it was always the wrong basis for any kind of relationship. But Johnnie had never learned to get past it, so she had, quite simply, put it away. She hadn't dated for over three years. The men she found appealing were all wrong, and the ones who seemed right didn't interest her. So that was that.

Recklessly hurrying away from the gardener, she finally made her way through the tropical confusion of the gardens to reach the great front doors of the keep. To her left was a covered passageway leading from the keep to the chapel, and she could see three arched doorways lining the passage. The first one had a small sign on it: *Office*. Smoothing her skirt once more, she opened the door and stepped in. Blinking in the sudden semi-darkness of the room, which was of the same stone as the outer castle walls, Johnnie hastily removed her sunglasses. A young man was in the room, although it looked as if he were just about to leave through a back door.

"Good afternoon," Johnnie said pleasantly. "I am Johnnie James, with Andrews, Smith & Wesley. Are you Mr. Ventura?"

The young man looked at her quizzically for only a brief moment before smiling warmly. "You are Johnnie James? The accountant?"

"Yes, I am."

"Please forgive me." He hurried forward to take her hand and lead her to one of the ornately carved Spanish chairs in front of the desk. "You certainly don't look like an accountant, Señorita James."

"Thank you," Johnnie said crisply. She'd heard that line before, and she didn't add the obvious: He didn't look like an inn-keeper. The man looked like a movie star, and he was much younger than she'd anticipated. He was twenty-three, perhaps twenty-four. "I hope I didn't arrive at an inopportune time?" she hinted, nodding at the door he'd been in the process of opening.

"Not at all." Instead of sitting behind the expanse of the rough oak, age-blackened desk, he sat in the chair across from her. "We're very glad you came so promptly, Señorita James."

"Certainly. It's my pleasure, and I can see that working here is going to seem more like a vacation."

"We'll try to make certain of that."

He studied her, and she studied him. His appraisal was open and friendly, while hers was guarded. He was handsome, with fine brown-black hair worn long, combed back from a high forehead and falling to his collar in that careless manner that indicated an expensive stylist. His eyebrows were as sculpted as a woman's—perfect long arches over dark Latin eyes. His nose was thin, and his mouth was wide over a faintly dimpled chin. His skin had the rich golden hue of a California tennis tan. He was slender and elegant, and no doubt wealthy and spoiled.

"It is *siesta*," he finally said in a low voice. "I'm sure you would like to rest this afternoon and have time to freshen up before dinner."

"That would be fine, Mr. Ventura," Johnnie replied with relief. "I am rather wilted. And I don't go on the clock until tomorrow anyway."

He stood and offered her his hand. Although she was somewhat taken aback—this was old-world manners, indeed—she took it and rose, collecting her briefcase as she did so. "I have a request to make of you, Mr. Ventura."

"Yes?" He opened the door for her, but she stopped to look up at him.

"Yes." It was difficult for Johnnie James to ask for *anything*, so she took a deep breath before plunging on. "The room with the balcony, overlooking the sea. May I have that room, please?"

His smile was as automatic—and just about as genuine—as all of the other charming gestures he'd made. "I'm terribly sorry, señorita, but that room is part of the family quarters and is not available."

"Ridiculous." The deep voice came from the passageway. "Give her the Ventura Tower Room, Diego."

Diego Ventura's smile froze while Johnnie turned to see who was issuing orders from the passageway shadows.

It was the gardener.

"*Buenos días*, señorita," he said evenly, offering her a freshly scrubbed hand. "I am Esteban Ventura."

Two

*E*steban Ventura's hand was warm, not hot, and certainly not
sweaty, though rough and work-callused. Johnnie was
speechless for a moment, her hand completely engulfed in his.
He'd taken off the sunglasses and was staring impassively down
at her with fathomless black eyes.

Johnnie swallowed and stood up a little straighter. "Mr.
Ventura, I believe I owe you an apology."

He waited.

With consternation Johnnie went on stiffly, "I apologize for
my rudeness to you in the garden. I didn't realize who you
were."

"You thought I was the gardener." He smiled coldly, a wide
smile displaying strong white teeth. "But you see, I am the gardener, so perhaps you don't owe me an apology after all."

While Johnnie was still working on this cryptic remark, Esteban Ventura seemed to dismiss her and turned to his younger
brother. "Show her to the Ventura Tower, Diego," he repeated
brusquely. "I'll send Pablo and Mateo up with her luggage and
some refreshments. Miss James," he finished by way of excusing
himself. He turned and headed back toward his empty flower
bed. Johnnie watched him go with wide, confused eyes.

"This way, please, Señorita James," Diego said resignedly.
"I hope you'll be comfortable in the Tower Room. It is three

floors up and isn't yet wired for electricity."

"No, no, it . . . if it's the room I requested, with the balcony, I certainly wouldn't be so rude as to complain," Johnnie said, recovering some of her spirit.

"Of course," Diego replied smoothly, slipping his hand under her elbow as they walked along the passageway. Johnnie glanced suspiciously up at him, but she decided that he was simply one of those courtly men who still believed in opening doors for women, standing when they entered a room, always allowing them to proceed in front. Diego belonged to that rare breed of people who could be charming without seeming overly familiar.

And maybe you're flattering yourself, Johnnie thought ruefully. *He is very handsome and probably is very spoiled—by women, too. Why should he want to get cute with me? I've got to remember that I'm getting old enough that politeness from men might simply be just that—politeness—unlike his brother . . . not very polite . . . or at least, it certainly was a sort of fierce, concentrated politeness. . . .*

With determination Johnnie yanked her thoughts away from the older Ventura brother. "I'm already confused and slightly lost," she told Diego. "Could you please give me some idea of where I am and where I'm going?" They had passed the keep and turned left into a completely enclosed passage. Electric lights in wrought iron sconces along the stone walls lit the way.

"The castle passages are confusing," Diego admitted. "They are all enclosed, few of them have windows, and many of them are built right into the outer castle walls. I should have given you a diagram. For right now, though, I promise you will be escorted until you get the layout firmly fixed in your mind. This passageway leads up into the stairwell of Ventura Tower. Neither of the sea towers has ground-floor entrances." The hallway went steadily upward. Johnnie saw three doors along the passage and one side passage to the left. It was very much like a tunnel, and their footsteps echoed eerily within the shadowed concave walls.

Finally Diego pointed ahead to a Norman-arched door. The

door creaked on its iron hinges as Diego opened it and looked back at her apologetically. "This is the second floor of Ventura Tower. Just inside, on this table, are two flashlights. You can take one to your room, but please always leave one here. In the drawer are a store of batteries"—he grinned engagingly—"and also candles and matches. You're certain you wish to take the Tower Room? The rooms in the keep are electrically wired, and there are elevators."

"I've always wanted to wander around a castle with a candelabra," Johnnie said lightly. "Somehow I just don't think the fantasy would work with electric lights hanging from the ceiling."

"Ah yes," Diego gravely agreed. "The castle ghosts would not be nearly as interesting by a seventy-five-watt bulb. Please, if you would allow me to go first—?"

"Please do."

The stairwell was narrow, jutting out from the inside of the tower wall and winding in a slow curve up the circular tower. Twice they passed arched doors, and Diego told her that they were armament storage rooms but had not yet been converted into guest rooms. "The only room in this tower that has been completed is this one. Esteban had it designed exactly like his."

"What? His room is near?" Johnnie asked with some alarm.

"No, no," Diego said hastily. "His apartments are in the west sea tower on the far side of the keep. Actually, the balcony you saw from our yacht was the one off of his bedroom. And for some reason, he had this room prepared at the same time and an identical balcony built—even though we had planned to finish the north and south towers first."

They reached another doorway, and Diego opened it without hesitation. This one didn't creak.

Johnnie stepped in and looked around in awe. The room was exactly as she'd pictured it, exactly as she'd hoped, and she felt a sudden, tremendous rush of gratitude toward Esteban Ventura, curt as he may be.

The room was round, of course, and very bright from the

three tall, narrow windows. Around all of the walls were bench seats with blue velvet-padded covers. Directly across from the door was the opening in the ten-foot wall leading to the balcony, and—forgetting Diego—Johnnie hurried out onto it. It was small, with a waist-high wrought iron railing. On both sides were planters containing lush hibiscus shrubs with deep scarlet blooms at least eight inches across.

But it was what was beyond the balcony that literally took Johnnie's breath away. On this late June afternoon, a great field of diamond lights strewed the aquamarine Caribbean. Over two hundred feet below, the surf crashed and roared as it threw geysers high in the air over massive boulders. There was no beach at this end of the island; the rocky ground fell sharply, straight down into the sea just beyond the keep and the two easternmost towers. The dangerous cliffs were covered with huge rocks nestled among small slippery stones and were honeycombed with caves.

Gulping great breaths of salt air, her eyes watered from the brightness, the heat enveloped her like a warm bath, the occasional breeze refreshed her.

If she could have, Johnnie James would have lived the rest of her life alone on the balcony and died happily there.

Eventually she wandered back inside and hesitated in the hallway to adjust her sea-dazzled eyes. Then she saw two doorways hollowed into the passage to the balcony, and eager to explore, she started toward the nearest one. Suddenly remembering Diego, she hurried back into the Tower Room. He was gone, but he'd left a note on a small table by the door. The console also held a pitcher of the red fruit drink, a bucket of ice, a box of chocolates, and a single exquisite orchid.

My dear Señorita James,

Dinner will be at nine o'clock, and I will come promptly to escort you, if I may. A housekeeper will check on you (and wake you, if you will indulge in siesta) at about six o'clock.

Please do not wander about the castle by yourself. The passages are quite intricate, and many of them are still unsafe. I would be devastated should you have some sort of mishap on your first evening here with us.

I remain your servant,

Diego Ventura

"Well," Johnnie told herself with amusement, "it seems I am a prisoner in the tower."

Still smiling, she hurried to see what the two passages off the balcony held. The one on the right, she saw, was a closet. Hooks had been inserted into the walls in two long, orderly lines.

The other was the bathroom, and Johnnie was amazed to find such an amenity in a sixteenth-century castle. But of course, the outside tower wall had been recently hollowed out to make one, which would have been a terrible breach in defenses then but was certainly a welcome sight now. It was fully plumbed—she checked both the sink and the commode—and then she admired the bathtub. As the walls, floors, and ceiling were of the same rough stones as all the original walls of the castle, the bathroom had been designed in keeping. The tub was kidney-shaped, about five feet across, and was set into a rock platform with three steps leading up to it. Completely surrounding the tub and on each end of the curved steps were pots of ferns and ivy. *A secret garden pool.* Immediately Johnnie started running a hot bath, and it took her two hours to finish it.

Dressing in a light shift, she decided to take a nap and was somewhat surprised at herself that she'd barely noticed the rest of the Tower Room. The bed was magnificent, a double-sized antique tester bed with an ancient tapestry hanging at the head. It was of a dark wood, elaborately carved, with two small steps to facilitate getting into it. Matching night tables were on either side, with a single drawer each. Curiously Johnnie checked the drawers and smiled. One nightstand held candles, the other held matches.

She lay back against sweet-smelling, satiny percale sheets,

wondering where she might find a candelabra. . . .

***

"Señorita?" *Tap, tap.* "Señorita? It is six o'clock."

"Yes, yes," Johnnie called sleepily.

The door swung open silently, and a woman entered, carrying a tray. "Buenas tardes, señorita. Here is *café con leche*. Sometimes you must have this for breakfast, to wake you up. Sometimes you must have it after siesta."

She bustled. Short, round, with her gray-sprinkled hair parted down the middle and pulled tightly back into a circular bun, she looked very capable. "Will you require help with your dressing, Señorita James?" she inquired, placing the tray on the bed beside Johnnie and patting the pillows behind her.

"No, no, of course not," Johnnie said hastily. At the woman's smile she added, "Americans are not accustomed to such personal service, ma'am. My name is Johnnie James." She stuck out her hand, feeling a little absurd as she did so.

The woman looked surprised, then pleased, and clasped Johnnie's hand in a firm grip. "I am Dolores Rosado. I am cook and housekeeper for Señor Ventura."

"I work for him, too," Johnnie told her. "Thank you for your kindness, Mrs. Rosado. I'm certain it must be a great deal of trouble to serve guests up here."

"De nada," Mrs. Rosado answered with a dismissive wave of her hand. She went to the door, then turned and folded her hands, returning to servant mode. "Will you be needing anything else, señorita?"

"Um . . . if I should, do I yell out the window?" Johnnie asked, winking at her. No telephone lines had been installed in Ventura Tower, and Johnnie knew before she arrived that Taíno Island was not in a "cell," so mobile phones didn't work here.

Mrs. Rosado looked startled, glancing at the long, thin rectangular window high above the courtyard. One foot wide, with small leaded panes, there were two other windows that also faced the castle grounds—one in the closet and one in the bath-room. The other five overlooked the sea.

Mrs. Rosado didn't smile. "Why did they put you up here, señorita?"

"Don't worry, Mrs. Rosado, I asked for the room with the balcony," Johnnie assured her, taking a sip of the hot, strong coffee liberally laced with cream. "Mr. Ventura explained the drawbacks to me."

"And you aren't afraid?" Mrs. Rosado asked quickly.

"Afraid? Of being without electricity and a telephone?" Johnnie laughed. "No, of course not. Now, a bathroom—I might've been afraid if I hadn't had that, but . . ." Her laughter faded out at the expression on the woman's honest face; it was something very close to fear. "What's the matter, Mrs. Ro-sado?"

Dropping her eyes, she turned to the door and pulled it open too quickly. "Nothing, nothing. Perhaps . . . nothing. Dinner will be at nine o'clock, Señorita James." She pulled the door shut firmly behind her.

"Every castle has its ghosts," Johnnie said with satisfaction. "Looks like I'll be needing that candelabra." She shook her head at the woman's superstition or fear or whatever it was. Johnnie had lived alone and traveled alone for twelve years. She'd never been afraid, not once, and she certainly wasn't afraid of any old forlorn castle ghosts.

The café con leche revived her completely; she felt full of energy and looked forward to dinner. Perhaps she could start all over again with Esteban Ventura.

Her suitcases were lying along the bench seats that sur-rounded the room, and impulsively she jumped up and hurried to them. She'd already emptied her garment bag and hung up her suits, but her lingerie and shoes were still packed. Zipping open her shoe bag, she began to take out the pair she would wear for dinner when she noticed for the first time that the over-stuffed, padded bench seats had definite seams, or sections, to them. Feeling underneath the slight ledge that the top formed, she lifted, and sure enough, the seats were built as cabinets for storage. Four wrought iron candelabras were stored in the bench. The next one was empty, and the inside was finished nicely, with a shallow inset drawer for lingerie, she supposed. The next one held extra towels and bed linens.

Mr. Esteban Ventura must be a very clever man, Johnnie thought. *He's refurbished this room to make it comfortable enough for Americans—the most demanding customers in the world—but yet it still retains the sixteenth-century atmosphere . . . this just might work! He might actually be able to make some money at this!*

Johnnie was shocked when she realized how very much she wished that Esteban Ventura would succeed at turning Taíno Castle into an exclusive hotel. *Just give him a good and fair accounting!* she scolded herself. *Treat him just as you do every other client! Don't . . . don't get personal!*

But it was already too late.

Three

S eñorita James, may I present to you Señorita Nuria Cristina
de la Torres. Nuria, this is Señorita Johnnie James."

"It's a pleasure to meet you, Miss Torres."

"I'm pleased to meet you, Señorita James."

After barely touching fingertips, Johnnie and Nuria sized
each other up in the way of women. Johnnie saw that Nuria was
eyeing her with slight hostility, and she wondered why. Nuria
Cristina de la Torres was around twenty years old, at least three
inches taller than Johnnie, and ultra-fashionably thin, with
waist-length satiny black hair and smoldering dark eyes. She was
wearing a little black sheath dress with a square neckline and a
choker of pearls.

For dinner Johnnie had simply replaced her white jewel-neck
linen blouse for a red one, worn the same gray skirt with a wide
red belt, and had changed her black heels for matching red ones.
She felt short, dumpy, and boring. But long ago Johnnie had
learned not to let such insecurities govern her. She couldn't stop
those feelings from coming over her from time to time, but she
could quickly put them out of her mind.

"And of course you know *Don* Serralles," Diego went on
smoothly.

Johnnie turned to the man standing slightly behind her.
"Mr. Serralles! What a pleasant surprise!"

He took her hand in both of his. "No, Señorita James, it is I who am pleased to see you again so soon." Antonio Serralles, at sixty-eight years old, was still sharp and energetic even though he was small and rather stooped. His hair, though completely white, was thick and luxuriant, as was his mustache. His smile was that of a much younger man. "Syntex-Serralles Pharmaceuticals had a conference here two weeks ago, and I refused to leave. Esteban and Diego have tried to make me go away, but I wouldn't until I got to see you again and perhaps have some more business lunches, hmm?"

"Mr. Serralles, I would be honored," Johnnie smiled. "Especially if Syntex-Serralles Pharmaceuticals pays for lunch."

"Ventura Enterprises would be happy to pay for Don Serralles' lunches for the rest of his life," Esteban Ventura put in, appearing at Nuria's side. He looked quite different in black jeans and a white shirt, open at the neck. Johnnie saw with fascination that his poet's shirt had French cuffs, and Esteban was wearing gold cufflinks. She hadn't seen a man wear cufflinks for years. He wore no other jewelry—no rings nor even a watch. Still he was quite intimidating; he towered over even Nuria. Johnnie decided he must be at least three inches over six feet.

"And Don Serralles may have the key to Taíno Castle at any time," he was saying. Turning his dark eyes on Johnnie, he gestured with his glass of sparkling water. "You did know, Miss James, that our old friend Don Serralles recommended you so highly that I couldn't consider any other accountant?"

"Y-yes, I mean, no—" Johnnie stammered. Good gracious, was she eternally going to act like a blooming idiot in front of Esteban Ventura? Was she never going to be able to carry on a simple conversation with him?

"What is this?" Nuria asked in a heavily accented, sultry voice. "An accountant? What is it?"

Esteban turned to her and answered softly in Spanish.

Nuria turned back to Johnnie, frowning. "You count things?"

"Yes," Johnnie answered with a smile. "Money, mostly."

"Esteban, you are paying her to count your money?" Nuria asked disbelievingly, turning to him and laying a long, slender hand on his arm. Her manicured nails were painted blood red. "Diego can do that!"

Esteban smiled down at her and patted her hand affectionately. "Nuria, you should have finished school. It's a good thing you are so beautiful." He turned and motioned to the heavily laden table behind them. "Shall we all sit down?"

As he had promised, Diego had knocked on Johnnie's door at precisely nine o'clock and had escorted her to the second floor of Esteban's tower for dinner. It was a combination dining room and study. A round oak pedestal table with lion's claw feet was centered on a magnificent Persian rug just to the side of the door. From the right side of the door and all around the room were bookcases from floor to ceiling, comfortably cluttered with everything from dusty old tomes with colorless covers to modern paperbacks with garish glossy covers. At the opposite side of the room in a cozy arrangement were two couches with a long, low table in between and two enormous overstuffed leather armchairs. Lamps with parchment-colored shades cast a warm, inviting light in the reading area.

Just on the other side of the dining table was a fountain, softly backlit, with two eight-foot areca palms waving gracefully over each side. Three water lilies floated serenely in the pool. The fountain held a most unusual life-sized statue. It was a young man, obviously Greek, with a tunic, sandals, and a headband about his thick, curly hair. A large jar was on one shoulder, and water came streaming out of it, splashing down over his back into a sizable pool. Posed as if he were running, the man was looking back over his shoulder, his eyes wide and wary, his well-formed mouth slightly open as if he were breathing hard.

Antonio Serralles was handing Johnnie into her chair when she registered the meaning of the statue. Abruptly she jumped out of the chair—she was only half seated—and hurried over to stand in front of the fountain. Wonder and delight washed over her as she stared at the statue.

Don Serralles and Diego exchanged perplexed looks; they couldn't very well seat themselves while a lady was still standing—or rather, wandering about the room. Nuria turned in her chair to give Johnnie's back an odd look, then she said, "It's a fountain, Señorita James."

"Yes . . . yes, I know. . . ." Johnnie said softly, half to herself. "But it's . . . it's—"

"Yes?" Esteban appeared at her side, staring down at her with penetrating eyes. "You recognize this?"

"I know a poem," Johnnie replied in wonder. "Is this . . . is this modeled after *Haunting the Winerunner*?"

"It is," Esteban said with surprise. "You know the poem?"

"No, I don't," Johnnie said. "I . . . I mean—oh, it's complicated. I've read the poem, yes."

" 'Poetry has always started here. . . . ' " Esteban quoted under his breath.

"Yes," Johnnie nodded. "The statue—the fountain—is exquisite."

"Yes, it is," Esteban agreed politely. "We will speak of this later, Miss James. Now would you do me the honor of joining us at dinner? My other guests are waiting."

"Oh yes, of course." Johnnie hurried back to the table, leaving Esteban Ventura holding his hand out to take her arm. With a sigh he followed her.

"Please forgive me, but the fountain is so striking," she apologized to everyone in a rather flustered manner.

"It is a fountain," Nuria repeated carelessly. "I've always felt sorry for the poor little scared winebibber."

"Winerunner, Nuria," Esteban corrected her automatically. Nuria shrugged with boredom.

Finally everyone was seated: Esteban, then Nuria, then Diego, Johnnie, and Antonio. To Johnnie's astonishment, Esteban bowed his head and prayed. It was in Spanish, so Johnnie understood not one word, but it sounded quite honest and natural, unlike the automatic blessings that people often muttered over dinner. When she peered up she observed that Nuria was studying her fingernails; Diego looked embarrassed, though he had bowed his head and closed his eyes; Antonio Serralles looked amused, watching Nuria and Diego.

"We serve ourselves tonight, Miss James. I hope you don't mind," Esteban explained. "Normally Mrs. Rosado doesn't work on Sundays, and we sort of fend for ourselves."

"It looks—and smells—wonderful," Johnnie said appreciatively. In the center of the table was a big stew bowl, and spicy steam curled up from it. On one side of the bowl was a sizable platter piled high with cubes of meat. On another side was a platter of tropical fruits: grapes, mangos, bananas, kiwi, chinaberries, pineapple, and coconuts. Two covered dishes held, Johnnie was sure, the ever-present corn *tortillas* instead of bread.

"This is *mofongo*, and this is *carnecita*," Diego explained, pointing to the big stew bowl and then the platter of meat. "If everyone will just pass their soup bowls, I'll serve."

Mofongo consisted of seasoned and fried plantains served in chicken stock. Carnecita was marinated pork cubes, very lean, and fried in olive oil. Johnnie liked mofongo, but the carnecita was so tender and flavorful, each bite made her mouth water. "It's delicious," she commented between mouthfuls. "I'll be certain to thank Mrs. Rosado tomorrow."

Both Esteban and Nuria looked rather surprised at that, and Johnnie couldn't understand why. She was still wondering about it when Mr. Serralles said, "It's the Ventura Olive Oil, of course. Superior in all ways. I think we should all have a glass of it after dinner."

Esteban and Diego smiled. "It is good, but not that good, Don Serralles," Diego countered. "But we will be sure to tell our father that you drink it for your health!"

"I will tell him myself," Don Serralles said with satisfaction. "I'm going to visit your family after I get bored here."

"So your father imports olive oil?" Johnnie asked Diego with interest.

"No, he exports it. And olives, of course," Diego answered. "From Spain."

Johnnie was confused. She knew that Antonio Serralles had been born in Spain, but he had come to Puerto Rico as a young man. When Antonio Serralles had told her of the Venturas, she had just assumed that they were in Puerto Rico. "But I thought you were Puerto Rican. Your family lives in Spain?" she asked.

"We are Spanish, Miss James," Esteban told her. "Our father has an olive farm about thirty miles outside of Lorca, in Andalusia. None of our family has ever lived in Puerto Rico until Diego and I came here about a year ago."

"Except for Roberto," Diego reminded him. "And his son."

Esteban shrugged.

"I knew this castle was built by your ancestor, Roberto Diego Ventura," Johnnie said. "And has your family managed to retain title to it all these years?"

"All these centuries," Don Serralles said with satisfaction.

"It's something of a miracle," Esteban murmured. "And I'm very grateful to God that Taíno Castle still belongs to the Venturas."

"You're the one who's paid for it for the past ten years, Esteban, and sweated blood to make it so beautiful," Nuria argued. "You deserve it."

"Whether or not that is true, I do love it," Esteban admitted.

"Like a woman," Nuria said acidly, turning to Johnnie. "Taíno Castle is Esteban's mistress. Did you know that, Señorita James?"

"No, I was not aware of that when Mr. Ventura retained my firm," Johnnie said with a half smile. "I'll be certain to make a note for the file."

"Yes, do that," Nuria said with a cat smile of her own. "So you will remember."

Antonio Serralles painstakingly stroked his mustache with his napkin. "Señorita James never forgets anything. That's one reason why she's such a good accountant."

Johnnie James had been the lead accountant representing Serralles Pharmaceuticals in a merger with Syntex of Panama. She had managed to make the merger both very lucrative and very smooth for Antonio Serralles.

Johnnie colored slightly. "Mr. Serralles, that is a gross exaggeration."

"What is 'gross'?" Nuria demanded. "I thought that was something that smells bad!"

"Nuria, I wish you would finish learning to speak English," Esteban growled, though his eyes lit with amusement.

She smiled brilliantly and leaned very close to him. "Then you finish teaching me, Esteban. You speak English better than Spaniards speak Spanish."

"So could you, little *gatito*. But who can make you sit still long enough?"

"You could, *gato*."

Esteban looked at Diego and winked. "Fine, Nuria. First go down to the library and look up the meaning of 'big tease.'" With determination he leaned away from Nuria, who looked disappointed, and said to Johnnie, "So you have a good memory, Miss James? I suppose that would make for a good accountant."

Inwardly Johnnie sighed. It might make for a good accountant, but it certainly sounded bland and boring. And Nuria Cristina de la Torres shimmered and glowed, like a fountain filled with flowers, rich and full of life.

"Señorita James has a flawless memory, Esteban," Don Serralles insisted. "Don't try to put anything over on her. She'll find out, and she'll never forget."

"Women never do," Diego sighed.

"I forget things all the time, Diego," Nuria argued, her eyes sparkling.

"Yes, but you are special, gatito," Diego laughed.

Oh yes, very special, Johnnie was thinking furiously, *but just exactly who the blue thunder are you?*

As if he were working hard to read her mind, Esteban studied Johnnie's face. Surely she must have glanced at Nuria with curiosity—she hoped with curiosity—because Esteban suddenly said, "I have been a terrible host. Miss James, I believe I didn't explain Nuria to you when you were introduced—"

"Who can explain Nuria?" Diego interrupted, casting long, teasing glances at the exotic young woman on his other side.

"—and I beg your pardon. She is from the same village in Spain, and our families are very close," Esteban went on, ignoring both Nuria and Diego as they made little faces at each other. "We have known Nuria since she was born."

"That's . . . nice—" Johnnie desperately cast around in her confusion to try to think of something polite to say, but all she could think of was *So she travels with . . . who? Both of you? Lives with you? What?*

"She is a flamenco dancer," Esteban went on gravely, almost reprovingly, as if he indeed could read Johnnie's thoughts. "She's here to help me decide how to best present the flamenco. Soon the rest of the company will arrive for the summer entertainment."

Nuria tossed her head, and her black hair shimmered softly back over her shoulder. She had left it long, with only a slim silver headband holding it back from her face. She had a perfect widow's peak that accentuated her smooth oval forehead and almond-shaped eyes. "You should build me a theater, Esteban," she said in the manner of reopening an old argument. "Tell him, Señorita James. He should build a beautiful theater for the flamenco. Perhaps where the chapel is. He has the money, and I will make him much more."

"I couldn't presume to advise Mr. Ventura on capital investments yet, Miss Torres," Johnnie said stiffly.

"Ah yes, you haven't counted his money yet, eh?" Nuria said softly. "When you do, we shall see."

Four

Early morning sunshine blazed through the east-facing window, illuminating the Tower Room as if a sun spotlight were trained on it. Johnnie stared at her reflection in the full-length cheval mirror.

She had chosen the cream-colored suit for this first day of work. *It flatters me*, she thought. *Even though I'm not fashionably stick thin.* Johnnie had curves, but she wasn't plump. One good thing her mother had taught her was that the anorexic appearance so much in vogue was not necessarily the only kind of beauty for a woman. Johnnie was generally satisfied with what she viewed as her clean and wholesome looks, in spite of occasional bouts of insecurity that plagued her when she met hothouse flowers such as Nuria Torres.

The jacket was single-breasted, with a peplum, and she wore a western belt that had a heavy silver buckle. The skirt was straight and came to an inch above her knees. It was her most ornate suit, and she rarely wore it. Frowning, she finally decided to wear the earrings that were patterned in the same beaten silver as the belt buckle.

At the door, Mrs. Rosado's voice sounded. "Señorita James! Buenos días!"

Johnnie hurried to let her in. The door to the Tower Room had no doorknob or keylock; it was an old door, with a black iron pull on the outside and a slide bolt on the inside. "Good morning, Mrs. Rosado. What is all this?"

"This is café con leche, señorita, and *el desayuno* for you." Mrs. Rosado set the tray on the table by the door and busily began to pour Johnnie's coffee.

"Mmm! It smells delicious! Is that gingerbread?" Johnnie lifted the linen cover from a small basket and saw two thick slices of sweetbread and two pastries.

"*Sí*, my own secret recipe," Mrs. Rosado said proudly. "A little ginger, some nuts . . ." Stirring the heavy cream into Johnnie's coffee cup briskly, she searched Johnnie's face. "Did you sleep well last night, Señorita James?"

"Oh yes," Johnnie replied. "The sound of the sea has always been most restful to me. And the breeze! I actually got a little chilly in the middle of the night. No, don't worry, I found the coverlets in that wonderful old chest at the foot of the bed."

"That is good, Señorita James," Mrs. Rosado said with ill-disguised relief. "Then—unless you wish something else for breakfast—"

"Oh no, this is fine, thank you."

Mrs. Rosado turned to leave, when a thought occurred to Johnnie. "Um . . . Mrs. Rosado—"

"Sí, señorita?"

"Have you seen Mr. Ventura this morning?"

"Oh yes, of course. I see him early every morning. He comes to the kitchen when I begin the baking." Watching Johnnie quizzically, she stood at the door, waiting.

"Yes, well . . ." At dinner last night neither Esteban nor Diego had made any arrangements to meet with her this morning. Esteban had been distantly polite. Diego had been charming but obviously preoccupied with Nuria. Once, Diego had mentioned in an offhand way that an office had been prepared for her, but Johnnie wasn't sure where—and she wasn't sure she could just walk out of the tower by herself without wandering through the honeycomb passages for half the morning.

Confusion and indecision flitted over Johnnie's face, while

sudden comprehension filled Mrs. Rosado's. In a neutral voice she asked, "Will an hour be enough time for you to finish el desayuno and to ready yourself, Señorita James?"

"Hmm? Oh yes, of course."

"Then I will return in an hour."

"Thank you," Johnnie said stiffly. It was an embarrassing and frustrating position to be in. *I already know that Puerto Ricans—and particularly Spaniards—are much more laid back than Americans*, Johnnie was thinking sourly as Mrs. Rosado left, *and so far it seems that neither of the Venturas is too anxious to get his system set up . . . but not to even have an introductory meeting. . . ?*

Another thought occurred to Johnnie that was much more unpleasant and presented a problem much harder to solve. *Suppose it's just . . . me? I already got off to a horrible start with Esteban. Diego is polite enough—but suppose they just simply have decided that they don't like me and would rather have another accountant?*

Johnnie's chagrined expression changed. She sat up straighter, and a certain determination, almost hardness, came into her tawny eyes. "It doesn't matter," she said aloud in a harsh tone.

With that she buttered a slice of the gingerbread and poured herself another cup of coffee. *I'm a good accountant, and I'm proud of my work. I can do this job. Personalities don't matter. I will show Esteban Ventura that whether he likes me or not, I'm the best accountant he'll ever have.*

By the time Mrs. Rosado arrived for the second time, Johnnie's appearance was perfect. She had pulled her hair straight back and French-braided the entire length, then added a leather bow at the nape of her neck. Her smile was warm, if impersonal.

"I need two favors, Mrs. Rosado," she said without preamble.

"Sí, Señorita James, I will help you if I can," she said uncertainly.

"I don't have any idea where Mr. Ventura has set up my office," Johnnie said matter-of-factly.

Mrs. Rosado's eyebrows rose, and she stammered a bit. "But . . . but it is next to Señor Diego's, I believe."

"Then take me there, please. And the second favor is that you show me, clearly, how to get there. I don't care if I have to leave a trail of bread crumbs," Johnnie fumed, "I'm going to learn to find my way around this castle!"

☙〰〰〰❧

Johnnie's office was indeed next to Diego's and was a carbon copy of his. The three offices Johnnie had seen—Diego's had the sign on it that said *Office*—were interconnected. Each had a back door that led into a lovely little shady courtyard with a small fountain surrounded by six tables, all in exquisite wrought iron, and chairs with comfortable cushions.

The offices were of stone and obviously part of the original castle. The floor was flagstone, but Johnnie's office had a plush area rug that covered the entire room except for a twelve-inch border around the perimeter. A copper and iron chandelier hung from the ceiling, and the desk was actually an eighteenth-century Spanish captain's table, scarred and work-worn, but made of fine mahogany sanded to a satiny finish. In contrast, the chair was a modern ergonomic, and the desk had a powerful halogen lamp. Also on the desk was a brand-new Macintosh computer, a laser printer, a modem, an expensive new calculator, and a telephone. Behind the desk was a sizable credenza fully stocked with office supplies and flanked by two filing cabinets.

Johnnie went right to work.

After a time the door opened, and Johnnie blinked cautiously at the bright sunlight invading the cool semidarkness of the room.

"Señorita James, it is time for lunch. Come out into the sunshine with me!" Antonio Serralles commanded.

"Mr. Serralles! It's lunchtime?" Johnnie checked her watch in surprise. It was, in fact, one o'clock; she had worked five straight hours without looking up.

"Come, señorita. You work too hard," Mr. Serralles grumbled. "Spaniards are not impressed with hard workers. They are only impressed with poems and sad songs and dancing."

"Wonderful," Johnnie sighed, then rose and gathered up her briefcase, which doubled as a purse. "No wonder I didn't make much of an impression."

Antonio Serralles gave her a look as cunning as a fox's. "Americans," he announced, "understand nothing. They are always quick to make a judgment, to reach a decision, to see things, to know things, to have things." He rounded her desk, offered his arm, and pointed to the back door.

Warmly she clasped his arm and sensed the wiry strength still vital in his aging body. "And Spaniards are quick to create what sounds like poetry when they haven't much to say."

"I have much to say," he retorted, "but young people never listen anyway. Do you like avocados?"

"Yes, very much."

"Good, because that is what I told Señora Rosado to fix us for lunch. Avocados, any way, with anything."

On one of the tables in the courtyard were set two places with heavy pottery plates, antique silverware, and red linen napkins. Both plates had covers, and Johnnie and Mr. Serralles lifted them to see quartered avocados on a bed of lettuce. On the table were salt and pepper shakers, lemon juice, mayonnaise, bacon bits, and an assortment of other condiments. Two heavy goblets filled with crushed ice stood by a large bottle of Pellegrino.

"Perfect," Johnnie said with satisfaction while he filled her goblet with the sparkling water. "I dislike heavy lunches."

"I love them," Don Serralles sighed, "but here at Taíno Castle Esteban and Diego have gotten into the despicable habit of eating like Americans. Small pitiful breakfasts, small pitiful lunches, elaborate dinners served too late. Did you know that in Spain one eats a light breakfast early, another breakfast at 11:00, and the largest meal is lunch, which is from about 2:00 until 4:00? And most often dinner is very light."

"No, I know very little about Spain, I'm ashamed to say," Johnnie answered, savoring her first mouthful of fresh avocado sprinkled with lemon juice and crisp bacon bits. "When I got this account, I studied more about Puerto Rico because I had no idea that Mr. Ventura was Spanish."

Serralles chewed thoughtfully. "So you believe you would have made a better impression on Esteban if you had studied Spain?"

Johnnie smiled bitterly as she looked down at her plate and toyed with a piece of lettuce. "No, under the circumstances I believe I would have made the same first impression on him, Mr. Serralles." Suddenly she realized how personal this conversation was getting and hastily asked brightly, "By the way, I noticed the Venturas call you 'Don' Serralles. I don't know what that means."

He shrugged carelessly, but his gaze on Johnnie's face was penetrating. "The strict meaning of the word is 'lord,' but that's archaic, as are those titles now. It's a courtesy phrase, I suppose you'd call it, but with Esteban and Diego it's really more a sign of . . . warmth, affection, respect for an old friend." Still eyeing Johnnie closely, he persisted, "So you don't know much about Spain. How much do you know about the Venturas?"

"I know they are my clients," Johnnie said shortly. "I know the history of Taíno Island and the castle. I know what Mr. Ventura wants to do with them. I can supply them with the financial information they'll need."

Mr. Serralles frowned. "You sound angry. In the two months we worked so closely together, every day, under such stress, I never heard anger in your voice or saw it on your face."

Johnnie closed her eyes tightly for a moment and took a deep breath. Then she looked back at Mr. Serralles and smiled, genuinely this time. "I am angry—with myself—because I was not adequately prepared for this job. I didn't do my homework, Mr. Serralles."

"Ah, I see. And what is it, exactly, that made you angry with Esteban?"

"What! I'm not angry with Mr. Ventura!" Johnnie exclaimed. "I don't even know him! People don't get angry with people they don't even know!"

"Of course they do, all the time, for all kinds of reasons," Serralles said mildly. Settling back in his chair, he took a long drink of Pellegrino, then smacked his lips with satisfaction.

Johnnie sat up stiffly in her chair, then clasped both her hands tightly in her lap. "Mr. Serralles, I appreciate so much your recommendation of me—and my firm—to Mr. Ventura. It is due to you that I got this client, and this is a good account. It's already helped me gain respect in my company, and that is important to me. Equally important to me is doing a good job, the best job that I can for my clients. All of them, large and small. And I will do a very, very good job for Mr. Ventura. It is nothing personal. It's business."

"Business," Serralles repeated with amusement. "I know business. I see business. But what I see is that you offended Esteban in some way, and so he is wary of you, and so you are— what do you say—defended?"

"Defensive," Johnnie told him rather petulantly. "Which I'm not."

Serralles laughed. "Oh no?" Then he sobered and eyed her speculatively. "Diego says you snubbed Esteban because you thought he was only the gardener."

"Oh, blue thunder!" Johnnie blustered. "Is that what Mr. Ventura told him?"

"No. Esteban has said nothing and would say nothing. What do *you* say?"

Johnnie stared at him, suddenly stricken. *How can I explain? I'm not a snob, snubbing the servants . . . I saw him, and I was instantly attracted to him, and I . . . I just . . . What a mess!* She couldn't think of one reply.

"So you don't want to talk about Esteban, eh?" Serralles went on as he saw her distress. "Fine. I will talk about him."

Johnnie opened her mouth to protest, but she could see that the older man was now grandly ignoring her, gazing innocently at the fountain, the sky, the flowers, and was going to have his say anyway, so she gave up.

"Did you know Esteban is famous?" He openly enjoyed Johnnie's look of surprise. "Yes, in Spain, and in many of the Latin American countries—Brazil, Venezuela, Costa Rica, Peru, Argentina—he is as famous as your movie stars. He was, perhaps, the most famous soccer player in the world for fourteen of the sixteen years that he played. He retired two years ago, when he turned thirty-four."

"I . . . I had no idea!" Johnnie stuttered. "I should've been briefed on this!"

"He is unpretentious," Serralles went on gravely. "That is one reason he longed to settle in Puerto Rico. Here he is little known, although he is better known than in America, of course."

"Of course," Johnnie agreed blankly, desperately trying to think of what she might do to remedy this absurd situation with her client.

"They called him 'The Lynx.' The Spanish lynx, you see, is very quick, very smart, and very dangerous. Esteban's athletic ability was almost supernatural, for he seemed much too large and muscle-bound to be so quick, so agile."

"I could kill every cappuccino-slurping Yuppie in the public relations department," Johnnie muttered, staring into the distance.

"I beg your pardon?"

"Never mind, sir. I just wish I'd known this."

"The most important thing I must tell you about Esteban Ventura is that he despises being treated differently because of his fame and fortune. He is an honest man and he dislikes insincerity. And so, Señorita Johnnie James," he asked slowly, "now that you know Esteban is a celebrity, how will you treat this client?"

Before Johnnie had a chance to figure out her answer to Serralles' question, Esteban came out of the back door of the last office. He was dressed, again, in faded jeans and a T-shirt, and he was wearing muddy black rubber Wellingtons. His bandanna headband was navy blue this time, and the same Gargoyle wraparound sunglasses were in place. Johnnie deliberately dropped her eyes. He was a most compelling man, with his cinnamon-colored skin, crisp black hair, and smooth, taut muscles.

"Here you are," he said, then turned back to lean inside the office and whistle a short, sharp note. An enormous dog came out and followed him at a dignified pace. Esteban made his way to their table, stopped, stuck his hands in his jeans pockets, and looked around at the huge white dog following him. "Sit," he softly ordered. Turning to Johnnie he said quietly, "She is a guard dog and very loyal. She's wary of strangers. She won't hurt you, but you must make friends with her. Her name is Isabella."

Johnnie, who had never been around a dog for more than five minutes in her entire life, looked uncertainly at the dog. She was huge, probably two feet high at the shoulder, and must have weighed close to one hundred pounds. Heavy bodied and strongly muscled, she sat watching Johnnie closely—not with hostility, but with caution.

"Isabella, you are a beautiful and frightening dog," Johnnie said, echoing Esteban's soft, even tone. "But I am prepared to like you if you will like me. Shall we be friends?" Johnnie put out her hand, loose, relaxed, palm up. Isabella looked at Johnnie, looked at her hand, then looked up at Esteban.

"It's all right, Isabella," he said.

Isabella got up and walked slowly over to Johnnie. She cursorily sniffed her hand—Johnnie got the impression that she did it just to humor her—then walked up close to Johnnie and studied her with surprising intelligence and clear decisiveness.

Yes, we can be friends.

Johnnie started rubbing her head and scratching her ears, which Isabella seemed to enjoy, though she was much more restrained and dignified than the nervous, shivering apartment-sized dogs owned by some of Johnnie's friends.

"Good," Esteban said with satisfaction. "May I join you?"

"Of course," Don Serralles said.

Esteban pulled out a chair and sprawled into it, crossing one muddy-booted leg over the other. Checking the two now-empty plates, he said lightly, "Miss James, Don Serralles, to a Spaniard an empty plate is not good; if you can finish your meal, there is not enough. Shall I go find Señora Rosado and ask her if there is any food on the island?"

"Thank you, but it was quite enough for me," Johnnie said stiffly, still petting Isabella, her eyes averted.

Only the slightest movement of his head showed that he noted Johnnie's cool tone. Don Serralles looked amused, in that special way of the older and wiser. Smiling, he turned to snap his fingers at the dog. "Isabella, come here and let me pet you. Esteban, I want you to give me this dog."

"You can have one of her puppies, Don Serralles, but you can't have my Isabella," he said, rather automatically it seemed to Johnnie, and she thought he might be looking at her. But with the sunglasses she couldn't tell; he might have had his eyes closed, for all she knew. "Where is Diego?" he asked abruptly.

It did seem that he was looking at her. "I don't know, Mr. Ventura," she finally replied after a moment's uncomfortable silence. *Well, here I am, having my usual sparkling, witty conversation with Esteban. . . .*

He stood, a bronze statue burnished in the sun; Johnnie was mute and stared at the table; Don Serralles was laughing, possibly at the dog, who looked very much as if she were grinning. Or perhaps the old man was laughing at the two young people behaving so oddly.

Esteban Ventura turned on his heel and stalked angrily back into the shadows of his office. Isabella abruptly jerked away from Don Serralles and ran after him.

"Just like a woman," Don Serralles said, shaking his head, his eyes sparkling with mischief. "Never can tell what they're thinking, so you never can tell what they're going to do next."

"Yes, Mr. Serralles," Johnnie agreed absently.

But it was no woman she was thinking of, and like a woman, she was trying to figure out what to do next.

Five

As it turned out, there was no need for Johnnie to try to figure out what to do with Esteban and Diego Ventura. Esteban took charge and reset the chess pieces of their working relationship.

Johnnie didn't see anyone else the rest of her first working day. At six o'clock she made her way back to the Tower Room—at least she had the passages figured out from her office to there—and took a long, hot bath. By the time she had finished she was so tired she could barely complete her usual evening reading: one article in the *Journal of Accountancy*, one article in *National Review*, a chapter from the Bible, and a poem. She fell asleep with the candles burning, and when she awoke in the morning, they had burned all the way down and gutted out.

Mrs. Rosado arrived with breakfast. Johnnie felt refreshed and energetic and was anxious to get to work, so she hurriedly sipped her café con leche and ate one slice of her ginger nut bread, then went to her office.

The back door leading into the courtyard was open, and she saw that Esteban and Diego were there with the remains of their breakfast. She hesitated in the doorway. Esteban looked up, and he and Diego hastened to their feet. "Please, Miss James, will you join us?" Esteban asked, coming to her.

"Certainly." They seated themselves in the shade of an ancient oak tree covered with bougainvillea.

"Did you sleep well?" Esteban asked politely.

"Very well, thank you. And thank you for giving me the Ventura Tower Room. I . . . it's perfect."

"You're welcome," Esteban replied smoothly, then got right down to business. "I would like to explain to you the areas of your responsibility here, Miss James, and how you will address those areas. Any and all papers, documents, and records you need have been, I believe, transferred and filed in your office."

"Yes, I looked through all the files yesterday, and I can't think of anything more that I need right now," Johnnie remarked.

"Should you need any records, ask Diego," Esteban said directly.

"All right."

"Diego will be handling all of the administration of Taíno Island and the castle. Every detail of paper work and computer work will be his area," Esteban went on, watching his brother closely.

Diego smiled at Johnnie. "Don Serralles says that you will make this very easy for me."

"I will try," Johnnie replied.

"Good," Esteban said with relief. "So you see that Diego will be working most closely with you?"

"Yes, Mr. Ventura." *And don't you sound relieved!*

"I care nothing for such things," Esteban admitted. "As I told you, I am the gardener. I take care of the horses and the dogs and the island and the castle."

Johnnie considered this for a few moments. "I understand, Mr. Ventura. But I'd like to tell you that if you should need any assistance with budgeting and forecasting for completion of the castle renovation, my firm would be delighted to help you. We have developed some excellent computer models, and they are based on the cost projections of actual luxury hotels. I just want you to know that this service is available to you should you wish to take advantage of it."

Esteban raised one eyebrow. "Thank you, Miss James. I am aware that you provide this service, and I am considering it. Before I get into capital budgeting, though, I want to get the administrative systems completed."

"Wise," Johnnie commented. "That's the way I would advise you to proceed."

"You are modest," Esteban said quietly, and Johnnie stared up at him in surprise. "I happen to know that you, Miss James, developed these models for luxury hotels, although you have only had one such client yourself. I also know that you are the expert in your firm at tailoring the software to fit each particular client's needs."

Johnnie actually blushed. She hardly ever blushed, especially when she was in the middle of a business discussion. "I . . . the models—that is, with help—they belong to Andrews, Smith & Wesley—" She despaired of making a coherent reply and finally murmured, "Thank you kindly."

Esteban smiled. "De nada."

Johnnie was as pleased as if he'd given her a million-dollar bonus.

Diego's eyebrows rose slightly, but when he addressed Johnnie, it was in the same normal, warm voice he used to talk to everyone from Nuria to Isabella. "You disappeared after leaving the office last evening, Señorita James. Shall we make some arrangements for your meals? Would you like to instruct Señora Rosado on meals in your room, or would you like to have them in the dining room?"

Johnnie could deal with Diego's smooth charm much better than the heat of Esteban Ventura's full attention. "Thank you, Mr. Ventura, but please don't concern yourself. I'm not familiar with the Puerto Rican traditions of hospitality for retainers, but in America I never expect my clients to make arrangements for my evenings. It's more than kind of you to provide me with the lovely room and breakfast and maid service. I intend to make my own arrangements for the rest of my meals."

Esteban and Diego exchanged surprised looks. "Very well," Diego shrugged. "I'm sure Mrs. Rosado will be happy to help you with anything you might need."

"And if you wish to go to Ponce, let me know," Esteban told her. "Pablo and Mateo work on Saturdays and Sundays, and I go over at least once or twice during the week."

"That's kind of you. I'll let you know," Johnnie said.

He was watching her so closely. *He never just looks at me*, Johnnie reflected. *He's so intent . . . he studies me every moment. . . .* But with a will Johnnie decided that it was just that his eyes were so dark, and his manner of expression so clear, that Esteban Ventura only seemed intense, his signals so *tangible* they could be felt.

At least that's what she told herself.

⟨⟩

For four days Johnnie worked hard, making enormous progress in getting every aspect of Taíno Castle's administrative functions on computer. She entered all the payroll records for the past year and five months, and for the first time, the staff received computerized checks with year-to-date information on the stubs. She coded all income, expense, asset, liability, and capital accounts. She generated monthly reports for test purposes and spent one day working out the odd little glitches that always happened when a computer lumped categories together and manipulated debits and credits. She began a preliminary inventory procedure, but with that she came to a dead end, confronting problems that could only be solved by Diego Ventura.

And that was a problem in itself.

Diego was rarely to be found.

Even before Esteban Ventura had explained his and his brother's various duties, Johnnie had her suspicions as to how the two brothers fit into the business scheme. In fact, she was getting to know a lot about the brothers; neither of them would have believed that checkbooks and payroll records and stacks of invoices would have told Johnnie James so much about their hearts—and their souls. Johnnie shrugged a little as she reflected on this. It was always the same. You didn't have to walk ten miles in a person's shoes to understand him. All you had to do was balance his checkbook.

Esteban Ventura was the money, the heart, and the soul of the business. Diego Ventura was a highly paid executive whose brother loved him very much. But Esteban Ventura was no fool, and he was a good businessman. He had retained fifty-one percent ownership of Ventura Enterprises, Incorporated, and his father and mother owned forty-nine percent. That was the first fact that had surprised Johnnie. Normally family-based operations such as this were partnerships, and Diego would have had equal standing. Esteban paid Diego a fine salary for management, but Diego owned no stock.

Johnnie saw Esteban Ventura at least once a day, usually in the late afternoon. Every day he and Isabella were somewhere in the gardens, and Esteban would speak to her for a few moments as she was going to her room after work. Three times during the week he came into the office to ask how she was progressing and if she needed anything. His inquiries were incisive, his questions to the point, his visits short. He was very cordial to Johnnie, though strictly professional in bearing.

But Diego Ventura took his managerial duties very lightly. Johnnie saw him once in the morning, usually early, for a perfunctory, polite five minutes. Twice he'd shown up to have lunch with her. He usually stuck his head in the door at about three o'clock and recited the same request to take siesta, which Johnnie politely declined, preferring to work through the day and be done with it at six o'clock or so instead of beginning again.

Now after five days of these "Hi, how ya doing?" meetings, Johnnie was going to have to pin him down. She frowned and looked at her watch. It was three-thirty on Thursday. For all she knew, Diego might take Fridays off, as did many higher-level executives.

Even as she was thinking of these problems, Diego opened the door and stuck his head in. "Señorita James, may I come in?" he asked as always.

"Of course, please do, Mr. Ventura," she answered as always. "I was just thinking of several things I need to discuss with you—"

Diego put up a slender hand of protest and smiled warmly. "Yes, I'm well aware that we must meet more often, Señorita James. But this week I am very busy, I'm afraid. In fact, that's why I'm here. Tomorrow night you must dine with us in the keep. We have a special surprise planned for everyone."

In spite of her pressing business questions, Johnnie was intrigued. "You extend an interesting invitation, Mr. Ventura."

"Call me Diego," he said, "and say yes."

"Yes, Diego," she replied.

"Bueno," he said with satisfaction. When he turned to leave, Johnnie opened her mouth to protest, but he preempted her once again. "Tomorrow we will dress for dinner," he instructed as he opened the door. "Someone will come to escort you at nine o'clock. Buenas tardes, Señorita James."

"Good afternoon, Diego," she said faintly to the closing door.

The world spoke sanity at them.
They didn't hear or choose to hear.
God became the enchanter
whose enchantments set one free.
The air grew alcoholic.

—From *Haunting the Winerunner*
by John Wink

Six

A *sound heart is the life of the flesh: but envy the rottenness of the bones."*

Johnnie leaned back against the mound of feather pillows on her bed and considered the verses from Proverbs. She stared out the open window, savoring the clear vision of the stars bathed in the cool aura of distant moonlight. The half-moon had not yet come around to angle the night glow into the Tower Room, but the sky turned royal blue as it rose above the distant horizon.

Sound heart . . . envy . . . envy means jealousy. . . .

Am I? I am! I'm jealous of Nuria Torres!

The realization shocked and dismayed Johnnie. She'd never been a malicious or spiteful person, and she considered herself to be emotionally healthy. But there was no denying it. She was jealous of Nuria Torres—her beauty, her grace . . . and probably Nuria's relationship to Esteban Ventura.

So in Johnnie's own businesslike way she made up her mind to face the problem and address it.

Johnnie prayed. She never seemed to be able to pray in a smooth and sincere manner without feeling self-conscious, but she had gotten into the habit of discussing whatever verses she'd read that night with her heavenly Father. What she was just beginning to realize was that these prayers had come to be very real, quite honest, and surprisingly unselfconscious. They were certainly moving her quickly along a journey she hadn't even realised she'd begun.

"Father, I see that I have envy for this woman. Please forgive me. Help me to put this sin away, Lord, because I want to have a sound heart and life. Thank you, Father, for your love and for caring for me. Amen."

Weary but at peace, Johnnie blew out the candles and settled down into her luxurious bed.

Johnnie was a Christian, but she had never felt very close to her Father God, or even her Savior, Jesus Christ. She loved God in the same distant way that she loved her own father, and mostly she felt very grateful—and obligated—to Jesus for dying for her sins. But the Lord was not a vital, energetic presence in her life. Rather, He was her hero, and she worshiped Him in that way.

The previous winter had been particularly cold and dreary in Atlanta, and she had spent a lot of time alone at home, generally staying warm and reading voraciously. During this time it had occurred to her that she was quite unable to comprehend poetry. This was unacceptable. Johnnie James was intelligent, articulate, and very well-educated. Her mind was incisive, quick, and analytical, and she should be able to read and dissect any poem she happened across.

She tried Emily Dickinson. She tried Lord Byron. She tried Yeats, Marlowe, and Shelley. To Johnnie all of them were bewildering at best and nonsensical at worst.

Then she tried King David of Israel and his son King Solomon the Wise. Now, here was poetry she could understand. Most of it, anyway.

Johnnie's study of biblical poetry had two tangible results. One was that she was slowly getting better acquainted with King David's Father God, and His Son—whom David seemed to know, too, somehow, even though it would be almost a thousand years before Jesus would be born.

The other result was that Johnnie found she could, haltingly and with some effort, begin to understand other poetry.

Now as she let her tired body relax and her senses bask in the warm, rich night and the smell and taste and sound of the sea, she thought again of Esteban's magnificent fountain and of the statue of the winerunner.

"So very odd . . . coincidence . . ." she said drowsily to the Gothic stone ceiling above.

Johnnie had decided to buy a book of poetry to take to Puerto Rico. She'd gone into Barnes & Noble and had immediately seen a provocatively titled book in the Modern Poetry section. The name of the book was *Haunting the Winerunner* by John Wink.

When a noise aroused her, she wasn't even sure if she had actually gone to sleep. She sat up, looked quickly around the room to get her bearings, then got up and went to the window. That sound—what was it? Where was it coming from? It was elusive, ill-defined, but loud enough to awaken her.

At the window all she could hear was the rhythmic booming of the sea below.

She went back to her bed and sat down; now she could hear it. The sound waxed and waned, but it was—

Johnnie flew to the door and opened it. Of course. Voices, loud, the timbre angry as they surged, an indistinct mass of human sound through the maze of passages in the castle.

One voice rose high above the rest, but it was not a shriek like a woman's voice, rather the harsh shouting of a man.

Johnnie thought it sounded like Diego Ventura.

"Nonsense!" she said sturdily. "How should I know what he sounds like shouting from a mile away! It could be anyone! Anything!"

But Johnnie did know it was a man. An angry man.

Johnnie sighed. "Here's my chance," she muttered with ill humor, "to fulfill my fantasy and to continue making a royal fool of myself. But really, the candles would be a bit too much. . . ."

Then Johnnie remembered that she'd come up the passage from the keep into the Tower Room when it was still daylight, and the stairway had been lit because the door at the top of the stairs had been left open. The flashlight she normally used was still in the little table at the entrance to the passage.

Smiling ruefully, she lit the six candles in the brass candelabra, put on her flowing silk robe and matching slippers, and went out into the passage.

She stood still for a long moment, listening. The sounds of voices continued; now she could distinguish the harsh croak of a man with a very deep voice, the smoother voice sounding like Diego's—though it was still raised in anger—and at least two other men's voices that were slightly higher. They were somewhere to her left and probably on the ground floor.

They must be on the first floor of the tower, she thought. *But I don't exactly know how to get there . . . and suppose they're just playing poker or having a party or watching a football game or something?*

But Johnnie knew this wasn't true. The voices were angry, and the sound of them portended violence.

"I'll just go a little way," she whispered as she nearly floated down the passage, her slippers making no sound, her robe billowing behind her in an airy silken cloud.

She took the left hallway, then took a passage that seemed to go down, then took a little stairwell that curved around to the left, hoping it would lead to the first floor. Then the passage bore to the right, and Johnnie tried to compensate by going up some stairs that went to the left and making another left-hand turn . . . and then she was lost.

But the voices were growing louder. She could even catch a word now and then, though they were Spanish. She had heard the words before but had no idea what they meant. Johnnie thought she heard the guttural voice shout something about Ponce, and barking. In any case there were definitely four— maybe five—very angry men somewhere in Taíno Castle.

One of them certainly sounded like Diego Ventura. Another of them—the one with the deep voice—sounded like Esteban. Well, not exactly like him, but Esteban did have a deep, rather hoarse voice. . . .

Johnnie was suddenly very tired, and her feet and hands were getting cold. The passages, she had discovered, were chilly at night. She walked to the end of the stone corridor and stood still, trying to decide whether to take the left- or right-hand passage or whether to try to retrace her steps.

The bitter clangor continued in her ears, now seeming to fill the stone hallway, roiling and thudding around the gently rounded walls. Johnnie decided she just wanted to go back to her room, to close her eyes, to hear nothing but the sweet music of the sea. She didn't care about the angry men; she didn't want to know why they were shouting; and she especially didn't want to find out for certain whether or not two—or perhaps one—of those men were named Ventura.

"I didn't pass a window getting here," Johnnie said softly to herself, mostly to have something else to listen to besides the disturbing din assaulting her senses. "I think I'd better just try to go on and try to get outside."

She took the right-hand passageway—it appeared to slope downhill somewhat—and came to the end, which turned sharply to the left. Unhesitatingly she turned the corner.

A whip of wind snapped her robe behind her. The candles blew out, plunging Johnnie into total darkness.

A small choked cry escaped, then she dropped the candelabra and flattened herself against the wall. Her heart thudded unevenly in her chest, and her breath became ragged.

Okay, calm down, just calm down . . . breathe . . . breathe . . . make it slow and even. . . . After a few desperate gulps, Johnnie managed to slow down her breathing somewhat. *Now just wait, don't strain, just let your eyes adjust, and then you can keep going. At least there's nothing in any of these passages to trip over. . . .*

Can the human eye adjust to complete darkness?

But before Johnnie had time to decide, she knew that she must not be in complete darkness. She couldn't be, because far down the passage she could see eyes. Yellow glaring eyes and a glimmer of white.

"Oh, Lord, I'm scared, I'm so scared," she whispered helplessly, shutting her eyes tight. Now her breaths were just tiny little moans, and her mind was full of red-hot flashes of panic. *Lord, please help me!*

Something cold touched her hand. Johnnie jumped and screamed.

Her eyes flew open, stark and wide and staring.

Before her was a huge white dog.

Johnnie sank to her knees, threw her arms around the dog's massive chest, and sobbed until the dog's leather collar was thoroughly soaked in one spot.

Isabella bore it patiently, Johnnie decided after a while. She stood still, her feathery tail wagging just a bit. Isabella felt warm and strong and safe, and Johnnie whispered, "Oh, thank you, thank you, Lord! Thank you for this wonderful, beautiful, noble dog!"

Finally Johnnie sank down to sit with her back against the cold, damp wall. Isabella didn't move, she only swiveled her head to look at Johnnie. "Isabella, I owe you, girl," she whispered. "Thank you kindly."

The dog padded silently down the hallway, back the way Johnnie had come.

Johnnie panicked again and scrambled up. "Isabella! Wait, please, wait!"

Stopping, the dog calmly looked back. Johnnie could see Isabella only as an outline, a shimmer of white in the blackness. Johnnie walked up to stand beside her and touch her smooth head, more to reassure herself than to pet the dog.

Isabella walked on and Johnnie followed. They walked, and Isabella turned this way, then that way. Soon she stopped at a door and scratched at it. Johnnie, as if she were in some strange dream, opened it without hesitation and the two walked through it. It led to a long, upward-winding flight of stairs; these stairs were treacherous. Carved out of a wall, they had no railing at the side. Isabella walked slowly and confidently up, and Johnnie hovered close behind her, feeling along the wall. Johnnie looked down, seeing nothing but darkness. Once, the stair seemed to crumble away as she stepped up. She stumbled and fell against Isabella, who immediately stopped. Johnnie steadied herself with both hands on the dog's strong back, and then the two climbed on. Cobwebs brushed against Johnnie's hair, and with a shaking hand she pulled them out. Finally they reached the top of the stairwell, where there was another door, another hallway, and yet another door.

The door to Johnnie's room.

She opened it in amazement and stepped in, looking around in wonder. Turning, she meant to invite—beg—her savior to come in and stay with her.

But the beautiful white dog was gone.

Seven

*B*uenos días, Señorita James." Diego rose from one of the chairs in front of her desk and came toward her. She couldn't see him very well in the dimly lit office, but she could see as he neared her that his expression changed from a polite greeting to concern. "Miss James, are you all right? You look . . . tired."

You mean I look like I was up all night? Johnnie thought wearily. *You mean I look red-eyed and pasty-faced?* "No, I'm fine, thank you, Mr. Ventura. I'm glad to see you this morning. I've gotten quite a lot of preparatory work done, but there are many things I need to discuss with you."

"Ah, you are working too hard," Diego said knowingly. He took her arm and escorted her to one of the comfortable old chairs in front of her desk, then seated himself by her. "Spaniards don't require anyone to keep up the pace Americans seem to set for themselves, señorita. Why don't you take the morning off?"

"Mr. Ventura—"

"Diego."

"Diego, I haven't yet worked one full week," Johnnie said with ill-disguised frustration. "Thank you for your concern, but I assure you I'm just fine."

Diego studied her with his brown velvet eyes. "Are you? Are

you comfortable in the Tower Room?"

Johnnie met his eyes squarely. "Yes, quite comfortable."

"Good, I'm glad to hear it, Señorita James. I've been concerned about you. Well—" he rose and walked to the door, "don't work too many long hours in the heat of the afternoon, señorita. We do have a reason for the custom of taking siesta, you know. And don't forget we have a special dinner planned for everyone tonight."

Johnnie jumped out of her chair. "But, Mr. Ven—Diego—there really are several issues we need to discuss—"

Diego smiled. "You're the accountant, and an expert one, I understand. I'm sure that any decisions you make concerning our bookkeeping will be fine. Please accept my sincerest apologies, but I have several important matters to attend to this morning. Perhaps I will see you at lunch." He left, quietly closing the door behind him.

Johnnie sank into her chair, propped her elbows on the desk, and rubbed her eyes. Her mind was cotton-woolly, and she was certain that somehow, in some way, she had mishandled Diego. After a few moment's study, however, she gave up. *It's almost impossible to think clearly after a lost night's sleep*, she admitted to herself, remembering the eerie events of the previous night.

After Johnnie had been safely returned to her room by Isabella, she was restless the remainder of the night. Dark, endless passages and ominous rolling thunder consumed her dreams. Once, she had even imagined she was the poor winerunner, forever running, forever haunted. . . .

Johnnie shook herself out of her nightmare review, took out a year's worth of bank statements on two accounts, some twelve-hundred-plus checks, and went to work.

After about an hour of punching in endless columns of numbers on her calculator, the telephone rang.

Johnnie stared at it blankly; it hadn't rung a single time all week long. It was a businesslike black telephone, with buttons for three lines—helpfully numbered #1, #2, & #3—and a hold button. Line one was blinking urgently. She thought it might be Diego's office, but she knew he wasn't next door.

How do I answer it? "Office" ... *"Taíno Castle"* ... *Puerto Rico, may I help you?"*

Making a face at her own foolishness, Johnnie snatched up the receiver and said simply, "Johnnie James."

"Perdóneme?"

Rolling her eyes, Johnnie said slowly and awkwardly, with a pronounced Georgian accent, *"No hablo español, señor."*

Sounds of fumbling and muted voices in the background came over the wires. Finally a male voice, young and southern, said, "Hullo? Hullo, ma'am?"

Relieved, Johnnie replied, "Hello, this is Johnnie James. May I help you?"

"I hope so, ma'am," the man replied. "Is this Taíno Castle?"

"Yes, it is."

"I'm Lieutenant Gregory Dyess of the United States Coast Guard, ma'am," the man said, now sounding older and much more businesslike. "May I speak with Mr. Esteban Ventura, please?"

Johnnie was suddenly nervous but replied smoothly, "I'm sorry, Mr. Ventura is not in the office right now. May I take a message for him?"

A short silence ensued, and Johnnie could hear crisp rattles of paper. Then: "Is Mr. Diego Ventura in, ma'am?"

"No, he's not in the office at this time, either, Lieutenant. I'm sorry, but neither Mr. Esteban Ventura nor Mr. Diego Ventura is in the office at regular hours."

"Ma'am, please excuse me, but who are you, exactly?"

Johnnie smiled wanly. "My name is Johnnie James, Lieutenant, and I'm with the accounting firm of Andrews, Smith & Wesley. I'm the Venturas' accountant."

"Oh," he said, sounding a little disconcerted for the first time. "Well, let me tell you my problem, Ms. James, and maybe you can help me or you can tell me who can. I'm circling Taíno Island right now in my cutter. Lieutenant Ray Leone of the

Ponce Police Department is with me, ma'am, and we need to make a landing at your island there. Could you tell me exactly where the devil I can do that?"

"No . . . sir . . . no—" Johnnie began, then took a deep breath and started over. "I'm sorry, sir, but I was brought to the island for the first time on Mr. Ventura's yacht last weekend. I wouldn't know a landing from a rattlesnake pit."

"A yacht?" He suddenly sounded urgent. "Where'd you dock, ma'am?"

"On . . . at . . . a little boathouse. A little cove. By the beach."

"All right, thank you, Ms. James. We'll probably be landing shortly, and I'm sure I'll meet you then."

"Yes, I'm sure," Johnnie echoed faintly.

"And, ma'am?"

"Yes?"

"If you should see either one of the Venturas," he said evenly, "we're coming to talk to them. Let them know we'll be docking at their boathouse."

"Yes, I will, Lieutenant."

"Thank you, ma'am. G'bye."

"Good-bye, Lieutenant."

Johnnie hung up the phone and stared at it blankly for several minutes, her mind working furiously but futilely.

Finally she rose and hurried outside, looking first at the keep—she knew Mrs. Rosado was in the kitchen in the back of the great hall—and at Esteban's tower. He might be in there, but she had no intention of walking up to his personal living quarters and knocking on the door.

So now what?

The answer came through the massive front gate. Esteban came dashing over the castle grounds on a fiery, prancing horse. The horse's hooves clattered loudly on the iron bricks. Esteban directed him to the edge of the gardens and nimbly slid off, disdaining the stirrup.

Johnnie, who had on her ever-present heels, still managed

to make very good time down the passage and across the bailey. Esteban was tying the horse's reins to an iron post with a ring half hidden in a fern. He looked up in surprise when he heard Johnnie's hurried, clicking footsteps. Taking a step forward he demanded, "Yes, Miss James? What is it?"

"A Lieutenant Greg Dyess of the Coast Guard just called, Mr. Ventura," she recited automatically. "He and a Lieutenant Ray Leone of the Ponce Police Department wish to talk to you and your brother. They'll be landing at the boathouse in just a few minutes, I think."

Esteban's head snapped up alertly. He was wearing his anonymous sunglasses, but Johnnie could see that his square jaw tightened perceptibly and his mouth hardened into a straight line. "Landing? Landing in what?" he demanded.

"A cutter, sir. Lieutenant Dyess's Coast Guard cutter—"

Esteban muttered something dire under his breath, whirled, and jumped—not mounted, *jumped*—into the saddle. The horse snorted and pawed the air, and Esteban grabbed the reins and jerked, but the slip knot didn't release. Johnnie hurried to the post and, without fumbling, untied the tangled knot and threw the reins up to Esteban.

He stared down at her for a minute, controlling the horse easily, who was trying to start. "Thank you—kindly," he said with obvious satisfaction at using her colloquialism.

"You're . . . kindly welcome, sir," Johnnie said in a low voice.

Esteban turned the horse and galloped furiously back through the gate.

∽◦◦◦◦

"Esteban is worried about the cutter, you see," Diego explained smoothly. "Taíno Island is surrounded by coral reefs. The landing in the cove is the only safe approach to the island, and only a boat of a certain displacement can make it without being in great danger of bottoming out. If the cutter is too large or too heavy, there is a possibility that it might not make it into the cove."

"But won't they just come onto the island on one of those little . . . rafts, or whatever you call them?" Johnnie asked.

"Yes, the landing craft. Inflatables, usually," Diego said with a hint of surprise that Johnnie would think of that. "Certainly they will. Nevertheless, the coral reefs are still dangerous for sizable boats up to three miles out from the island."

"I see," Johnnie said thoughtfully.

Outwardly she was calm, but her mind had been racing furiously ever since Esteban had flown out of sight on his magnificent horse.

She'd returned to her office and had seen Diego and Nuria, arm in arm, coming out of the keep, evidently going for a walk in the gardens. After intercepting them she'd quickly told her tale to Diego. He had decided to come back to her office to wait for the men, sending Nuria back to the keep.

Diego was calm and seemed unsurprised that the police wanted to talk to him and his brother. As they waited he'd spoken idly of the weather and some of the improvements to the island, then he had asked Johnnie if she was feeling better. Finally Johnnie had mentioned as casually as she could that Esteban had seemed upset that the Coast Guard and the police were landing on the island in a few minutes, and Diego had explained to her about the difficulty in navigating the waters surrounding the island.

At last the door opened. Esteban came in and stood aside, motioning two men to follow him.

Lieutenant Greg Dyess of the Coast Guard was no more than twenty-five years old. Of medium height and stocky, he had thick brown hair, brown eyes, and dimples, but his expression was grave. Lieutenant Ray Leone was older, short, with a narrow, intense face and darting eyes. Both men stopped to study Johnnie, who was seated behind her desk, and Diego, who rose to greet them with his hand extended.

Esteban came forward and made businesslike introductions.

Short greetings were said all around. Then Johnnie said, "I'll be leaving now, Mr. Ventura. If you should need me, I'll be out in the courtyard."

Esteban studied her. "Will you stay?" he asked simply.

Johnnie drew a sharp breath but said clearly, "Of course." She sat back down.

There were only two other chairs in the office. Esteban seated himself casually on the corner of Johnnie's desk. "Please sit down, gentlemen. Diego, you wouldn't mind standing, would you?"

"Not at all. Please, gentlemen, sit." Diego leaned casually against the wall and crossed his arms.

Lieutenant Leone began speaking in Spanish, but when Esteban held up his hand, the man faltered and stopped.

"Please pardon me, Lieutenant Leone, but Miss James speaks no Spanish. Do you speak English?"

"Yes, Mr. Ventura," he replied politely, though his quick eyes narrowed as he stared at Johnnie. Nevertheless he went on in an accent so thick Johnnie could barely catch every other word.

"A yacht was stolen from my port last night, Mr. Ventura. It is the second time in six months."

"I've heard," Esteban said.

"Have you?" Lieutenant Leone asked quickly. "What is it that you have heard, Mr. Ventura?"

"That two yachts have been stolen from the port at Ponce in the last six months," Esteban replied patiently.

Lieutenant Leone visibly deflated. It was likely hard for him to catch innuendo or to play cat-and-mouse games in English. He looked at Lieutenant Dyess with frustration, and the Coast Guard officer nodded slightly and took over.

"This yacht was a forty-footer and very expensive. It was owned by a company based in New York, and two of their executives and their wives are stuck in Ponce without a boat. They're not too happy."

"I'm sure it is a terrible inconvenience for them," Esteban said politely.

"It's more than that, Mr. Ventura," Lieutenant Dyess countered. "It's a loss to their company of over a quarter of a million dollars."

"Must have been a nice little craft," Diego commented, his eyes wide.

"Yes," Lieutenant Dyess agreed.

A silence fell over the room. The two lieutenants and Johnnie fidgeted and shifted in their chairs, while Esteban and Diego seemed perfectly at ease.

Finally Lieutenant Dyess blew out a frustrated breath and asked abruptly, "Do either of you know anything about this theft?"

Esteban didn't move, his voice remained exactly the same tone and quality as before. "No, Lieutenant, I know nothing other than what I heard on the radio this morning: A yacht was stolen." He looked at Diego expectantly.

"I know nothing about it," Diego shrugged, though his handsome face tightened with just a hint of anger.

"And you, Miss James?" Lieutenant Dyess asked perfunctorily.

"This is the first I've heard of it," Johnnie answered quietly.

"Where were you last night, Mr. Ventura?" Lieutenant Dyess asked neutrally.

Esteban answered steadily, "I was here, at the castle."

"Where exactly, sir?"

With a shrug Esteban replied, "I stayed down in the stables last night. My dog had puppies, and one of them was a little sickly—"

Johnnie's sharp intake of breath was audible—even loud, roaring, *thunderous*—to her ears. But no one else seemed to hear, though she clearly saw the muscles in Esteban's folded arms knot perceptibly. His voice, however, never wavered or changed tone.

"—so I stayed with Isabella all night. At dawn I came back

and slept a few hours in my room."

As if from far, far away, Johnnie heard Lieutenant Dyess ask Diego where he was last night, and Diego answered that he was alone in his room, sleeping. Johnnie's head seemed to be roaring, and though her eyes were wide open, she actually saw nothing. *He's lying. Esteban's lying! Oh, Lord, why did he have to lie? And . . . did I hear them say "Ponce" last night? And barking . . . Isabella wasn't barking, she rarely makes a sound . . . oh no, it wasn't "el barco" was it? That means "boat" . . . or "yacht". . . .*

"Did you see anything last night, Mr. Ventura? Hear anything? Anything at all that might be connected to this theft?" Lieutenant Dyess doggedly asked Esteban. Lieutenant Leone's dark eyes seemed to burn as they rested on Esteban, then Diego, as they each answered the question.

"I saw nothing and heard nothing at all that would help you," Esteban said calmly.

"Nothing," Diego said shortly, his eyes now sparking with anger.

Johnnie's mind started spinning and then screeching. *What if he asks me? What do I say? If I say nothing about hearing the voices last night—is that lying? Is it possible that Esteban and Diego are—No! No! I might not have heard—it was probably nothing at all! I don't even know who it was—or could I possibly have imagined the whole thing? Dreamed it? But what about Isabella . . . did I dream her, too? No, it was too real, too frightening—*

Suddenly something in Johnnie's mind seemed to cut the confusion of half thoughts and unformed ideas bouncing haphazardly about in her head. She knew two things and understood them with great clarity:

She desperately wanted to lie to protect Esteban Ventura.

And Johnnie knew she could not.

"Señorita James?" Lieutenant Leone impatiently repeated, waiting for an answer to a question she hadn't wanted to hear.

"I beg your pardon?" Johnnie said in a low tone. For the first time Esteban turned to look at her with concern, and she met his eyes, pleading for something he obviously didn't understand.

"Where were you last night, Señorita James?" the police lieutenant repeated, his gaze boring into her.

"Really, Lieutenant Leone, is it necessary to question Miss James?" Esteban asked smoothly. "She's an accountant from a highly reputable firm in Atlanta, and she only arrived here last Sunday."

"I only was wondering if she'd seen or heard anything," Lieutenant Leone said to Esteban defiantly, but then he nodded with a quick, sharp jab of his head. "But I suppose that even if she'd heard a boat, it would mean nothing. . . ."

"True. Thank you, Miss James," Lieutenant Dyess said, nodding to her and rising to his feet. "We may want to talk to you again, but I think that is all for today."

Johnnie stared at him, mute and nearly paralyzed with relief.

"You'll take us to the staff?" Lieutenant Dyess asked Esteban.

"Of course," Esteban replied. He motioned toward the door. "Please . . ."

The two lieutenants and Diego filed outside, but Esteban paused at the door to look back at Johnnie.

"Are you all right, Miss James?" he asked neutrally, but his dark eyes were smoldering.

"Yes . . . yes, thank you," Johnnie replied with difficulty.

Esteban hesitated in the doorway. "You will still have dinner with us at the keep tonight?"

"Hmm? I . . . oh yes, tonight . . . yes, I suppose—"

"Good." He looked back over his shoulder, obviously considering something. Then he turned back to Johnnie. "May I call for you a little early? At seven, perhaps?"

Again Johnnie had to make an effort to stop her wildly spinning thoughts and form the words, "Yes . . . yes, Mr. Ventura—perhaps that will . . . be best."

Esteban hesitated, his eyes unfathomable, his expression unreadable. The voices of the men waiting outside floated into the room.

"At seven o'clock," he finally murmured quietly. "I will come to you."

After he closed the door, Johnnie buried her face in her hands.

Eight

When Johnnie finally roused herself from her misery, she saw that it was only two o'clock. "I've got to take a break," she whispered dully. "I'm so . . . tired."

Slowly, as if her muscles were stiff and sore from running, she put several papers in her briefcase and went outside. The afternoon sun, which usually seemed so cheerful to Johnnie, was today like fiery darts in her eyes. She put on sunglasses, and, head bowed, she made her way along the walk to Ventura Tower.

As she passed the keep, one of the heavy wooden doors swung open and Nuria hurried out. "Señorita James!" she called. "Come here!"

Johnnie stopped and looked at her in disbelief. *Come here! How dare she?* Then reason took over. *She probably doesn't know how to say it politely in English. . . .*

But Nuria had stopped, propped her hands on her hips, and glowered at Johnnie from the steps of the keep. "I said for you to come here!" she shrieked.

"I beg your pardon?" Johnnie said as politely as she could, yelling over a distance of a hundred feet.

Nuria stood and watched.

Johnnie stood and waited.

I have neither the time nor the patience for this right now!

Johnnie nodded curtly to her and began walking again.

She heard Nuria make an indignant sound, then footsteps sounded behind her. With resignation, Johnnie stopped and turned around. She noticed that Nuria was wearing a black body leotard that clung to her body like a second skin. A light sheen of sweat lay on her forehead and throat. She was wearing ballet slippers, and Johnnie reflected with a tinge of shame that perhaps she couldn't walk very well across the iron flagstones with such soft-soled shoes. *She is a flamenco dancer*, said a malicious little voice inside Johnnie's throbbing head. *If she can stomp that hard, a few little bricks aren't going to hurt her precious little tootsies. . . .*

"Señorita James! I called you!" Nuria said petulantly.

"I heard you, Miss Torres," Johnnie said blandly. "Good afternoon. How are you?"

But Nuria was still not interested in social niceties. "Where is Esteban and Diego?" she demanded, putting her hands on her hips.

"Do you mean 'Where *are* Esteban and Diego?' " Johnnie asked innocently.

Nuria narrowed her stormy eyes. "I do not think that is funny. Answer my question."

Johnnie sighed. She was really too tired to fight with this melodramatic girl. "I'm sorry, Miss Torres, but I don't know their whereabouts. I believe they were going to take Lieutenant Dyess and Lieutenant Leone to interview the staff. Maybe they're in the keep."

Maintaining her angry stance, Nuria grated, "I was just in there! No one is there!"

"Then I do not know where they are," Johnnie said very clearly. "Good afternoon."

She turned to walk away, but Nuria, like a puff of smoke, suddenly appeared right in front of her. "Wait!" she snapped. "You were with them, weren't you?" she said accusingly. "You were with them when the police questioned them! Tell me what happened!"

"I beg your pardon?" Johnnie said with clench-jawed politeness that translates itself into any language.

As if a genie had snapped his fingers and changed her into someone else, Nuria's voice lowered, and she made a graceful, placating gesture. "No . . .no . . . you see, I'm worried about Esteban and Diego. They are my very oldest and my very best friends, Señorita James. And I don't know how to . . . ask . . . or say it right in English."

Johnnie, through headache haze, studied her. Her expression was pleading, apologetic, but something about her stance and the shadowy depths of her eyes told Johnnie that she was completely insincere. It was as if she'd realized that being rude was getting her nowhere, so she would try politeness.

At this point neither of those tactics was going to work with Johnnie James.

"Oh, I think you know very well how to be polite in either Spanish or English," Johnnie said so mildly that Nuria blinked several times, not instantly comprehending what Johnnie was saying. "And if Mr. Ventura and Diego are such good friends of yours, I'm certain they'll tell you everything . . . as soon as you can chase them down. Good-bye, Miss Torres."

Johnnie literally whirled on her heel and marched away, and this time Nuria didn't stop her. But the back of Johnnie's neck crawled as she walked away, knowing that Nuria was watching her. On some deep gut level Johnnie knew how dangerous it could be to turn your back on an enemy such as Nuria Cristina de la Torres.

But by the time Johnnie was wearily pulling herself up the curved flight of stairs to her room, she had forgotten all about Nuria's childish spite. She was thinking, again, about Esteban Ventura.

"What am I going to do?" she asked herself hollowly as she walked into her room. Her Bible was open on the table by her bed, and Mrs. Rosado had placed her daily flower—she always had a fresh blossom on her breakfast tray—on the open pages. Today it was a creamy yellow daffodil, and its simple beauty and sweet scent somehow cheered Johnnie up a little and lessened the throbbing in her head. "A bath," Johnnie breathed. "The longest bubble bath in the history of mankind!"

Thirty minutes later, as she lay in the luxurious bathtub allowing the almost-hot water to soothe her knotted nerves, Johnnie's mind also worked out some of its knots.

"Did he lie? Could he possibly be involved with thieves?" she asked the steamy, perfume-heavy air. She closed her eyes.

Be logical, she ordered herself. *What's the problem here?*

After a long time of calm reflection, Johnnie's mind was clear on one very simple solution. *I am Esteban Ventura's accountant, and I have a duty to do the very best work I can for him.*

I can do that.

I have absolutely no obligation to do, say, or imply, in any way, anything dishonest on behalf of or to benefit any client.

Have I done that?

Yes, I have. I know Esteban was lying! The thought disturbed Johnnie so much that she jerked one knee angrily in the bath, sloshing bubbly water all over the stone steps. Still she kept her eyes closed and willed herself to relax. *So now, tonight, I will tell him that I know he lied about Isabella. I don't have to tell him how I know. He knows the truth. What he says to the police is his affair. But I will make it perfectly clear to him that I will never, in any professional capacity, tolerate dishonesty—and I certainly will not be an accomplice to it.*

Like I was today?

"The trouble is," Johnnie said, rising and stepping out of the bath, "that Esteban lied, so I'm guilty by omission. If he hadn't lied, then all that weird wandering around in the passages last night wouldn't have been important at all. In fact, it would have been irresponsible of me to tell the police and allow such a vague story to implicate Esteban and Diego." She dried off briskly with a marvelously huge, thick towel, looked in the mirror, and uncertainly asked her foggy reflection, "Is that right?"

It was right, but the knowledge did little to ease the turmoil still churning through her thoughts.

The light knock on her door came precisely at seven o'clock. Johnnie was ready.

Since she'd brought no formal dinner wear, she'd chosen to wear her black suit, which her secretary called her undertaker's uniform. Johnnie preferred to think it was dignified, though she admitted to herself that it was quite severe. On this night she wore sheer black hose, which she deemed evening wear, with black heels. She took extra care with her makeup, particularly her eyes, which always made her feel confident. Her hair was pulled back into an impeccable French twist.

Finally, after much debate, she'd decided to wear her diamonds. She believed they were frivolous and too ostentatious, but somehow she always found herself taking them with her when she traveled. Her father had given them to her, and she did love them. The marquise-cut one-carat ring, the two-carat necklace, the one-carat diamond studs; Johnnie decided to wear all of them at once, which she'd never done.

Opening the door, the sight of Esteban Ventura made her take a deep breath. He was wearing a tuxedo, and Johnnie marveled that he was the kind of man who could look at ease wearing either a T-shirt and worn blue jeans or in black tie. He looked vital and strong as he leaned against the doorframe in a relaxed stance. "Good evening, Miss James. Are you ready for me?"

Johnnie reflected that though Esteban's English was excellent, it was a devil of a language when it came to learning all the inferences. With some confusion and rather high color she managed to mumble "Yes" while wondering to herself if she was even going to be able to form a complete sentence with a subject and a predicate while she talked with Esteban Ventura, much less have a complex conversation with him.

"—that be all right?" he was asking. He had preceded her on the stairwell, holding the flashlight so she might best see, but Johnnie was too flustered to remember what he had said.

Johnnie James, get a grip on yourself! her mind cried out desperately. *I've never been this gaga, this stupid, this horribly attracted to a man so fast! If I don't straighten up and grow up, I'll just have to leave here!*

That last thought completely appalled her. Though Johnnie had had several emotionally charged and difficult relationships in the last ten years, not one single time had it ever affected her professional life. Never.

And this man is not going to, either!

"Mr. Ventura, I have a request," Johnnie said in a coolly professional voice.

"All right," he said in an equally cool manner. "Watch here, please . . . last step." They walked out into the warm evening. The sun's heat still radiated from the stones of Taíno Castle, and in the west the sky held tinges of maroon.

Esteban stopped and turned to look at Johnnie. She looked back up at him, and it seemed that she saw—in his face, in his entire countenance—only kindness. But she cleared her throat and went on. "I think that before we have any . . . social niceties . . . we should discuss some business matters."

To her surprise, Esteban looked relieved. "That would be good, Miss James. There are several things I need to bring to your attention, and I would like to get them out of the way." He chewed on his bottom lip for a moment. "Would you like to go to your office?"

"Yes, that would be best," Johnnie answered. Neutral ground would be better than Esteban's warm and intimate rooms.

In silence they walked to Johnnie's office. When they entered, Johnnie hurried to sit behind the desk. She could see Esteban's look of disapproval—it was a blatant power play—but Johnnie didn't care. She needed to put space—both physical and mental—between herself and this man.

"Please, sit down," she said.

He looked thinly amused. "Thank you. Since my great-grandfather made this chair, I believe I will take this one."

Johnnie sighed. This was not going well, but she plunged ahead anyway. "Mr. Ventura, there is something that I must make clear to you."

"Yes? And what is that?" He was beginning to look wary.

Johnnie faltered for only a moment, then gathered up her strength and said quietly, "I am an accountant, and in that profession I follow a very strict set of rules. The first rule is, of course, my most important rule."

Esteban waited and watched her with narrowed eyes.

Swallowing hard, Johnnie went on. "Honesty. I am always honest. That means that my clients must be honest, because I will not in any way make a concession in any of their financial representations that will allow them to be dishonest."

Ever so slowly, Esteban Ventura crossed one leg over the other and rested one strong, scarred brown hand on his black dress boot. The other hand he lifted to his chin, resting two fingers lightly on it. He never dropped his gaze from Johnnie's eyes, and he now looked appallingly angry. His voice was whisper-soft, filled with warning. "Speak plainly, please, Miss James."

Johnnie's mouth felt numb, and she was suddenly very thirsty, but she never dropped her eyes. "I know that you lied to the police, Mr. Ventura."

Esteban Ventura looked startled, but then, inexplicably, he relaxed. Though Johnnie didn't understand it, she could actually feel his lessening tension. "You are mistaken, Miss James. I told the truth to the police. Now, is that all? Or are you trying to tell me that you've seen something in my records of which you disapprove?"

Johnnie was dumbfounded; of all the reactions she had expected, this calm refutation was not one of them. Her confusion was so profound that for a long moment she simply couldn't speak. Esteban watched her, his eyes flickering with some emotion she couldn't read. Finally she managed to stammer, "But . . . but . . . Mr. Ventura, I'm telling you that I know you lied!"

The anger in Esteban rose again. Johnnie felt it rather than saw it or heard it, but she felt totally out of control and helpless. In the sharpest tone she'd heard him use, he ordered, "Miss James, answer my question. Have you found anything in my financial dealings that offends your honor?"

"N-no, no, nothing at all," Johnnie replied desperately. "They . . . they . . . your records are quite straightforward and meticulous."

"That is good," he said, his jaw clenching tightly. "Now I will address your accusation. My belief, Miss James, is that I owe you no explanation, no justification. I need not defend myself to you because I am guilty of nothing."

A long silence fell. Johnnie dropped her eyes and studied her hands. They were clenched together so tightly that the blood had strangled out of them. "As long as you understand that my accounting will always be completely honest, Mr. Ventura," she said in a subdued voice.

"Since you are so dedicated to brutal honesty, Miss James," he said in a curt tone that made Johnnie's head snap up, "with your permission we'll now talk about the problems I have with *you*."

"What?" Johnnie cried. "But . . . what problems?"

Esteban's eyes narrowed to cold stone gunports. "While you seem to have an obsession with professional standards, Miss James, I have a problem with personal integrity. You were quite rude to me when you thought I was only the gardener. I was willing to forget that because I do believe that you are an expert in your field, and so it was a good business decision to retain you. I could ignore your pretentious behavior with me—I even thought, for a while, that there must be some misunderstanding, some mistake. . . ."

He faltered for only a moment, then the granite in his jaw and voice returned. "At any rate, I have no intention of allowing you to insult anyone else, Miss James, because you think they are not your social equals. Nuria might be just an ignorant little dancer, beneath your notice, but I cannot tolerate you offending my guests, my friends, or my servants."

Johnnie's eyes opened wide with dismay, and her lips parted in surprise. She licked them; even with her perfect lipstick, they were dry. "But, Mr. Ventura," she began, and her voice sounded like a child's plea. She cleared her throat and began again. "Mr. Ventura, I have never insulted Miss Torres! I don't understand!"

One black wing of an eyebrow went sardonically upward. "Miss Torres says you were very rude to her today. Since I've already seen that tendency in you, I must believe her."

Johnnie was silent, stricken by his words.

Esteban went on relentlessly. "I was considering requesting another accountant from your firm, Miss James, but I have decided against it for this reason: I know that Don Antonio Serralles is a wise man, and I cannot believe that he was so mistaken about you. He speaks very highly of you, both professionally and personally. So I will bow to his wise counsel and ask you to remain our accountant."

Numbly, Johnnie whispered, "I appreciate you being willing to reconsider your . . . opinion . . . of me." She was looking at him much as the little field mouse looks up at the circling eagle.

"That is more than you seem to be willing to concede to me," Esteban growled, "which is another reason I must ask you to stay. If I asked you to leave now, I would appear to be guilty and afraid."

He stood, put his hands on the desk, and leaned over close to Johnnie. He was immense, and the very tautness of his hands and the muscles in his wrists were a sign of danger. "I fear nothing on this earth, Miss James, except my God. And before Him I tell you that I am guilty of nothing."

Johnnie shrank back in her chair. As usual, when she faced Esteban Ventura, she could think of nothing at all to say.

Nine

*A*fter forcing a long, scorching gaze upon Johnnie, Esteban started out of his chair, stalked to the door, and flung it open. Johnnie thought he would leave her sitting in the office, pinned down in the harsh circle of halogen light at her desk, confused and morose. But he leaned against the doorjamb, his back to Johnnie, and she could hear him taking deep, even breaths. Crossing his arms, he stared out into the sultry night.

Johnnie looked down at her tortured hands and willed herself to relax. Such scenes—regardless of why they took place or who was right and who was wrong—were stressful and depressing. She sighed.

To her surprise, when she looked back up, Esteban had returned to his chair across the desk and was studying her intently. She hadn't heard a sound as he'd closed the door and crossed the room.

The lynx . . . Spanish lynx . . . agile and dangerous . . .

"This is most discomfortable," Esteban muttered darkly.

"Yes," Johnnie wearily agreed, "it is very discomfortable."

He eyed her critically. "I said it wrong, didn't I?"

Smiling wanly, Johnnie replied, "Yes, I think you did, and so did I. Would you accept an apology, Mr. Ventura, and an assurance from me that from now on I will confine my dealings with you to the accounting systems of Ventura Enterprises, Incorporated?"

He cocked his head, leaned back in his chair, and crossed his arms. "No, that won't do, Miss James."

With a frustrated sigh, Johnnie went on. "And if I apologize to Miss Torres for my alleged rudeness, will that be sufficient?"

"No."

"What must I do then?" Johnnie demanded.

"You must accept my apology for losing my temper and speaking so harshly to you," Esteban said, his voice low. "I'm sorry."

"Oh, my . . . I . . . of course I accept, Mr. Ventura. And I . . . I'm sorry."

"I accept."

They stared at each other, Johnnie uncertainly and Esteban with a glint of humor. "We are still discomfortable, hmm?"

"Not exactly. I personally have upgraded to merely being uncomfortable."

"Ah. The word is 'uncomfortable' then?"

"Yes, that's the word."

Restlessly Esteban rose and paced in front of her desk. "English is difficult. Uncomfortable," he repeated thoughtfully. "I dislike such angry—" He stopped and stared at Johnnie. "Or is it 'unlike'?"

"Unlike?" she repeated blankly. "Unlike what?"

"Unlike or dislike?" he said impatiently.

"They're both words, Mr. Ventura," Johnnie answered quietly, "and I believe the one you're looking for is 'dislike.' "

"Thank you. I dislike such angry scenes." He checked his watch, then asked, "Shall we go on over to the keep? Everyone else will be there, even though dinner won't be served for another half hour or so."

Johnnie stood, smoothed her skirt, and nodded. "That will be fine. I will speak to Miss Torres first thing."

"I would consider it a personal favor if you would," he said formally, coming to offer her his arm.

Johnnie barely touched his arm as she replied evenly, "I won't do it as a personal favor to you, Mr. Ventura, but I will offer Miss Torres an apology for my own satisfaction."

Quietly he said, "Then that will be satisfactory to me."

They walked in an uneasy silence to the front doors of the keep. The first floor was the original great hall, and the second, third, and fourth floors had been converted into rooms and luxury apartments.

Esteban was in the process of remodeling the cavernous great hall into a dining room. He had partitioned off almost a third of it and converted it into a modern kitchen. Still, the great hall was huge, the ceiling thirty feet high, with the original gallery still running around the entire circumference. Two fireplaces were at each end of the room, the mantels eight feet high, the openings six feet wide. Because of the huge open space of the room, Esteban was sectioning it off, with two groupings around the fireplaces defined by Persian area rugs. One set of dining tables was centered around an exquisite fountain twelve feet high. Another partition was in an arbor, planted with china trees and exotic potted plants. In one corner of the arbor three great earthenware olive jars were arranged. All of these partitions lent a much more comfortable intimacy to the room.

A long table was set in the arbor, which was a three-sided alcove with torches flaming at one end. The table had the most sumptuous centerpiece Johnnie had ever seen, with a big basket of ivy in the center. Shasta daisies, red geraniums, and orange straw flowers were entwined in the curling tendrils of the ivy, along with red, green, orange, and yellow peppers, red and green lady apples, bananas, chinaberries, and pomegranates. The table was set for ten.

Antonio Serralles, resplendent in black tie, hurried forward as Johnnie and Esteban entered. "Señorita James! I was wondering where you were. Esteban, go away. I want to escort her."

Esteban made a mock bow. "As always, I defer to your greater wisdom, Don Serralles. Miss James."

Mateo had followed Mr. Serralles and now slipped close to

Johnnie's side. "Buenas tardes, Señorita James. May I escort you, too?" His hair was carefully combed, and he wore black pants, a white shirt, and a black tie.

"I would be honored," Johnnie said gravely. "I shall be escorted by the two handsomest men in the room."

Don Serralles eyed her with appreciation. "You look stunning, my dear. But tired, perhaps?"

"Perhaps."

Mateo edged closer to Johnnie and pulled lightly on her arm to get her attention. "Señorita James, you look stunning," he said somberly, pronouncing the word carefully. Johnnie was certain it was the first time he'd ever heard it.

"Thank you so much, Mateo. You are quite a gentleman."

"Señor Ventura says I must be," he told her. "He's teaching me and Pablo how to be true gentlemen, he says."

"He should be an excellent teacher," Johnnie murmured. "But he doesn't have to teach you two. Both you and Pablo are already charming."

"Gracias."

"You're welcome." Johnnie looked around the room. "My goodness, everyone is here tonight, aren't they?"

Esteban was talking quietly to Mrs. Rosado, who nodded and then hurried over to the table to make some minor rearrangements. Nuria, striking in a long, slinky red dress with spaghetti straps, was sipping a glass of champagne and talking to Mrs. Rosado's two daughters, who worked at the castle as maids and assistant cooks. The older was Rita, who was an attractive girl of about twenty, but was rather empty-headed, it seemed to Johnnie. The two times she'd spoken with her, Rita had only been interested in knowing who cut Johnnie's hair and who did her nails. Evidently Rita had plans to be a hairdresser and manicurist.

Mrs. Rosado's younger daughter was Consuela, who was perhaps not as pretty as Rita but seemed brighter and much more intelligent. Her manner was more similar to her mother's. She was, however, hanging on to Nuria's every word, staring raptly up at her with shining brown eyes.

Diego and Pablo stood a little apart from the three girls, watching them with amusement. Johnnie noted that Diego's manner was relaxed, and he seemed interested in whatever Pablo was saying. She was impressed by Diego's courtesy and thought it was unusual for a man to treat a young boy, and an employee, with such respect.

"Have you met Mrs. Rosado's daughters?" Mr. Serralles inquired politely as he led Johnnie to a small table set up with a silver ice bucket, glasses, and assorted drinks.

"Yes, I have. They've been quite helpful, you know, because I'm always raiding the kitchen in the afternoons, and Consuela stashes little snacks for me," Johnnie told him. "She found out I prefer light suppers—fruits and crackers and cheeses—and she brings me some fresh fruit from Ponce when she sees something that looks particularly good."

"Consuela's nice," Mateo said decisively, "but Rita's silly. Like my sisters. I have four."

"Oh, you poor thing," Johnnie sympathized.

"How many do you have?" Mateo asked her.

"I don't have any brothers or sisters. I'm an only child."

Mateo's dark eyes widened. "You are? How'd that happen?"

Johnnie smiled, and Don Serralles laughed out loud. "You, my boy, ask too many questions. Maybe Señorita James is so special that her parents only wanted her. Look—Señora Rosado is bringing the food in. Why don't you go help?"

"Yes, Don Serralles," Mateo begrudgingly replied, then bowed to Johnnie. "Excuse me, señorita."

"Hmm? Oh, of course, Mateo." Johnnie was still thinking about Mr. Serralles' clever reply to Mateo's question. It was odd, Mateo asking why she was an only child. Johnnie had often wondered that herself. Though her parents had always been dutifully loving, when Johnnie got older she thought that perhaps she'd been unplanned, and that they hadn't actually wanted children—though she had never spoken of it to them. Johnnie shrugged inwardly. It didn't really matter.

Rita and Consuela hurried to help their mother. Mrs. Rosado was wheeling in a three-tiered cart full of plates and bowls. Nuria turned to speak to Diego and Pablo, but Johnnie decided she wouldn't get a better chance to speak to her tonight.

"Would you please excuse me, Mr. Serralles?" she asked. "I must speak to Miss Torres."

"Here, come with me, I want to talk to Diego anyway," he replied, leading Johnnie toward them. Diego and Pablo watched them approach, but Nuria had her back turned. As Diego smiled, Nuria turned and looked Johnnie up and down with a bland expression.

Johnnie decided to jump right in and be done with it. Out of the corner of her eye she saw Esteban, who was directing Mrs. Rosado on how to place the salad plates, look up and watch them. "Good evening, Miss Torres," she said pleasantly. "May I have a word with you in private?"

Nuria's dark eyes shifted toward Esteban, then to Johnnie's face. "Of course." She walked over to stand by the fountain, then turned to Johnnie, her expression now guarded.

"I apologize for my rudeness this afternoon, Miss Torres," Johnnie said briskly.

Nuria's full mouth curved upward in disdain. "Did Esteban make you apologize?"

"No, he didn't," Johnnie answered shortly. "And he couldn't. He did, however, inform me that you considered me to be rude this afternoon. I repeat, I am truly sorry. Will you accept my apology?"

Again Nuria's eyes cut toward Esteban. Johnnie was certain he was watching, though she now had her back turned to him. Suddenly Nuria smiled brilliantly and extended her long, thin hand. "I accept your apology."

Johnnie shook her hand in a businesslike manner, then turned away. Nuria muttered, "But I don't think we will be friends."

Looking back over her shoulder Johnnie smiled wryly. "Neither do I, Miss Torres. But you may be certain that I will never say anything to you again that could be construed—even by someone with such an imagination as yours—as rudeness. That way I will never be obliged to apologize to you again.''

To Johnnie's satisfaction, Nuria looked utterly confused as Johnnie walked away. *It'll take her a while to work that out. And even if she doesn't know what 'construed' means—I hope she doesn't think it's a cuss word—there's no way she can say that I was rude. Unless, of course, she lies . . . like she already did. Liars— Nuria and Esteban are two of a kind. . . .*

But the thought was halfhearted; Johnnie couldn't make herself view Esteban Ventura in the same class as Nuria Cristina de la Torres. They were so completely different. Nuria was petty and a little cruel, while Esteban was—

What? Esteban is what? Muscular and bronzed? Yes! So what! That's a real character reference!

But it wasn't that simple for Johnnie to dismiss. Though reason told her that Esteban Ventura was a liar, her heart told her otherwise.

⟐

Though the dress was formal, dinner was served informally, as Mrs. Rosado and her daughters were seated at the table with everyone else. Esteban was at the head of the table, with Nuria at his left and Mrs. Rosado on his right. By Nuria was Pablo, then Rita, then Consuela by Diego, who was seated at the opposite end of the table from Esteban. By Mrs. Rosado was Mateo, then Mr. Serralles, and Johnnie, with Diego on her other side. Johnnie thought it was curious that they weren't seated in the traditional male-female arrangement, as the complement of men to women would have allowed.

Then, as they were taking their seats, Mateo said loudly, "One moment! I was supposed to sit by Señorita James! Who changed my flowers?"

Everyone hesitated, and even Esteban looked nonplused for a moment.

Johnnie stared down at the seat into which Mr. Serralles was handing her. There was a small card, written in careful script, that read "Señorita James." Next to it was a white rosebud. Each place had a card, and the men had red carnations. As she glanced around the table, she realized what had happened. Mateo had probably set the table, arranging them in man-woman order as Mrs. Rosado had directed.

I was probably going to be seated on Esteban's right . . . and directly across from Nuria, Johnnie thought bleakly, *but he must have told Mrs. Rosado to change the seating after we came in. . . .*

A glimpse of Esteban's perturbed expression—he was looking at her—confirmed Johnnie's suspicions.

Don Serralles looked around the table in surprise, then comprehension flitted across his lined face. He shook his head slightly, then he grinned widely at Mateo. "Normally I would not give up a place next to so gracious a lady," he said expansively, "but as I will be able to sit by the charming Señora Rosado, I will offer to change places with you, Mateo."

"Thank you," Mateo said with dignity, carefully picking up Mr. Serralles' place card and carnation and exchanging them with his, arranging them just so.

Everyone seated themselves, and Johnnie recovered enough from her embarrassment to smile at Mateo. "Thank you, Mateo," she whispered. "I'm glad at least that you want to sit by me."

"If you're worried about that old Nuria," Mateo scoffed in a hoarse whisper, holding his hand up to his face, "then don't. Maybe she didn't want to sit by you, or maybe she just didn't want you to sit by Señor Ventura. But did you really want to sit by her anyway?"

Johnnie was surprised, and then she laughed. "No, I didn't. I'm so glad I get to sit by you. And you are one smart little boy!"

The dinner was wonderful. It only consisted of three courses, and those were already served up. The salad was a delicious fruit concoction of bananas, cherries, pineapples, mangoes, and almonds in a coconut sauce. For the entrée Mrs. Rosado had prepared *pollo en adobo*, which was chicken with red sauce; *tortilla de papas*, a potato omelet; and *arroz con chorizo*, a rice dish with spicy, succulent bits of sausage. Johnnie couldn't eat much because she'd eaten all but one ladylike bite of the delicious fruit salad, but she was careful to sample everything and compliment Mrs. Rosado on each dish.

Most of the conversation around the table was in Spanish, but Diego was careful to speak to her often, as he painstakingly split his time between Consuela and Johnnie. Johnnie noted that Consuela was polite to him—even warm—but she didn't seem to be infatuated with him. Her sister Rita, sitting on her other side, watched Diego adoringly throughout the meal, and Rita often strained forward to talk over her sister to Diego. When she did, shifting forward in her seat, Consuela's eyes often wandered to Pablo on the other side.

Seems like the seating is unsatisfactory to Consuela and Rita, too, Johnnie thought dryly. Then the thought occurred to her: *So what am I thinking? That I'm upset because I wanted to sit by Esteban? That I'd really, really like it if Nuria were seated somewhere else—Antarctica, maybe?*

With determination Johnnie roused herself from her unhappy reverie. In a week, she'd more than likely be finished with her work at Taíno Castle, and she'd go back to Atlanta and be done with it. Brightly, she spoke to Mateo, asking him about school, trying to ignore her emotional state concerning one Esteban Ventura.

After about an hour everyone was finished with dessert, which was a refreshing coconut sort of pudding called *majarete*. Esteban stood and raised his glass. "To Taíno Island and Taíno Castle, and to each of us who are a part of it. I pray God blesses us always." Everyone raised their glasses, then Esteban went on. "If you'll all come this way, Pablo and Mateo are going to gather chairs around the fountain. Everyone be seated there, please, and give us a few minutes."

With a little confusion, along with much laughter and teasing, everyone helped Pablo and Mateo arrange the chairs in a semicircle around the fountain, which was surrounded by flag-stones with potted plants in a half circle border around it.

When everyone had been seated, Johnnie noticed that Esteban, Diego, and Nuria had disappeared. A moment later the lights went out, which made Rita scream and her mother scold her severely in rapid Spanish. Then two spotlights, hidden behind two stone pots holding lush ferns, came on.

Nuria came slithering around the fountain, looking over her shoulder into the darkness, and then searching ahead as if looking for someone. She had changed into a sensuous, clinging yellow-green dress. The bodice was tight, with a V-neckline and deep cut in the back. The skirt was made of hundreds of ruffles and had a long train. A high slit in front revealed her long, slender legs and the traditional flamenco dancer's heeled shoes with an ankle strap. Her hair was tucked into a lacy black net with orange rosebuds anchoring it. She was breathtaking.

Out of the darkness behind Nuria a shadow moved, and then Diego stepped into the small circle of light. He was dressed like a *vaquero*, with a short, fitted jacket, tight breeches with a black velvet stripe down the side, and boots with two-inch heels. With a ballerina's rhythm, Nuria turned to face him, slowly, turning her head first, then her body.

Suddenly she threw her head up, arched her back, and raised her arms to a graceful arc over her head. Diego stepped forward on one leg, then raised one hand to lightly touch her fingers.

The flamenco began.

Johnnie was enchanted. Nuria was an exquisite dancer, each motion deliberate yet graceful. Diego was agile, his movements strong and well-defined. They had no musical accompaniment. Both of them clapped their hands and snapped their fingers—and of course, there was the heart cadence of their intricate steps on the flagstones.

Even though there was no music and certainly no words, Johnnie understood the story of the flamenco perfectly. The young couple were very much in love, but the girl's family disapproved of the young man. She was to be married to another man, and the lovers were devastated. Not only was Nuria's and Diego's dancing a clear conveyance of the story, but their expressions seemed to be choreographed, executed with precision, grace, and tremendous realism. In fact, if Johnnie hadn't known the two, she would have been certain the story they were telling must be true.

Nuria and Diego danced, and Johnnie was so enthralled she was almost startled when the dance came to an end. Then Esteban came forward and seated himself on a high stool just to the left of Diego and Nuria. He played the guitar, a mournful but intricate piece in a minor key. Then the tempo began to speed up, and Nuria danced alone. Johnnie guessed it was a continuation of the story—now the girl was preparing for her wedding, but she was thinking of her lover, and she would, forever.

When the dance ended, Johnnie had tears in her eyes.

They filled the world
With imprecisions of the world.
They warmed death over,
Rearranged the flowers,
Rebuilt joy's engines.

—From *Haunting the Winerunner*
by John Wink

Ten

*J*ands propped on her hips, her head cocked to one side, Johnnie muttered, "No, no, this isn't quite right, either. Maybe over by those boulders. . . ?" Looking in both directions, then turning to look behind her, Johnnie giggled. "Now, what did I do with those boulders, anyway?"

She decided they must be somewhere to her right in the sumptuous gardens of Taíno Castle. Picking up her lunch, which was wrapped in a kitchen drying towel, and her book *Haunting the Winerunner*, she headed off to where she thought the great moss-decorated boulders might be. The landscaping, in its tropical profusion of greenery and its winding, aimless little paths, was bewildering. But in her wanderings on this bright, lazy Saturday morning, she distinctly remembered a grouping of three or four boulders surrounded by cool ferns by a small clearing.

Strolling along a path that looked promising, she soon caught a glimpse of the boulders through some thick shrubbery just to her left. She hesitated. The walkway she'd been following had no side paths to the clearing, she was sure, and ahead the single row of adoquines seemed to curve away from where she wanted to go.

"Drat on these bushes!" Johnnie fumed, staring at the tantalizing peeks of the boulders just on the other side of the thick greenery.

With an impatient grunt, Johnnie pushed aside the leaves and branches, enough for her to stick her head through. Now she saw that the shrubbery was actually some kind of big plant with thick stalks, rather like what her grandmother had always called "elephant ears," but they were entwined and entangled by some kind of vine with purple flowers.

But Johnnie James was a determined woman, so she stepped into the confusion of vines and eight-foot-high nodding stalks and waded through. A vine caught at her ankle, but she broke it easily as she stepped. Two or three of them managed to wrap themselves securely around her arm and tied themselves in knots around her linen sack. They were too strong for Johnnie to break, so she patiently unwound them. More vines pulled at her, and she did break one of the thick but brittle stalks. Finally she was on the other side of the hedge.

Setting down her lunch and her book, Johnnie methodically brushed off her khaki pants, swiped at her loafers, and pulled out two or three tiny little tendrils that were in her hair. She'd left her shoulder-length hair down, and she hoped fervently that there weren't any bugs in it.

She then stalked over to the boulders and resumed her observation, hands propped on hips, head cocked just so. "Yes . . . yes," she murmured with satisfaction. "This would be perfect."

A gnarled oak tree that must have been two hundred years old towered behind the boulders, and smaller trees on either side of it made a shadowy backdrop. Slowly Johnnie turned, searching the ground around the little clearing, testing the firmness of the earth with her foot, noting that the nearest landscaped beds were about twenty feet away.

And so was Esteban Ventura.

His muscular arms were crossed, resting on the handle of a shovel. He was wearing a white T-shirt that was smudged with the rich black earth and blue jeans with grass and earth stains at the knees. A red bandanna was jammed into his pocket, and as he was in the shade, he wasn't wearing his sunglasses. He was making no pretense of working; he watched Johnnie with open curiosity.

"Ohhh!" Johnnie groaned when she caught sight of him. She must have made quite a sight, bursting through a hedge, pointing to things, talking to herself. In frustration she buried her hands in her face, rubbed her forehead, then stiffly marched over to him. "Good morning, Mr. Ventura," she said with resignation.

"Miss James," he said cautiously, bobbing his head.

Johnnie took a deep breath. "I know I must look a little . . . odd," she muttered, "but I'm not dangerous."

"Aren't you?" he murmured so quietly that Johnnie almost didn't hear and wasn't certain that's what he'd said anyway. But quickly he went on. "Miss James, I hate to intrude upon your privacy, but I must know what you're doing. Please."

Johnnie saw that the corners of his mouth were creased and his eyes sparkled. She smiled with relief. "I was looking for a place to have lunch. This would seem to be the perfect place."

"Let me know the next time you want to have lunch in my gardens," Esteban said wryly. "I'll have the surveyor's report and landscape architect's rendition sent to you."

"Thank you," Johnnie replied with a deep sigh of mock relief. "That would make my job so much easier."

Esteban stared at her for a few moments, then laughed, and Johnnie couldn't help but laugh with him. He had such an inviting laugh.

"May I join you for lunch, Miss James?" he asked suddenly.

Johnnie was off guard and stammered, "Why . . . why . . . y-yes, of course." He looked pleased, which made Johnnie feel bright and confident. "Oh, dear, there is one thing . . ." She shot Esteban a sly look. "Now I shall be obliged to search for a new place for lunch. For two, you see."

"I was hoping to eat sometime today, Miss James."

"Then I suppose this will have to do," Johnnie relented, "even though it's not been properly examined."

Johnnie went over to pick up her book and knapsack, then

went to sit down beneath one of the smaller trees behind the boulders. Esteban went back to the flower bed he'd been working on and retrieved a small ice chest and a liter bottle of water, then joined Johnnie.

"I hope you don't mind my clothes and my hands," Esteban said apologetically. He poured water over his hands and rubbed them briskly. "This is why I usually just bring a lunch out here when I'm working in the gardens. It takes too long to wash up decently enough to eat in the keep, and I don't like to interrupt Mrs. Rosado to bring me something in my apartments."

"Don't apologize, please," Johnnie said hurriedly. "As a matter of fact, my hands are not exactly lily-white, either." She held them out, and Esteban poured some water over them. For some reason this made Johnnie blush, and she ducked her head.

"You have a vine in your hair, with two flowers," Esteban said in a low voice. "I would ask your permission to remove them, but actually I think they're pretty."

"Oh . . . oh, dear," Johnnie murmured in embarrassment, hesitantly feeling of her hair. She couldn't feel anything and looked up at him helplessly. "But . . . I feel so . . . silly. . . ." Her voice trailed off because he was staring at her so intently.

"Don't," he said shortly, sinking to a cross-legged position across from her. He opened the ice chest and held out a green bottle. "Water?" he asked politely.

"Thank you," Johnnie said, still uncomfortable, but she took the bottle and drank gratefully. "I forgot to bring something to drink. If I ever found the fountain again, I was planning on stealing some of that water."

Nodding, Esteban busily laid out a blushing Golden Delicious apple, saltine crackers, a chunk of sunny yellow Gouda cheese, two of the fat sausages that Mrs. Rosado made herself, and a small jar of Ventura olives. "The water here is very good," he said idly, "and you could drink right out of the—What is it?"

Johnnie was staring at his food in the oddest manner. "Well . . . it's . . . it seems we can hardly trade different lunch items," she finally stammered. Untying her knapsack, the towel opened to reveal an apple, crackers, Gouda cheese, half of a chorizo, and a small jar of Ventura olives.

Esteban burst out laughing. "You have gourmet tastes, Miss James! Especially in olives."

"They're very good," Johnnie said defensively, which she felt for some obscure reason.

"Yes, they are," he agreed, popping one into his mouth. "You would think I would be tired of them, but I'm not. I suppose it's because I didn't like them as a child. I only started eating olives when I became an adult." He searched her face, chewing contemplatively, and Johnnie averted her eyes.

"I suppose they are rather an adult taste," she mumbled. Her perpetual uneasiness in Esteban Ventura's presence was returning in full force. He was so close and seemed so relaxed and was such a magnetic man. He wasn't as handsome as Diego; Esteban's face was more rugged, with sun creases radiating out from his eyes and two or three laugh lines at the corners of his mouth. His size alone was intimidating, and Johnnie was very conscious of the powerful bulk of his body.

As she reacted to his nearness, she sternly began to remind herself that Esteban Ventura was an unknown quantity. It was very likely that he had lied to the police about a most serious matter, and he might—possibly—be a criminal. And besides, Johnnie painfully told herself, he really didn't seem to like her very much anyway.

She looked back up. Esteban had picked up her book and was reading it. They ate in silence for a few moments, then Esteban asked curiously, "Did you go buy this book after you came here?"

"No, I bought it a week before I arrived," Johnnie replied.

"I remember, when you saw my fountain, that you knew the poem, but I didn't know you had the book. Do you read much poetry?"

"Not much," Johnnie answered reluctantly, taking a contemplative bite of the sweet apple.

"Quite a coincidence," Esteban remarked.

Johnnie was silent. It was not only a coincidence, but it was a very strange coincidence that Johnnie had chosen that particular book of poetry—and Esteban had chosen the title poem as a theme for his fountain.

After long moments Esteban insistently went on, "My favorite is the title poem. And your favorite, Miss James?"

Looking down, Johnnie carefully made a little sandwich with two crackers, a slice of cheese, and a little piece of sausage. "I . . . suppose the title poem. I picked up the book and opened it right to the poem *Haunting the Winerunner*. The first line: 'Poetry has always started here . . .' appealed to me." She glanced at him, then studied her cracker. "But I've never been able to quite figure out the poem."

"No?"

"No," Johnnie said more firmly. "In fact, I don't really understand much poetry at all."

"Then why do you read it?"

Johnnie took a bite of her little sandwich, savoring the spicy burst of flavor of the sausage. "I'll never learn if I don't read it. So I always try to include a poem in my nightly reading."

Esteban's dark eyes sparked with interest. "What do you read in your nightly reading?"

"An article from the *Journal of Accountancy*—"

"A dedicated professional," Esteban commented with a smile.

"An article from *National Review*—"

"Conservative politics," Esteban said.

"One poem—"

"A curious mind."

"And the Bible."

Esteban's eyebrows flew upward. "You're a Christian?"

"Yes," Johnnie said, again defensively. Then she realized the absurdity of her belligerent tone and smiled halfheartedly. "People are not always what they seem, are they?"

"No, we are not," Esteban said quietly. "Nor are we always what we wish to be. . . . *For that which I do I allow not: for what*

I would, that do I not; but what I hate, that do I. . . . '"

Johnnie was startled. Was this some sort of admission of guilt? Was he guilty? Of what, exactly? Johnnie opened her mouth to say something—she wasn't sure what—but Esteban was in a deep reverie and spoke first.

"I saw you crying last night after the flamenco," he said in a low voice, then waited for Johnnie to answer his unspoken question.

But Johnnie was confused, and her emotions were in turmoil. She was so drawn to this man—he was a total enigma to her—and this situation made her thoroughly nervous. When Johnnie was nervous, she always retreated into cool professionalism. Standing up and brushing herself off, she replied in a businesslike manner, "I found it moving, Mr. Ventura, and I'm glad you brought up the flamenco. Because that's why I'm blundering around in your shrubbery today."

Esteban's face closed, and his expression of warmth was replaced by polite inquiry. He stood and crossed his arms. "Oh? For the flamenco?"

"Yes. I was thinking about what Miss Torres said about building a theater . . . and I just thought . . . that is, my belief is . . ." Johnnie faltered, suddenly doubting that she was in any position to advise this man about the art of flamenco.

Esteban sighed. "Just speak plainly, Miss James. In spite of our difficulties with . . . effective communication, I do respect your opinions."

"Yes, well . . . thank you. I was just thinking . . . the flamenco originated with Andalusian gypsies, didn't it? And wasn't it traditionally—until a few decades ago—performed only in their camps?"

"Yes," Esteban answered, his eyes alight with interest.

"And many times those camps were in caves, weren't they? I just was thinking, last night, how much it added to the flamenco—to the atmosphere, to an observer's understanding of the dance—for it to be performed in a natural setting instead of in a cold, impersonal theater. And then I thought of the gardens and how a small pavilion could be set up, without destroying the effect . . . torches, you see, and some very discreet lighting in the trees, shining down like moonlight, maybe . . . or maybe a fire! Could you do a big campfire here? Without burning down the castle?"

Esteban was grinning at her mounting enthusiasm. "Miss James, I am not the fraud. You are."

Johnnie asked stiffly, "I beg your pardon?"

"You understand much about the flamenco," he said warmly. "Much more than most Americans—or most Europeans, for that matter. It's an old and intimate art form, and many Spaniards feel that no Caucasian can ever comprehend it."

"I . . . didn't realize. The meaning has always seemed so clear to me. Though the form—the song, especially—is sometimes obscure. But even though I don't understand all of it, the underlying themes are represented so uniquely."

" 'They filled the world with imprecisions of the world . . .' " Esteban quoted softly from the poem.

"Exactly!" Johnnie agreed. "The form of the flamenco is stylistic, but the intricacies of the song and dance always illustrate simple, universal themes of loss and tragedy and sorrow."

Esteban smiled at her. "I thought you didn't understand poetry, Miss James."

Johnnie was amazed, both at herself and at his insight, but she was resolved to retain her dignity and not let him fluster her again. Finally she stammered, "Anyway, I . . . I . . . just thought that the grace and beauty of the dance would be shown to the best advantage in a natural, rather wild setting."

Esteban studied the scene in front of them. "I think you are right, Miss James, and I think you are a very intelligent woman." He turned back to her. "By the way, it was very generous of you to offer such praise to Nuria last night."

Johnnie shrugged. "Not really. I only told her the truth. She dances exquisitely, and I did enjoy the performance more than any I've ever seen."

Esteban studied her face closely, then took a step toward her.

He was very near. "I don't understand you at all," he murmured under his breath, as if he were talking to himself. "Why can't I understand you, Miss Johnnie James?"

Johnnie stared up at him, her eyes wide. The heat from his body warmed her, he was so near. Slowly he reached out both his hands—he was going to touch her—

"No!" Johnnie cried and stumbled backward, desperately trying to get as much distance between them as possible.

Esteban blew out a frustrated breath. "Sometimes your vocabulary is extremely limited, Miss James!" he muttered with savage politeness. "As that word was our initial conversation upon meeting, today it can be our closing conversation!" He turned on his heel and stalked away, back toward his flower bed.

Johnnie snatched up her book and the remains of her lunch and stalked in the opposite direction. With each step she grew angrier. *Why can't I just have one polite conversation with that man?* she raged inwardly, then thought again, *Why can't I just stay away from him?*

Because you work for him? a tiny timid voice of reason responded.

"Oh!" Johnnie grated, then did an about-face and walked back toward Esteban. This foolishness must stop now, or else Johnnie was going to have to leave Taíno Island. And at the moment she really didn't care if Andrews, Smith & Wesley lost this lucrative account or not.

She started talking while she was still ten feet away from him. "Mr. Ventura, if you would like to retain another accountant, or another firm, please tell me now. If you would like me to stay, I will make sure that—whatever just happened—won't happen again."

Johnnie never found out what Esteban Ventura was going to say because at that moment a big white dog appeared on the pathway by her. Johnnie turned and smiled in spite of the tension of the situation and the turmoil of her emotions. "Come here, Isabella, you darling," she said, moving toward the dog.

"No . . . wait . . . Miss James—" Esteban said with alarm.

But he stopped abruptly and stared at Johnnie with amazement as she went down on one knee to pet the dog and scratch its ears.

"What is it?" Johnnie asked him, nonplused. She still roughly petted the dog, and it moved so close to Johnnie that she almost fell over.

"That's not Isabella," Esteban said.

"What do you mean? Of course it's Isabella," Johnnie retorted, rather stupidly she realized.

"That's Ferdinand," Esteban insisted. "See? He has the collar. Isabella doesn't wear one. Ferdinand usually guards the stables and the grounds outside the castle. But I've been training him to do guard duty inside the castle at night while Isabella's with the puppies. I didn't think you'd seen him yet, and he's not as friendly as Isabella."

Johnnie stopped petting the dog; indeed, she froze almost as if she'd turned to stone. She stopped breathing and stared up at Esteban in horror. "Would . . . would you repeat that, please?"

Esteban still looked perplexed, but he walked over to pet the dog, kneeling down by Johnnie. "This is Ferdinand, Miss James," he said slowly and patiently. "I thought you hadn't yet met him, and he's a highly trained guard dog. He won't attack without provocation, but he shouldn't be approached by strangers. But I can see that you aren't a stranger. When did you meet Ferdinand?"

Johnnie stared at Esteban, stricken with shame and sorrow to her very soul. "I . . . I met him in the tower, when I was wandering around in the passages! I was lost! And I thought he was Isabella, and he took me back to my room! And I thought you were lying!"

The two stared at each other for a long, long time.

Then Esteban began to laugh.

And Johnnie began to cry.

Esteban sighed deeply and shook his head. "Why are Americans so embarrassed at having emotions? This I cannot understand," he said to the sky, his Spanish accent suddenly more pronounced. Then he turned to Johnnie and spoke in his usual calm, well-modulated English, "It's very difficult for me to understand you, Miss Johnnie James."

"I know!" Johnnie sobbed. "I've been so . . . so peculiar ever since I got here! Usually I'm very professional and . . . and sophisticated and . . . and neat!"

This made Esteban laugh again, which made Johnnie cry harder. She was now utterly embarrassed, totally confused, and completely unable to get control of herself.

Suddenly she felt heat and a comforting heaviness as Esteban laid his hand on her shoulder. "Miss James, as of this moment we begin again. And please don't apologize. I'm tired of us apologizing to each other. I'm going to leave you now so that you can get . . . fixed . . . or whatever you need to do." He stood up, but Johnnie sat back cross-legged in the grass, her head bowed, scrubbing her face with both hands.

"There's just one more thing, Miss James," Esteban added.

"Y-yes?"

"You may be a difficult woman to understand," he said softly, "but you certainly are interesting."

Johnnie watched his Wellington boots as he walked away. He disappeared into the verdant plants of his garden.

Eleven

*L*ife was simple on the balcony.

Nothing touched her but the sweet sea breeze. Her eyes were filled with the serene, majestic line of sea and sky. No sound reached her ears but the continual bass cantata of the waves far below.

Johnnie stayed out on her balcony until sunset, watching the colors of the sky turn from cerulean to royal to indigo. She talked to the Lord in her matter-of-fact way, and by evening she felt at peace. Still, she was reluctant to go back inside and leave her private platform halfway to the heavens.

But a knock at her door summoned her back to the world.

Opening it, she found Esteban smiling down at her. "Good evening, Miss James. I hope I'm not intruding."

Johnnie returned his smile with a weary one of her own. "No, not at all, Mr. Ventura. Won't you come in?"

He shook his head. "No, I can see you're tired, and I know it's been a trying day for you. So I just wanted to bring you something." He offered her a silver bucket with a close-fitting lid and a book.

Johnnie took the bucket and was startled to find that it was freezing cold, with a light sheen of ice on the outside. She lifted the lid and looked inside. A pint of pecan praline ice cream and a silver spoon nestled in a layer of shaved ice.

"Oh, how kind of you!" Johnnie exclaimed, smiling more brightly now. "It's my favorite!"

"Mine too," Esteban declared. "I always eat the entire pint when something's bothering me. It makes me feel better. It has some wonderful medicinal properties."

"I know I'll feel much better when I eat this—all of it," Johnnie agreed. "Thank you kindly, Mr. Ventura."

"You are kindly welcome, Miss James. And here is a book I thought you might like. It's a favorite of mine."

Johnnie took the book from his outstretched hand and murmured, "*The Honorable Imposter* by Gilbert Morris. Provocative title."

"Yes. And applicable."

Johnnie stared at him, trying to discern who the title applied to—her or Esteban himself—but he was already moving on to a different subject.

Abruptly he asked, "Do you ride?"

Johnnie set the cold silver bucket and the book down carefully on the table by the door. "No, I'm afraid not. I barely know the upside of a horse from the backside."

Esteban chuckled. "Your speech is colorful. I like it. Anyway, I can certainly teach you the . . . ah . . . upside from the backside, Miss James. Would you like to go riding tomorrow? Diego and I usually ride every Sunday afternoon, and tomorrow Nuria is coming with us."

Johnnie's face changed, and Esteban watched her shrewdly. He added, "I would like you to come."

Still Johnnie was hesitant, but finally she decided that she wanted to go, and why not? "I'd love to," she responded enthusiastically. "But please promise me that you'll teach me everything so I won't make an idiot of myself . . . again," she added dryly.

"I'll teach you all you need to know in about three minutes," Esteban promised. "You'll be a good rider. I can tell by watching you walk."

Johnnie's eyes widened, her eyebrows winged upward, and she blushed furiously.

Esteban seemed unaware of the implications of his comment, until he muttered almost inaudibly, *"Norteamericanos,"* and Johnnie saw a glint in his dark eyes. *"Buenas noches,* Señorita James.'' He turned and walked down the passageway.

At last Johnnie recovered enough to call after him, "Thank you again for the ice cream!"

Though he had disappeared into the shadows, she heard a deep echo: "You're kindly welcome!"

⚬⚏⚬

The night was kind to Johnnie. When she awoke she felt more energetic, more refreshed, more at peace, than she'd felt since she first came to Taíno Castle. After a long, luxurious bath, she spent extra care on her makeup and hair and then chose a dress to wear.

Johnnie didn't have many dresses; she wore suits. Not pantsuits. She didn't like them. Skirts, jackets, and sometimes vests. But she had about half a dozen dresses that were softer, more feminine than her work suits. Since Johnnie didn't date anymore—she'd sometimes worn them when she had a date for the movies or a play—she now thought of them as her church dresses. This morning she chose a peach-colored shirtwaist with a delicate circle skirt. The bodice had a "shirt" pocket, and a white silk scarf with peach polka dots was cleverly folded to peep out of the pocket. Johnnie had matching heels and a clutch, and with this dress she always wore a silver bracelet and earrings of turquoise and coral stones that her mother had bought her on a trip to Santa Fe.

Gathering up her Bible and purse, Johnnie went to church. The chapel at Taíno Castle was the original sixteenth-century structure, with no modifications. It had required very minor restoration. Esteban had told Johnnie and Mr. Serralles that though most of the rest of the castle needed extensive repairs, and some of it was positively in ruins, it was as though God had miraculously spared the little chapel from the impersonal cruelty of time, wind, and water.

Johnnie paused in the entrance portico to let her eyes adjust to the semidarkness. The only light in the chapel was from a delicate stained-glass window that depicted Jesus' Transfiguration high above the entrance doors.

The chapel was two stories high. The nave was divided horizontally; the upper part, where the castle lord and his family normally sat, could be reached by passages from the great hall and what was now Esteban's tower. Johnnie could dimly see the gallery above, with four long, padded benches and two great chairs—resembling thrones—where, presumably, the lord and lady of the castle sat during Mass. The lower story had two rows of four benches each, though to Johnnie they seemed much like modern pews because they had gently curved backs and padded seats.

Johnnie sat in the front row, savoring the hallowed silence that always pervaded churches and the musky scent of ancient wood. The stone walls of the chapel had been lovingly wainscoted with precious *ausubo*, a fine ironwood native to Puerto Rico but now almost extinct. For a long time she merely looked around, her mind idle, as she let her eyes dwell on the intricate carvings of the pulpit, the magnificent detail of the bas-relief illustrations on the altar railing. She studied every facet of the chapel, not with an architect's or historian's eye, but as a child loves to look at beautiful things, and as a child of the King loves the chambers of her Father's house.

I just cannot believe that Nuria wanted to tear this down and replace it with a theater! Johnnie reflected. *There is a mystical holiness to consecrated ground. This is a holy place, and it seems that anyone could sense it. I think that if an evil man were blind and deaf, and if he were led into this place, he would immediately know he was on holy ground. . . .*

It was too dark to read her Bible, so Johnnie quoted to herself the only extensive passages of Scripture she had memorized:

Psalm 19 and 23, and 1 John 1.

Kneeling at the altar, Johnnie ran her hand over the etched figure in front of her on the altarpiece: St. Peter, as he cut off the Roman's ear at Jesus' arrest in the Garden of Gethsemane. She knew that many old churches and chapels had numerous such carvings in order to illustrate Bible stories to people who couldn't read. The thought suddenly made her overwhelmingly grateful for all of the countless and eternal blessings that the Lord had given her, and she prayed for a long time.

She went back outside almost reluctantly; she regretted that she hadn't come to the chapel earlier, so she could stay longer, but it was almost noon, and she had to change to go riding. Then the thought occurred to her: *Well, silly, the chapel's right here . . . you can have church anytime you want to! How nice to have a castle with your own church right across the yard!*

The prosaic thought made her smile, and her steps grew lighter as she hurried toward Ventura Tower. She was looking forward to her afternoon of learning to ride and seeing the rest of the island. That she greatly looked forward to being with Esteban Ventura was a thought that she reluctantly acknowledged, then managed to put away.

⁓

"Mr. Ventura—"

He turned on the passage stairs and playfully ran the light over her face for a microsecond. "Miss James, do you think we've come far enough—and been through enough—that you might call me by my given name?"

"All right. And you may call me Johnnie."

"Thank you, Johnnie." He turned and began negotiating the stairwell again.

"Esteban," Johnnie began again rather shyly, "could I see Isabella's puppies?"

Johnnie could hear the pleasure in his voice. "Why, certainly! I would have offered to show them to you before, but I wasn't sure you really liked animals."

"I like Isabella and Ferdinand. But I don't really know much about animals," Johnnie said honestly. "I've never been around them."

"I think that's sad," Esteban murmured. "Animals have been one of the greatest pleasures of my life. I imagine you'd like to have a pet, if you were around them enough to grow comfortable with them."

"Hmm. You prefer dogs, I assume."

"Yes, I do," Esteban replied with a mischievous shading to his voice. "I also prefer cats and horses. I'm partial to sheep and goats. And lizards. I really like birds. Monkeys are a particular favorite of mine—"

"I think I understand," Johnnie laughed. "You prefer some animals in general, and all of them in particular."

"Exactly," Esteban genially agreed.

They went outside, blinking rapidly in the sunny afternoon. "Isabella lives in the gatehouse," he told Johnnie, pointing toward the far end of the castle grounds. "Would you like to walk around the outside passageways instead of through the gardens?"

"Yes, I would," Johnnie replied enthusiastically. "So far I've only seen Ventura Tower, the keep, and the chapel."

Esteban glanced at her reproachfully. "And all of the passageways in between?"

Johnnie replied spiritedly, "No, not all of them, but about forty or fifty of them, it seems like. And you don't have to tell me again not to wander around in the passages. That night cured me. If it hadn't been for Ferdinand—" She shook her head regretfully.

"There are ghosts," Esteban said, only half jokingly.

"There are no ghosts," Johnnie retorted.

"There are ghost stories."

"Are they scary?"

"Yes. But I won't tell you any of them until one dark night, stormy, black . . ." Esteban whispered, embellishing his words with lavish gestures, "when the wind is howling and the fire begins to die down to sullen red embers. . . ."

"It's a date," Johnnie teased.

But evidently Esteban wasn't familiar with this particular colloquialism and stared at her in surprise. Then he smiled. "It's a date," he repeated owlishly. "It's a date."

Johnnie tried to think of some way to extricate herself from this silly situation—after all, she'd just inadvertently demanded a date from her boss—but Esteban dismissed the subject.

"These are some of the original quarters built by my ancestor," he told her, pointing to two doorways on their left. "Do you see these narrow passageways? There are three more rooms behind these, built as a part of the castle walls. At the back is a door that leads to the east side of the castle grounds—the narrow strip above the cliffs."

"Most all of the structures are merely extensions of the castle walls, aren't they?" Johnnie mused.

"Yes, they are," Esteban said with surprise. "The towers and the keep, of course, are separate structures, but the quarters, the stables, the chapel, and the garrison are connected to the original outside walls."

"Fascinating. And a most impressive plan for defending a fortress without weakening the outside walls," Johnnie murmured, staring down at the forbidding darkness of the passageway between the quarters.

"The southern part of the castle—these quarters, the south tower, the stables, and the quarters on the other side of the stables, are still in disrepair," he warned Johnnie. "They're unsafe, and I don't allow anyone to go into them at all."

"Don't worry about me," Johnnie said lightly as they continued their walk. "I have enough forbidden pathways in Ventura Tower to keep me lost for ages."

"Miss James—"

"Johnnie," she reminded him, "and I was just joking."

"You have a peculiar sense of humor, Johnnie," Esteban said with mock gravity. "Now, these are the stables, but of course I plan on eventually converting them to rooms. Down here are more quarters, exactly identical to those we just passed. You might have realized already that our offices were originally quarters like this—three wide and two deep—but I converted them to three rooms."

"Yes, I see," Johnnie said thoughtfully. "I have a question. Why did your ancestor build so many quarters? I assumed that his men lived in the garrison, and it's huge, and I know that the entire basement of the keep was the servants' quarters. Did he allow the Taíno Indians to live here?"

Esteban hesitated before anwering, and he looked away from Johnnie, around the immaculate castle grounds. "Some of them," he finally muttered.

Johnnie was curious, but Esteban seemed reluctant to answer the question, so she decided to let it drop.

But a few moments later in a low voice Esteban continued. "The women, you see. This is where the . . . Taíno women were kept. They were slaves, and my great-great-and-so-on-grandfather made them into prostitutes. He killed off all the men and young boys after they built this castle. The young women he kept as prostitutes for his men."

"That's certainly nothing for you to be ashamed of, Esteban," Johnnie said in a reassuringly practical tone. "All of us have a history, all of us have things in our past that are painful to us, and most of us have family members with problems. We may grieve for our families, but we don't have to bear their shame."

He met her eyes directly then. "I do grieve for the things he did," he admitted, "and it is hard not to feel shame. I am surprised you understand such things. Most people are impatient with the notion of longing for an honorable history."

"I think it's a noble wish," Johnnie declared, "but we can only choose our own honor." Grinning slyly at him, she went on in a lecturing tone. "It's a solid principle of accounting that without authority there is no responsibility. If you don't have authority to use the money, you have no responsibility for what happens to it. If you don't have authority to make decisions for your great-great-so-and-so's life, you have no responsibility for what he did with it."

"You are kind," Esteban said formally. "Did you, perhaps, have an ancestor who did terrible things?"

Johnnie laughed. "You should know that most Americans have no idea who their ancestors are. My family is no different. I knew my grandparents, and they told me some stories about their parents. But beyond that I have no idea. Of one thing I am certain, though. Since my ancestors were human beings, I'm sure all of them sinned." She shrugged.

"Sometimes I am happy that my family knows so much of our history," Esteban commented, "but sometimes I wish I didn't know every detail. Anyway, here is the door that leads into the south gatehouse tower." He turned to Johnnie and stepped close; although he seemed impervious to the invasion of her "personal space," Johnnie definitely felt it. Still she merely looked up at him politely.

"Isabella is, naturally, very protective of her babies," Esteban told her. "She already knows you and seems to like you, but don't speak loudly or make any sharp gestures. Talk in a soft tone—you already do that anyway—and move slowly."

"I do that, too," Johnnie joked. Then, growing more serious, she asked, "Do you think I shouldn't go in to see them? Maybe this isn't such a good idea."

"Don't be afraid," Esteban murmured, and it seemed to Johnnie that he moved even closer to her, though he didn't actually take a step. The fine hairs on Johnnie's arm rose, and unconsciously she crossed her arms and rubbed them as he went on, "Isabella will never hurt anyone who isn't overtly threatening. But we don't want to upset her, do we?"

"N-no," Johnnie said, then took a step backward. His nearness was just too disturbing.

Esteban didn't seem to notice. He turned to the heavy Norman-arched door and opened it.

"Isabella's house is nice," Johnnie said softly as they entered the ground floor of the south gatehouse tower.

Esteban had covered the flagstone floor with fresh, sweet hay. In one corner was an enormous, newly painted doghouse, with a clean blanket folded neatly on the floor. Several potted plants were grouped together by one wall, mostly ferns, along with one sizable palm. The walls were hung with old pieces of tack and some dog collars that Johnnie suspected were antiques. Across from the door they'd entered was another door that was ajar and led into the gateway, so Isabella could come and go as she pleased.

By the doghouse was a thick pallet made of several horse blankets. Isabella and the puppies were lying there, and as Johnnie and Esteban came in, Isabella raised her head. She looked suspiciously at Johnnie for a few seconds, then visibly relaxed. Her tail thumped once, twice, and she lay back down.

"Come on, it's all right," Esteban said quietly. Six round balls of white fur lay next to Isabella.

Johnnie knelt on the pallet, watching Isabella closely, but she seemed unconcerned as Johnnie reached out and gently poked one tiny ball of fur. It unrolled a little—Johnnie was reminded of little English hedgehogs—and wiggled. "Could I pick it up?" she asked Esteban.

"Sure." He crouched on the floor by the pallet and petted Isabella, whose eyes slowly closed.

The puppies were only a week old, so their eyes weren't opened yet. The little one that Johnnie picked up and held close was asleep, and though he grunted a tiny little "hmph" when Johnnie picked him up, he immediately relaxed against her. "What darlings!" Johnnie whispered. "They're so cute they don't even look real! They look like little candy-store toys!"

"Not when they're grown," Esteban said affectionately, ruffling Isabella's thick fur. "I think these are the most intelligent, most loyal, and most trustworthy dogs in the world." He looked up at Johnnie and frowned. "Do you know what kind of dogs Isabella and Ferdinand are?"

"No, I don't. I've always meant to ask you."

"They're Great Pyrenees," Esteban explained. "An ancient breed. They are believed to have originated in Central Asia or Siberia. Migrating Germanic tribes brought them to Europe, and herders in the Pyrenees Mountains between France and Spain came to rely on them, to respect them, and to love them as part of their family. That's their secret, you know. Their herding instinct is phenomenal, and it extends to the families who own them. They make you a part of their family, and you must make them a part of yours."

Johnnie smiled. "It would seem that some of your family has a long and noble lineage, Esteban."

He looked delighted. "True. Very true. Isabella and Ferdinand come from long lines of dogs who always work hard, who protect their family and friends, and who would gladly die in order to defend those principles. What more could you ask for?"

"What more, indeed?" Johnnie agreed. Esteban was watching her speculatively, and she bent her head to kiss the tiny puppy. "You're adorable," she whispered. "I wish you were mine."

"Would you like to have one of them?" Esteban asked.

Johnnie's head snapped up, her tawny eyes lit with hope, but then her face fell. "I couldn't possibly. My apartment—" She shook her head sadly. "It would be cruel for dogs like Ferdinand and Isabella to be cooped up in that apartment." She looked up again and said ruefully, "I don't even like that apartment."

Johnnie couldn't believe she'd blurted that out. Indeed, she hadn't even really realized until she'd said it out loud that she really didn't like her new apartment much. For the last eight years, as her income had steadily increased, she had regularly upscaled her living quarters. Six months ago she had leased a spacious, airy penthouse in a fashionable part of Atlanta and had decorated it in black-and-white and glass. But it was so modern, so sleek, so angular, so . . . cold. Johnnie suddenly realized she really hated that apartment.

Esteban watched the changing expressions on her face with some amusement and some sympathy. "Well, Johnnie, I'm one of those people who believe that we shouldn't live in a place where we're unhappy. Where would you like to live?"

Johnnie stared at him in faint alarm, and her cheeks drained of all color. As soon as he'd asked the question, that stubbornly honest voice in her mind had shouted, *Here!* "I . . . I don't know," she finally said faintly.

"Then think of what you want," Esteban said prosaically, "and then ask the Lord for it. He'll give you the desires of your heart."

The desires of my heart. . . . Johnnie's mind echoed as she stared at Esteban Ventura. *My heart desires—*

Johnnie jumped up as if she'd been electrified. "Shall we go now?" she asked brightly. "I want to see your horses."

Esteban rose more slowly, a curious, almost knowing half smile on his face. "*Ciertamente*, señorita. If that is the desire of your heart, then today I have the power to grant it."

Johnnie sighed deeply. *You certainly do.*

Twelve

A cart was waiting for them in the gateway.

"It's about a mile down to the stables," Esteban explained as he helped Johnnie into the cart. "Long walk."

Looking down onto the rocky plain falling away from the castle, Johnnie asked, "Where are the stables, anyway?"

"Down there." Esteban pointed left, toward the south end of the island. "Just at the edge of the woods. There's a bridle path from here to the stables. But as I said, it is about a mile, and I thought that you might be too tired from the walk for much riding." He made a clicking sound and snapped the reins lightly. The horse started down the path, which closely followed the irregularities of the coastline. The cliffs fell away to about one hundred feet; Johnnie knew that the lowest points of the island's coastline—except for the small beach—were still about eighty feet high.

Breathing deeply of the salty air, Johnnie commented idly, "I always thought it seemed a little absurd to claim to be tired from riding a horse. After all, one does ride the horse. It looks like the horse is the one who should be tired."

Esteban laughed. "You'll see. You'll probably be more tired than Peru."

"Peru?"

"Yes, that's the name of the mare you'll be riding. You'll like her." He gave Johnnie a sidelong look. "And she'll like you."

"I hope so."

From the castle the plain sloped down gently to about the middle of the island and leveled off into pine glades, which gradually thickened into a tropical forest. Esteban had tamed some of it, cultivating an avocado grove and a mango grove and landscaping around a natural pool. He also planned to put a *pasadía* with a covered patio and a *cantina* for horseback riders and hikers. Throughout the gentle jungle were orchids, banana plants, aloe, bamboo, tamarind, and cashew trees. Coconut palms fringed the northernmost borders of the forest.

At the western end of the island the land fell sharply, and a small waterfall led into the rain forest.

"I found two ausubo trees there," Esteban told Johnnie. "I'm trying to reproduce them. So far I have two small saplings and six seedlings. Most of the rest of the rain forest is mahogany, a hardy evergreen similar to teak, and Sierra palms."

"I have one question—probably a dumb one," Johnnie said ruefully. "How can it be called a rain forest if it hardly ever rains here?"

Esteban grinned at her. "This is not a dumb question. You know that southern Puerto Rico gets very little rain? That's because most of their fronts come from the north, from the Atlantic, and are stopped by the Cordillera Central mountain range. Our weather comes from the southeast, from the Caribbean. This island, only eighteen miles south of Puerto Rico, has a definite rainy season that begins in March and goes through November." He frowned up at the unblemished sky. "It's odd that we've had so little rain this month, so few of our usual picturesque storms in the afternoons. Strange . . . I wonder . . ."

Johnnie was curious. "Wonder what?"

He shrugged carelessly. "Old tales, ancient superstitions. The Taíno Indians believed that if the weather was unusually fine during the rainy season, it was because the god of the winds,

Huracán, was inhaling deeply, and soon would pound the earth with his angry breath."

"Huracán?" Johnnie repeated. "As in 'hurricane'?"

"Yes."

"Have you listened to the radio or read a paper in the last couple of days?"

Esteban was puzzled. "As a matter of fact, I haven't."

"There's a tropical storm just off of Cape Verde. It's gathering strength," Johnnie said quietly, "and it's heading due west."

Esteban and Johnnie looked at each other, but before either could say anything, Diego and Nuria came galloping up on two dancing horses.

"Hola!" Diego called merrily.

"You're late, Esteban," Nuria cried, her eyes sparkling. "Diego and I don't wait no more." The two let the horses prance around and around the slow-moving cart as it bumped along into the trim stable yard.

"What's your hurry?" Esteban said leisurely. He stopped the cart in front of a long, low building that was made of native stone halfway up and topped with whitewashed wood. All down the length of the building the wooden sections were cut and hinged; one pair was swung open, and two horses stared out at them curiously.

"I want to go to the beach," Nuria insisted. "I want to swim and eat and be lazy in the sun!"

"Go ahead," Esteban replied as he helped Johnnie down from the cart. "We'll be along soon. Diego, don't let her drive poor Caparra mad so that she gallops right off the cliffs."

"I'll try," Diego promised.

"You two old ladies," Nuria pouted. "No offense, Miss James."

"I am an old lady," Johnnie laughed. "But Esteban might take offense."

Nuria's left eyebrow rose a tiny bit at Johnnie's easy usage of Esteban's name, but her excited expression remained the same. "You'll like Peru," she told Johnnie. "I wanted to ride her, but Diego wouldn't let me. She's much more fun than poor old Caparra!"

"She is?" Johnnie gulped. Nuria's mare looked quite spirited as she skittered around the cart, her front hooves cutting the air high up by her chest, sometimes sidling to one side or the other. Nuria handled her easily, but Johnnie wasn't so sure she wanted to try a horse that was more energetic than 'poor old Caparra.'

"If you talk about Caparra that way, Señorita Torres," Esteban said sternly, "she may find a low coconut palm to gallop beneath. And then where will be your pretty head?"

Johnnie chuckled; Esteban's English was masterful, but the syntax could be tricky.

Nuria must have thought that Johnnie was laughing at her, because she gave her a hard look but quickly turned it into a smile and tossed her long, glossy hair. "Caparra wouldn't do that to me," she declared, rubbing the mare's neck affectionately. "Hurry up, Esteban!" She cantered a little way past the wagon, stopped, and turned the horse. Then, in a breathtaking display, Caparra raised her front legs, reared up, then leaped so that both of her hind legs left the air at the same time.

"Oh!" Johnnie breathed.

With a look of triumph, Nuria turned the horse and sped away.

Grinning, Diego saluted them jauntily and followed her.

"Her horse," Johnnie sighed. "That was wonderful! Did you train her to do that?"

Esteban shrugged. "A little. But these are *Paso Finos*, which means 'fine gait.' They like to show off."

"Sounds terribly modest of you."

"No, it's true," he insisted. He pointed to the two horses as they sped across the plains toward the beach. "Look—can you see? That is a distinct gait, known as the *Paso largo*. It's the fastest. These horses also have two other natural gaits, the *Paso fino*, which is a showy, collected walk, and the *Paso corto*, which is a little faster. You don't have to teach these horses these special gaits. It comes naturally to them."

"Like showing off?" Johnnie teased.

"They do show off. You'll see."

"Esteban, I don't think I want a horse that's showing off. I just want one that will figure out how to keep me in the saddle," Johnnie fretted.

"Peru will," Esteban said confidently. "Paso Finos are smart, but they aren't sly or mischievous. They have unusually kind natures. Peru is, in many ways, one of my best horses. The other is Araña. But she just foaled, so it'll be a while before she's ridden again."

At the end of the building a set of double doors swung open. Pablo came out of the stables leading two horses.

"Buenos días, Señorita James, Señor Ventura," he greeted them. "Here is Peru and Cacique."

Esteban's stallion Cacique was a sturdy bay, with muscular quarters and tough legs. He was quite a bit larger than Peru, who was a pretty dappled gray. Even as Pablo led them just the few steps out of the stables, Johnnie was enchanted by their proud, high-stepping gait.

"Here is Peru, Johnnie," Esteban said by way of introduction as he ran his hand down the mare's soft muzzle. She whinnied softly and tossed her head. "Pablo, why don't you tell Miss James about Peru?"

Pablo looked proud that Señor Ventura entrusted this responsibility to him. "Peru is a sweet and patient girl," he told Johnnie enthusiastically. "She has the smoothest pace of all of the horses, except for maybe Araña. Peru will do anything you tell her." He looked doubtful for a moment, then forged ahead: "You won't have to hit her or kick her very hard, señorita."

"Don't worry, Pablo," Johnnie smiled. "I have no intention of insulting this horse. She's going to have to teach me to ride, you know."

"She will do that," Pablo nodded. "She even puts up with Mateo, and he lays all over her and stands up on her and hangs over to one side with both his feet in one stirrup."

"Gracious!" Johnnie laughed. "Peru won't have to worry about me trying any of that!"

"You might," Esteban said, his eyes sparkling. "Thank you, Pablo, for saddling up for us. Have you finished cleaning the stables and polishing the tack?"

"No, sir, not yet," Pablo replied. "I still have to polish Señor Diego's dress saddle."

"Don't worry about that. He won't be needing it today or tomorrow. When you finish unharnessing Iglesias and putting away the cart, you may take Jennet out for a while."

"Gracias, señor."

"De nada."

Pablo hurried back into the stables, and Esteban turned to Johnnie. "Now for your first lesson."

"I'm ready," Johnnie declared. "What do I do?"

To Johnnie's surprise—and breathless pleasure—Esteban walked around to stand close behind her, then rested his hands lightly on her hips. "Here is the whole secret, Johnnie. Keep your lower back straight but not stiff. Let your hips follow the horse's natural movement. If your hips are relaxed, your whole body will learn to flow smoothly with the horse."

He moved his hands up to brush her shoulder blades, then rest lightly on her shoulders. Johnnie gulped. "Keep your spine in a straight line, but keep your shoulders loose," he casually continued. "Don't strain them."

Now he stepped close in front of her and made a careless gesture. "That is it. And you see, it'll be easy for you, because this is your natural posture. You keep your back straight and your shoulders relaxed as you walk. You'll ride the same way, and Peru will be happy."

Johnnie's breathing was a little shallow, and her color was high, but she managed to ask, "And . . . mounting and the dismount?"

Esteban grinned mischievously. "You've seen American Western movies, haven't you?"

"Of course."

"Can you copy how they get on and off a horse?"

"I . . . think so. Why not?"

"It's as easy as it looks."

He stood by Peru, gathered her reins, and made a motion to Johnnie.

After only a moment's hesitation, she came over, stuck her left foot in the stirrup, made a little jump, and swung her right foot high.

In a moment she was sitting easily in the saddle. "I did it!" she said with real pleasure.

Esteban carelessly tossed her the reins and mounted Cacique. "How do you say it? You are a maid in the shade?"

Johnnie laughed with delight. "That's close enough!"

"Then just relax and have fun," Esteban instructed her. "Peru will do the rest."

Sure enough, Peru seemed to understand that when someone was in the saddle, she was expected to take them somewhere. Johnnie and Esteban dawdled out of the stable yard and across the plains toward the beach. With each step the horse took, Johnnie could feel herself relax as she came to understand the natural rhythm of the horse.

"It's not as jouncy as I thought it'd be," she told Esteban happily.

" 'Jouncy'? What is this word?" Esteban demanded.

"I just made it up."

Esteban gave her a playfully disapproving look. "You're teaching me bad English. It's hard enough to learn the real words, without people making up words to learn."

Johnnie grinned. "Esteban, you speak better English than I do. And I could have lied, you know, and told you that in the dictionary it's a word meaning a cross between 'bouncy' and 'jarring.' "

"You are not a good liar, Johnnie," he retorted, then scoffed. " 'Jouncy!' I wouldn't have a jouncy horse in my stables!"

"Of course you wouldn't," Johnnie said soothingly, then ran her hand slowly down Peru's neck. "Peru is graceful, and I'm thankful to learn to ride on such a gentle lady." She looked back at Esteban, who was watching her with such open appreciation that Johnnie was almost embarrassed. "Do you think we might try the Paso corto now?" she asked hesitantly.

"Yes, because it's just as I said," Esteban replied warmly, "you are a good rider."

Johnnie, mimicking Esteban, gently tapped Peru and obediently she flowed into a faster pace that somehow seemed even more fluid than the Paso fino. Johnnie was elated and felt her heart pounding in excitement. She thought she'd never been so happy, or felt so free, as at this moment; it was like a fairy tale, gliding along on a dream horse on a tropical island paradise—with a gorgeous man.

Before they reached the crown of the slope that led down to the beach, Diego and Nuria came riding back up. "Now where are you two going?" Esteban asked.

"We were coming to look for you," Diego replied. "Would you like to go to the beach to sun, Miss James? Or did you want to ride for a while?"

"I'd like to ride," she answered quickly. "Can you ride all around the island?"

"We can't go down through the rain forest yet," Esteban told her. "But we can go to the falls, then cut over to the edge of the island and ride around the perimeter."

"I'd like to do that," Johnnie decided. "If it's all right with everyone else."

"Of course," Diego said cordially.

Nuria looked stormy. "I want to swim!"

"We'll ride, then go to the beach," Esteban said indulgently. "The days are long and the sun rides high, little gatito. You'll have plenty of warm afternoon left for swimming."

Nuria looked mollified, so the four turned to ride back down the plains to the green forest horizon below.

They rode slowly and were an amiable company. Sometimes

Diego rode with Johnnie and talked to her, sometimes he and Nuria cantered around in circles and teased each other in Spanish. Esteban rode with Johnnie some, and Johnnie told him how much she was enjoying *The Honorable Imposter*. They talked about the book, the weather, poetry, the flamenco. But truth to tell, Johnnie enjoyed just riding along and drinking in the beauty of the island, and Esteban seemed to realize this and respect it; in fact, he seemed to enjoy intervals of solitude and silence himself.

They rode through the cool pine glades, the horses' hoofbeats softened by the carpet of needles. Johnnie breathed deeply of the sharp evergreen scent; it was so strong she could almost taste it on the back of her tongue. Soon some hardwood trees were intermingled with the pines, and ferns grew at the base of the trees. Johnnie began to see pale, delicate wild orchids here and there. They passed the edge of the avocado grove, but the mango grove bordered it on the far side and wasn't visible from the forest.

A steady consonance reached their ears, faint at first, but growing more pronounced with each step. When they finally reached the cliff where the river plunged merrily down to the rain forest below, Johnnie was surprised that the falls were no higher than about sixty feet, and not sheer, although it was a slightly steep incline. At one point the cliff was undercut, and a curtain of water rushed headlong down into the pools below. But on either side of the water curtain, the falls wound onto rocks and through gullies. The differing velocities of the water made the sound harmonic, with the sheer falls a baritone and the gentle rushing sides a lyric contralto.

Esteban rode Cacique close beside her. "We call it *Cascada del Cante Jondo*."

" 'Waterfall of the Deep Song,' " Johnnie translated softly. "From the *cante jondo* of the flamenco . . . it's splendid. It fits."

"I didn't think you knew any Spanish," Esteban said with mild accusation.

Johnnie shrugged. "I don't know much. I've been studying

it, but my pronunciation is so atrocious I would never try to speak it. So I just read the dictionary."

"You're a surprising woman and an interesting one, Johnnie. I think you and I—"

Nuria came galloping up, chattering in Spanish, and Johnnie could have cheerfully strangled her.

Esteban nodded and said something to Nuria, then turned to Johnnie, evidently having forgotten his last provocative words. "We have to ride over there"—he pointed to their left—"to skirt the island. Are you ready?"

"Yes," Johnnie said a little sullenly. *I suppose those words are forever lost in the Waterfall of the Deep Song . . . blast that girl!*

"Let's race," Nuria baited Esteban after he gently reminded her to speak English.

"Cacique can beat all of the rest of the horses, gatito. Race Diego. Hidalgo is about an even match for Caparra."

Without replying, Nuria wheeled Caparra and rode past Diego, calling out to him, and Diego took after her as if devils were chasing him.

"I don't want to ride like a hot locomotive," Johnnie said wryly, "but I would like the Paso corto again."

"That's good," Esteban said approvingly. "The Paso corto is the natural gait for covering long distances steadily and quickly. You learn fast, Johnnie."

They covered the perimeter of the island in three hours. As they skirted the rain forest, Johnnie couldn't see enough, and she longed to wander through it. She'd never before seen a real rain forest.

Somber and primeval, the borders of it were abrupt. Only a few feet beyond the sudden barrier of sky-high palms and mahogany trees and gigantic ferns the verdant shadows darkened to mysterious dark purples and indigos.

Diego rode beside her. "We have seen Puerto Rican parrots in there," he said softly, staring at the secret depths only a few yards from the brightly benevolent afternoon sun. "They are almost extinct. There are ugly iguanas; Esteban once found one that was three feet long. A colony of mongooses live in one place. And boa constrictors. We have seen two that were close to six feet in length."

Johnnie shivered. "Sounds dangerous."

"Not really. None of the animals are dangerous to humans. Not even Esteban's lynxes."

"What? Lynxes don't live in the rain forest!"

Diego smiled. "Two of them do. They belong to Esteban. Their names are Miño—she's the female—and Metido. Some fool woman in Madrid gave them to him. I guess she must have spent thousands of *pesetas* tracking down a male kit and a female kit of different bloodlines."

"Some . . . fool . . . woman?" Johnnie repeated with difficulty. "Were they . . . that is, did Esteban—"

Diego eyed her knowingly. "No, Señorita James. She was just a fan. He'd never met her until she gave him Miño and Metido. It was on the television, and the City of Madrid gave him some kind of medal." He shrugged. "She was an *alcade*'s wife, and she was very much in love with Esteban."

Johnnie stared at him, shocked at this matter-of-fact revelation. Diego didn't seem to notice; he merely smiled at her politely.

I don't know if it's a difference in translation or a difference in culture, Johnnie reflected. *Their world is so different from mine. It seems that their blood is warmer, their hearts beat more slowly, their outlook is kinder, their soul is much more attuned to poetry and song and dance and art . . .*

And love. . . .

Thirteen

*A**repas*** was a sweet fried bread, originating on the Spanish island of Culebra, where Dolores Rosado had grown up. She'd graciously offered to make it for the four of them when she'd learned that they were planning a picnic on Sunday. Johnnie loved it; she found that it gave the wholesome satisfaction of bread along with a delicious sugared crunchiness. When they had passed the mango grove, Esteban had reached up while still mounted and easily picked six fat mangoes. Johnnie had tried mangoes from American supermarkets and had found them to be stringy and tasteless. Fresh-picked mangoes, sun-warmed and sweet, were heavenly. She ate two of them and two sizable pieces of arepas.

She had declined to swim—mainly because she hadn't brought a bathing suit—and was prepared to find a stump or a rock in the shade to sit upon because she sunburned quickly and painfully. But they had stopped on the beach very close to the boathouse, and Esteban had brought out blankets and towels and a soccer ball that were stored there. So Johnnie lazed on a cool cotton quilt under a stand of coconut palms, watching Nuria swim and splash around in her tiny neon-orange bikini. Diego and Esteban had stripped down to the swimming trunks they wore underneath their clothes and were playing soccer half on the beach, half in the lively surf.

The men had unsaddled the horses and left them untied. To Johnnie's surprise they didn't immediately return to the stables. Cacique and Hidalgo were wandering around behind Johnnie, always staying close, munching on tender stems of new monkey grass. Peru and Caparra ran up and down the beach, splashing wildly through the waves. Sometimes they reared and pawed the air, neighing and wheezing, just for the fun of it. Once, they even seemed to be playing soccer with Esteban and Diego. Peru chased the black-and-white ball once, and then somehow kicked it solidly with a front hoof. Esteban and Diego shouted with laughter at the frisky horse.

It seemed to Johnnie that Nuria swam entirely too far out from the beach, but then she turned easily and swam back, evidently as an exercise. When she stood up she ran up to the blanket where Johnnie sat, shaking jewel-like water droplets from her long hair. She wasn't even breathing hard. When she reached the blanket, Johnnie courteously handed her a towel.

Nuria took it, surprise on her face, and said hesitantly, "Gracias, Señorita James."

"You're welcome." Johnnie wished that she and Nuria could be—not friends, perhaps—but at least civil to each other. She had no desire to be enemies with this girl, and Nuria had definitely been more pleasant to her today.

After toweling her hair and then her stiletto-thin body, Nuria threw herself down on her back, crossed her long brown legs, and propped herself on her elbows to watch Esteban and Diego. In spite of herself, Johnnie felt a moment's envy. Nuria was lean, her stomach perfectly flat, her skin smooth and warm-colored. Johnnie felt more like the underbelly of a rather chubby fish, but she quickly stifled this and said amiably, "I understand Esteban was a champion soccer player. Did Diego play soccer too?"

Nuria shook her head with a touch of impatience. "No, Diego wouldn't play soccer, even though he was good enough. He could be a champion tennis player, which is even better, because he could have been a champion in America. But he is too lazy. He only played for not a year, and then quitted."

Johnnie didn't try to correct Nuria's English; she had only recently come to appreciate the complexities of her native language, and Nuria really didn't seem too interested in polishing her skills anyway.

Johnnie followed Nuria's line of vision to where the two men played in the sand. Esteban was holding his hands behind his back, and he kicked the ball toward Diego. It sailed far past him, bouncing in the surf, and a playful wave picked it up and began carrying it out to sea. Esteban called out in Spanish, gesturing, and Diego yelled something back to him. Then Esteban ran headlong toward his brother. Diego waited until he was close, then neatly stepped aside like a matador and gave Esteban a light push, which made him fall in the knee-deep water.

Esteban then jumped up and grabbed Diego, and Johnnie could hear them both laughing raucously. Esteban threw his arms around his brother, hugged him hard, and then kissed him on the cheek.

Johnnie's surprise must have been mirrored on her face, for Nuria said blandly, "I hear American men don't kiss each other. Not even fathers and sons."

"No, I guess they don't very much. At least not in public," Johnnie said a little lamely.

"Not in public," Nuria mocked. "Esteban says Americans hide everything they feel, as if it is shameful to have feelings."

Johnnie doubted that Esteban had said that—at least in such a critical manner—but she merely commented, "I suppose we are a little . . . reserved." She half smiled, her eyes still on the brothers. The soccer game had resumed, and it seemed that Diego had scored. Johnnie, though she knew nothing of soccer, suspected that Esteban had allowed him to.

When Nuria spoke, her voice suddenly sounded angry. "You know nothing!"

Johnnie's head snapped around. "Wh-what?"

Nuria pushed herself up to a sitting position and crossed her legs. "You think you understand Esteban so much! You think

he loves you! He does not! He's nice to you, just like he's nice
to all those stupid fans and the silly women who chased him all
over Spain, and just like he's nice to Señora Rosado and her two
silly daughters, and just like he's nice to Peru and Caparra, and
just like—''

"He's nice to you?" Johnnie said blandly.

Nuria's onyx eyes flashed. "I am the only woman Esteban
has ever loved. Can't you see that?"

Since she was managing nicely to keep her temper in check—
Johnnie found the conversation to be mildly irritating, but not
infuriating—she gave the question serious consideration. After
a long moment she answered slowly, "Yes, I think Esteban does
love you. He seems to feel a special protectiveness toward you,
and he treats you with an easy respect that only comes with being very close to someone. I would say," Johnnie finished decisively, "that he loves you very much as he would a little sister."

To Johnnie's surprise, Nuria laughed, and it wasn't a pleasant sound. "You know nothing," she repeated, now disdainfully. "Esteban has three sisters. I know their names. Do you? I
know how he treats them. Do you?" She jerked her head savagely toward the two brothers who roughhoused in the aquamarine surf. "You don't even understand how he loves his own
brother! How do you know how he feels about me?"

Johnnie felt a horrible uncertainty come over her. She
shrugged halfheartedly.

The younger woman could see it and moved in for the kill.
Leaning closer to Johnnie, Nuria warned, "He'll never love you,
Señorita James. He couldn't even if he wanted to. You are a little
mouse, a little white mouse, with a little pink nose and weak eyes
and thin skin. Your soul has no music; your heart has no passion.
You are cold." With slow, langorous movements she lay back in
her original position and stared at Diego and Esteban with a
spoiled kitten's smile on her full red mouth. "Esteban is hot-
blooded and strong. You could never have him."

Johnnie's heart was beating unevenly, and her breath caught
in her throat. Her hands were nervously clenching and flexing;

she stared down at them, her cheeks flaming. She thought of
several retorts to make to this cruel woman—some savage, some
icy, some venomous—but with an inhuman effort she swallowed
her anger and jumped up. With stiff, awkward steps she hurried
away, away from the sun-glittering beach, away from the two
golden brothers, away from the hateful woman.

She didn't look around at Esteban and Diego, but she did
register that their rowdy shouting stopped. Hurriedly she
stepped up the pace, willing herself not to run, and aimed for
the blessed shelter of some rocks just on the other side of the
boathouse. When she finally reached them and stepped around
them, she heard Esteban shout. He might have been calling her,
but the hot wind was brisk and carried the words away. She
found a depression in one of the boulders, where its flat base
almost formed a chair, and Johnnie sat down heavily.

Disciplining herself to breathe evenly and slowly, she began
to stifle the firebrand anger she felt. She decided not to play
Nuria's words over and over again in her mind, as was typical
after such a humiliating scene. She decided not to worry about
the implications of the conversation, not yet. In fact, she decided to think of something else entirely for a while. Later, when
she was alone in her room she would think about it and pray
about it. It surprised Johnnie a little that she was anxious to talk
to the Lord about it; normally she analyzed and made decisions
on difficult matters all by herself. As she was reflecting on this
curiosity, the verse in Proverbs she had read the previous night
sounded clearly in her mind: *"He that handleth a matter wisely
shall find good: and whoso trusteth in the Lord, happy is he."* Johnnie reflected ruefully that she was neither wise nor happy, so she
would do well to consult with Almighty God on this matter.

After a few moments she was calm. Rising again, she looked
around curiously.

The rocks were just a few yards from the edge of the cliff,
and cautiously Johnnie looked over the edge, surprised to see
that it wasn't really perpendicular, as all of the cliffs appeared to

be from her balcony. In fact, right by Johnnie part of the cliff sloped easily down to a small plateau with more great rocks, and then seemed to curve a bit toward the cliff wall, and then descended a little farther to another shelf. She couldn't see beyond that. But she was looking at a definite pathway. Not man-made, perhaps, but it was a perfectly suitable walk.

Esteban rounded the stand of rocks at a dead run, with Diego and Nuria close behind. He slowed down a bit but still hurried to Johnnie and grabbed her arm. "What are you doing!" he thundered, glancing over the edge of the precipice. "Are you insane?"

Gently Johnnie dislodged her arm from Esteban's firm grip. "No, I'm not. I was just wandering around, Esteban. I'm sorry if I startled everyone, but I'm really all right."

Esteban looked relieved, though his eyes still were narrowed with something akin to anger. "These cliffs are dangerous, Johnnie. I thought you had more sense than this."

"I am sorry," Johnnie said with only the slightest edge to her voice. "But really, that doesn't look too dangerous. See? It looks like a path. That's what I was looking at, Esteban."

He turned to search the fairly gentle walkway to the staggered plateaus below. After a careful scrutiny he muttered, "I've never noticed this before. It doesn't look too bad, does it?"

"Want to walk down?" Johnnie asked lightly, with only a very slight challenging glance at Nuria. But to her surprise, Nuria wasn't glowering at her and Esteban. She was staring at Diego, who was watching her as if waiting for her to say something.

"Why not?" Esteban replied. "We might get no farther than that second little shelf"—he grinned at Johnnie mischievously—"but the view should be good!"

"I don't think you should, Esteban," Diego said uneasily. "Or you, Miss James. You don't have good shoes for walking."

Johnnie shrugged. "It's only a couple hundred feet. And the ground looks pretty solid. Some of it's even grassy."

"It'll be slippery," Diego insisted. "Esteban, I don't think—"

"No, let's go," Nuria suddenly said, and Diego looked surprised. "Maybe we'll find a cave with some of old Roberto Ventura's treasure!" She hooked her arm in Diego's and pulled. "Come, gato *pequeño*."

Esteban had already taken a few steps down the path. He turned and offered his hand to Johnnie, for the first step—right off the edge of the cliff—was about eight inches down. She took his hand and savored the rough strength of it, the heat, the security of it. Nuria's hurtful words were kept safely at bay.

After Johnnie got her footing, she and Esteban continued on while Diego and Nuria negotiated the first step. Esteban asked her in a low voice, "Are you upset about something?"

With determination Johnnie answered, "No, not at all. It's been a wonderful, magical day, and nothing can spoil it."

He searched her face. Johnnie met his penetrating gaze squarely, hoping that no trace of the turmoil she had felt, but was holding strictly in check, showed. Esteban looked up at the sky and asked casually, "You are sure?"

"Yes, quite sure."

Esteban nodded and walked a little ahead. They reached the first plateau, and he stood on tiptoe to stare over the rocks that lined the cliff side of the path. "Do you know, it looks from here as if you might be able to go over there . . . is that a cave? If it is, it must be a big one. But it might just be shadows."

"Are there many caves in the cliffs?" Johnnie asked.

"Yes, many. No one really knows how many entrances there are to them. I found one on the other side of the beach, and I had the entrance filled up with stones. I don't want anyone, or even any of the animals, wandering into a cave and getting lost."

They made their way a little farther along, and Johnnie glanced back to see Nuria and Diego walking some way behind them. Nuria was whispering in Diego's ear, gesturing furiously. Diego looked puzzled, and he shrugged.

Johnnie turned back around and let her eyes wander over the

glorious sky and the graceful sea gulls wheeling and soaring, their insistent cries bandied about by the wind. High above them Taíno Castle brooded, and Johnnie was surprised, and somehow pleased, to see a tiny outcropping from the sea tower. It was Esteban's balcony.

They reached the second plateau, and Esteban considered the rocky path below them. "We could go that way," he suggested. "It looks like it winds all the way down to the water, and we could probably get back to the beach from there. Or we could try that"—he pointed to their right—"and see if we could get over there. You see? Is that a cave, do you think?"

"It's hard to tell," Johnnie said, shading her eyes and squinting. "It might just be black rocks or shadows."

Diego walked up behind them. "This is too much like work to me, brother. To you this is fun, Miss James?"

"I—"

Johnnie's words were cut off by a shrill scream. Diego turned, and Johnnie could see Nuria behind him, sprawled awkwardly at the base of a rock. "Esteban, help me!" she cried plaintively. "My ankle—my back—"

She was halfway lying on a sharp rock. Esteban flew to her, knelt down, and gently lifted her upper torso. Diego knelt by her other side, his face twisted with as much pain as Nuria seemed to feel. "What is it?" Diego demanded, his voice tinged with fear. "What is it, Nuria? What hurts?"

Nuria clung to Esteban, throwing her slender arms around his neck and leaning on his chest. "Oh, Esteban, my ankle! It hurts, it really hurts!"

"Let me see, gatito," he murmured, gently trying to pull Nuria's arms away.

"No, no!" she wailed. "Diego, my ankle!"

Johnnie stood over the three, watching helplessly. At first she had coldly thought that Nuria was pulling a highly theatrical stunt in order to get Esteban's attention. But now she could see that Nuria's slender ankle was twisted at an awkward angle, not so badly that it looked broken, but badly enough for a sprain.

Diego was running sensitive fingers over her ankle and foot, while Esteban had given up on trying to disentangle himself from Nuria's embrace. She was crying now, and her face was distorted with pain.

Diego seemed grim. He looked up and said something softly to Esteban in Spanish.

Esteban whispered to Nuria, and her bowed head nodded slightly. Esteban shifted, sliding one hand under her knees and the other under her back, and then he stood, holding her close. She nodded again, and now her fingers caressed the back of his neck. Easily Esteban started back up the path. Diego trotted alongside him, awkwardly stroking Nuria's hair and murmuring a soothing monologue in Spanish.

Johnnie, forgotten and forlorn, followed behind them.

Nuria's head slowly relaxed, coming backward just a little, just enough for her to look past the bulging muscles of Esteban's arm.

She stared at Johnnie with tear-stained eyes, then smiled.

Fourteen

As soon as they climbed back up onto the plain, Esteban headed toward the boathouse, still carrying Nuria. "Johnnie, would you please go get Nuria's things and bring them to the boat?" he asked over his shoulder. Diego was so distraught he hardly seemed to know where he was going as he stumbled along beside Esteban, talking softly to Nuria.

"Of course," Johnnie answered and ran to the cotton quilt where Nuria's bag and clothing lay. Quickly gathering up all of her things, Johnnie hurried back to the boathouse. Diego and Nuria were evidently already below. The yacht's engines were purring, and Esteban was untying the moorings.

"Thank you. We're going to take her to Ponce to get her ankle X-rayed."

Johnnie nodded. "What can I do to help?"

Esteban gave her a grateful look. "It's kind of you, Johnnie. I'll come catch Peru and—"

"No. There's no need. I know you're in a big hurry, and Nuria's ankle is already swelling. Can't I just walk to the stables and find Pablo?"

Shaking his head, Esteban murmured, "It's three miles to the stables, and he's probably not there now. Then where would you be? Another mile from the castle." He considered for a few moments, then instructed Johnnie, "Don't worry about the horses. They'll wander back to the stables when they get ready. So you just go on back to the castle and find Mateo. He's probably in the keep or with Don Serralles. Leave word with him to send Pablo down to the beach with the cart to pick up the tack. Would you mind doing that?"

"No, of course not. It seems very little to do. Are you certain I can't do anything else?"

"I hate to make you walk back to the castle," Esteban said hesitantly.

Johnnie turned to leave. "I don't mind, Esteban. In fact, I'll enjoy the walk because this island is about the loveliest place I've ever seen." She turned back around and added confidently, "Be careful. And don't worry. I'll take care of everything."

He smiled a little. "I believe you will, and I thank you."

As Johnnie started up the long hill toward the castle, she watched the yacht as it knifed through the glassy sea. *"Vaya con Dios,"* she whispered and was surprised to find that she meant it for all of them—Esteban, Diego, and even Nuria—in spirit and in truth.

It took her two hours to walk to the castle. Though the grade leading up to it was gentle, it was still uphill. Johnnie exercised regularly and was in good shape. Actually she enjoyed the walk, though she was terribly hot and thirsty when she finally made it through the great castle gates, feeling a little like Jack entering the beanstalk giant's house.

Pablo and Mateo were playing soccer on the bailey, and a saddled horse was tethered to the iron ring at the garden walkway, Johnnie was relieved to see. She wanted more than anything to make sure that she attended to the matters Esteban had entrusted her with, and then to have a long, refreshing bath.

She told the boys what had happened and instructed Pablo about the horses and saddles. Hesitantly she asked Mateo if he would mind bringing a pitcher of ice water and some fruit juice to her room. He was chattering "Sí, señorita" before she finished her sentence. Pablo jumped on his horse and galloped off as wildly as if it were a desperate matter of life and death, and

Mateo ran toward the keep with equal enthusiasm. Johnnie trudged wearily to Ventura Tower.

After drinking thirstily of the warm tap water, she ran a bath. Soon after she'd sunk gratefully into it, she fell asleep, but was awakened only a few minutes later by tapping at her door. Groggily she tried to get up, but she could hear Mateo's reedy little-boy voice shouting, "I will leave this outside your door, señorita!"

"Thank you!" she managed to call back, though it took an enormous effort. Johnnie couldn't remember ever being this tired.

After her bath she retrieved the tray outside her door. It held a pitcher of water, a bucket of ice, and a pitcher of Mrs. Rosado's special fruit drink made of mango, papaya, and cherry juice. Mateo had also added a basket of *arepas* and a rather sticky-looking chocolate bar, which Johnnie suspected came from his pocket. Instead of the flower that Mrs. Rosado always included on her trays, Mateo had laid a delicate white conical seashell on her linen napkin.

Johnnie was delighted and thought that she had probably never received a more precious gift. She went to sleep holding it in her hand.

Monday morning she awoke with a start, precisely at six o'clock, though she hadn't set her alarm. In fact, she had fallen asleep on top of the covers, in her terry cloth bathrobe. Sometime during the night she'd burrowed into the cool sheets and light coverlet. She smiled. She must have been taking care even in her sleep because Mateo's seashell was carefully laid on top of the pillow beside her.

As she readied for work, she hummed and talked to herself, as was her habit. Mrs. Rosado brought breakfast, and they exchanged polite good-mornings, but Johnnie didn't question her about Nuria. She was certain that she'd see Esteban first thing, and he would tell her everything.

She was wrong.

After working through the morning and through lunch

without seeing a soul, or even hearing anything on the grounds, Johnnie decided she'd better go over to the keep and eat something—and ask about Esteban. And Nuria and Diego, of course. But even as she was gathering up her briefcase, Antonio Serralles stuck his head in her door.

"Am I interrupting?" he asked jovially. "I hope so. It's one-thirty, and I happen to know you haven't eaten yet. Do you have time to lunch with a boring old man?"

"If I knew one, I probably wouldn't have time to have lunch with him," Johnnie answered pertly, coming to take Serralles' arm. "Are you buying?"

"No, Esteban is," Serralles said with satisfaction. "He can afford it. You know that, eh? Esteban has been smart with his money, hasn't he?" He squeezed her arm as he led her out into the gardens.

"You know that I won't discuss his financial affairs, you scoundrel."

Serralles sniffed. "I know it anyway. I know everything," he intoned, glancing at Johnnie intently.

"Do you? Then perhaps you know how Miss Torres is today?" she asked politely.

"Her ankle is not broken. A mild sprain only. No ligaments torn."

"That's wonderful news."

"The way she caterpillars, you would think she had lost a limb," Serralles said scathingly.

Johnnie grinned but managed to say blandly, "I believe the word is 'caterwauls,' Mr. Serralles. And I guess it was painful."

"You're so sympathetic toward her," Serralles observed. "How generous of you."

"Just keeping an eye out for my client's investments," Johnnie said mischievously. "If she had ligament damage, it would be months before she could dance again."

"You'd better keep both eyes on that investment," Don Serralles grumbled. "Don't let her sneak around behind you."

Johnnie glimpsed the entrance to the chapel on their left and reflected jubilantly, *What do I care what Nuria Cristina de la Torres says or thinks about me? I am a child of the King!*

It was such a pleasant surprise to Johnnie that she could view the ugly scene with Nuria yesterday so lightly, that she laughed. "One thing about Miss Torres: She doesn't say bad things about me behind my back!"

He eyed her knowingly. "So, she says them in front of your back, sí?"

"Something like that!"

Serralles nodded, then scowled up at the seamless azure sky. "It is not good, this sky. I ought to go back to San Juan. I miss the rain."

"I think the weather has been marvelous. Luscious!" Johnnie declared.

Still Serralles frowned. "Today we eat in the keep. Maybe if we don't stay outside, it will rain."

"Ah, so Huracán won't see us and will stop taking his deep breath?" Johnnie teased.

Serralles shrugged. "In 1989 I was minding the island and the castle for Esteban. I came every week, sometimes twice a week, even though nothing was here except iguanas and frogs. In September of that year we had the usual weather in San Juan, but here on Taíno it was sunny and hotter than July." He shook his head sadly. "On September the eighteenth, Hurricane Hugo struck."

"Mr. Serralles, don't tell me you believe in the angry god of the winds," Johnnie scoffed.

Idly he ran his eyes over the outline of the fortress above them. "Did Esteban tell you that his ancestor, Roberto Diego Ventura, recorded a similar event—cessation of rain, followed by a devastating hurricane—in 1582?"

"No."

"Did he tell you about the *coquí*?"

"The what?"

"The little tree frogs that sing all the time," Serralles said, waving one blue-veined hand in an all-encompassing motion around the gardens. "They are called coquí. It is said that the tones they make are a perfect seventh."

"Oh, really? How interesting."

"It is also said that just before Huracán blasts out his breath, the coquí cry instead of laugh."

"Ah," Johnnie said indulgently. "And how does one tell if the coquí are crying instead of laughing?"

The old man shrugged. "The Arawak legend says that only the wise and pure of heart hear the coquí weep." He smiled at her. "So perhaps, señorita, you will tell me."

Fifteen

*T*hat night Johnnie dreamed she was listening to the mellif-
luous little tree frogs, the coquí, as they sang. It seemed
their cheerful notes slowly deepened into a minor key, and then
their song turned sad, and they began to weep. Even in her sleep
Johnnie's judicious mind asserted itself, and she reminded herself that she couldn't hear the thousands of coquí in the castle
gardens when she was in her room.

Suddenly Johnnie opened her eyes and sat up. It wasn't the
sad warnings of the coquí that had invaded her sleep. It was the
sounds again, the mutterings, the rise and fall of human voices
carried in the lonely passages. Punching her pillow, Johnnie
snuggled back down under the covers and squeezed her eyes
shut.

After five minutes she got up again. The faint light of the
stars through the open windows made the room shades of indigo, and she could see well enough to throw on a pair of jeans,
a sweater, and a pair of tennis shoes.

"No nonsense about candles this time," she mumbled,
grabbing the flashlight she now always remembered to bring to
her room since that night.

As Johnnie opened her door, she noticed that the sounds
became louder, but at the same time more nebulous. They were
indistinct, fuzzy, as if Johnnie were hearing them through a

thick layer of cotton. Perhaps the men were farther away this time. Or maybe they weren't shouting now.

Or maybe it's not voices at all. . . .

The modulations seemed to be artificial and yet held the same difference in quality as human voices. But as Johnnie stood quietly outside her door, straining to hear, she was now not so certain. It could be echoes of the sea, the waves, melded and enhanced by the intricacies of the passages. Certainly it wasn't the same defined undulations made by human speech that Johnnie had heard the other night.

Did I? she asked herself cynically. *As soon as it grew quiet the other night, I thought I had been imagining things! How can I be sure I even—*

A thought struck her with the force of a baseball bat.

Usually the passages were quiet. Not just quiet, but eerily silent, echoing hollowly at any sound—a voice, footsteps— made within the halls.

Why should they be filled with the sounds of the rushing sea right now?

After considering this for a few moments, Johnnie decided that there must be a door opened somewhere in Ventura Tower, or in the connecting passages, that let in the rhythmic wave sounds, which Johnnie could now distinguish even though it was as if they were amplified and repeated.

She started to go back into her room, but had only half turned when she thought, *Wait a minute . . . how could it be this loud? On my balcony I stand right out over the surf, and it's barely an audible thumping and booming. . . . How could it be so loud two hundred feet above the sea?*

Even before Johnnie had finished forming the question, she knew the answer. There must be a tunnel or passageway that went all the way down to the sea, and somewhere between here and there a door, or maybe even several doors, were open.

That makes sense, she decided, still hesitating at the entrance to her room. *What I'm hearing does sound like a reverberation, or echoes of echoes. A long series of passages might have that mag-nifying effect on the waves. . . .*

Still Johnnie was not satisfied. She was curious, but she was certainly not going to try to negotiate the passages again. Ferdinand might not show up to save her tonight, and she had no desire to spend the night wandering . . . haunted . . . like the little winerunner. . . .

Johnnie shook herself out of this half trance and with mea-sured gestures stepped into the hallway, closed the door behind her, and switched on the flashlight.

"I know the way downstairs and out of the tower, at least," she announced, though her words seemed curiously muffled as they were overlaid by the murmurings in the passages. "I'll just go downstairs and . . . look around."

Exactly what this would accomplish, Johnnie hadn't the faintest idea, but she was dressed and wide awake, so she went.

Johnnie knew the way to the exterior passageway very well. She could probably have gone with her eyes closed. But she was nervous and unaccountably jumpy and clasped the flashlight tightly in a slightly clammy hand. She kept jerking her head around, straining to see something she thought was behind her. The sounds surrounding her were not menacing. They were cer-tainly coming from a distance. But because they were so vague and ill-defined, they were deceitful. It was easy for Johnnie to imagine some sound, some artificial resonance, some sly noise, some whisper or hiss . . . maybe something sliding along the pas-sage behind her . . . or was that a step, a furtive shuffling, only a microsecond behind her own step on the stairs? Somewhere back there—in the dark, where no matter how hard she tried she could see nothing except blackness?

Or was it close . . . just behind her, perhaps . . . only a step behind her. . . .

Johnnie reached the outside door, fumbled with the heavy iron handle, and almost sobbed. After several seconds' desperate rattling she finally remembered to push it vertically, and she heard the bolt *snick*. Bursting through, she pushed hard on the heavy, well-balanced door to shut it, then leaned against it and swallowed deep draughts of air.

"Johnnie!"

She jumped, her feet literally leaving the ground, and screamed, then struck out with the flashlight.

The blow was stopped. Her wrist was instantly enclosed in an iron vise. "Johnnie, please don't do that," Esteban said mildly.

Like a deflated balloon, Johnnie sagged. "Oh . . . it's you, Esteban," she gulped. He released her wrist, and unconsciously Johnnie rubbed it. The flashlight was still on, and the rod of light made peculiar circles in the air as she torqued her arm back and forth.

Esteban looked rueful. "I'm sorry if I hurt you. I didn't mean to."

Abruptly Johnnie stopped rubbing her wrist. "Yes, a . . . a true gentleman would have . . . let himself get brained," she joked shakily.

" 'Brained'?" he repeated, bewildered. "What is—never mind." Reaching over, he calmly switched off the flashlight. The light was trembling. "Would you mind telling me what you're doing, Johnnie?"

"Um . . . I . . . I came out for a walk," Johnnie stammered nervously.

"It's three-thirty in the morning," he blandly informed her.

"I couldn't sleep."

"Why not?"

Johnnie sighed and answered almost inaudibly, "Noises. I heard . . . sounds and . . . noises. Woke me up." She bowed her head and saw the white blur behind Esteban for the first time. "Good evening, Isabella," she said faintly, holding out her hand. The dog's cold, wet nose touched it lightly in greeting, and Johnnie knelt down to pet her and then hug her desperately. The dignified dog endured it stoically.

Esteban crossed his arms and watched. He stood like that

for a long time, watching Johnnie and Isabella without saying anything.

Finally, when Johnnie stood up, Esteban moved close to her side. "Would you still like to walk?" he asked politely, as if they were in the park on a Sunday afternoon.

"Yes . . . yes, I think so."

"May I walk with you?"

"Y-yes, please do."

Esteban took her arm. Johnnie shivered, but he seemed not to notice as he took measured steps to accommodate Johnnie's shorter stride, leading her into the gardens. Isabella followed them.

The half-moon was luminous, the night sultry. They walked for several minutes. Johnnie let Esteban lead her, unquestioningly walking with him this way and that way along the narrow iron-brick paths that looked like a shiny black satin ribbon under the mellow gleam of the moon.

Finally Esteban stated evenly, "You heard noises, and they frightened you."

"No," Johnnie replied quickly. "The noises—sounds—didn't frighten me. The noises in the passages and on the stairs frightened me."

Esteban nodded and squeezed her arm ever so lightly. "Ah. I see. The *noises* didn't frighten you, but the *noises* frightened you."

"Mmm. I think I'll begin again," Johnnie said good-naturedly. She was recovering quickly. Walking in this fragrant garden in the moonlight with Esteban Ventura was definitely having a bracing effect on her. Certainly not a calming effect. She smelled everything—the dirt, the flowers, the green things, Esteban's outdoorsy scent of cologne—and heard the chatter of the coquí and saw the surreal detail of a landscape colored only in shades of gray, lit by sterile moonlight.

She explained, "I woke up because there was a sort of . . . roaring in the passages. It's unusual, you know. Of course you know, don't you; your rooms are in a sea tower, too. Anyway, I just got up and walked out in the passage."

"But . . . never mind, just tell me the whole story."

Shrugging, she continued, "I heard this . . . these . . . sounds, these echoes, so I decided to walk downstairs, to come outside and look around."

For a long time he was silent. Then he asked in a carefully controlled voice, "And so what frightened you so much, Johnnie?"

She looked away and murmured, "I don't know. Nothing. My imagination, I guess."

"You heard something else. Something besides just the roar of the sea. Voices, maybe?" he asked quietly.

Her head jerked around. "What? Voices? You hear them, too?"

Esteban sighed and stopped on the path. They were standing in an open space, and he turned her so that they were facing each other. Clasping her upper arms gently, he smiled. "No, Johnnie, I don't hear voices."

She tried to step back and pressed her cold hands to her cheeks. They were hot. But he moved lightly with her, keeping his hold on her arms. Johnnie could hardly breathe.

In a kind voice he went on. "I'm sorry, Johnnie, I didn't mean to tease you. What I'm trying to say is that you're not the first person to think . . . that is, to hear voices in this castle at night. Has Mrs. Rosado or Rita spoken to you, by any chance?"

"What do you mean?"

"Never mind," he amended hastily. "There's no need to talk about this tonight."

With a deft movement Johnnie pulled her arms free and stepped away from him. In a precise voice she declared, "Esteban, I am not a child. Neither am I delusional. I merely woke up because of the roaring in the passages, then felt wide awake and decided to come downstairs for some fresh air or to take a short walk. That's all."

"But, Johnnie," he said gently, "there are two things wrong with this."

"Oh yes?"

"Yes. One is that there is no sound of the sea in the passages. For eight years they've been silent. That's when I found the entrances that lead down into the caves and had them walled up. With native rock and stone and a retaining wall six feet thick."

Johnnie's defiant stance softened a little. "I was afraid of that."

Again Esteban stepped close to her and reached out to take both of her hands. "The other is that you were scared, Johnnie. Really scared. This is not like you. You are a little—"

"Weird?" Johnnie suggested dryly.

"I was going to say 'high-strung,'" Esteban demurred. "But to see you so badly frightened like that—" His voice became deeper, richer, and Johnnie stared at him wordlessly.

"It was nothing," she whispered.

The silence grew long and tense, and Esteban's grip on her hands grew tighter. Then abruptly he grinned and dropped her hands. The spell was broken.

"We must learn to compromise," he said blithely. "First you tell me it is something, and I insist it's nothing. Now I'm saying there is something, and you decide it's nothing."

Her fingers were still trembling a little, and on her fingertips she could still feel Esteban's warmth. He gestured back toward Ventura Tower. "Do you want to go back now?"

"I suppose so," Johnnie said diffidently.

He mistook her reluctance to leave him for fear of walking back to her room by herself. "Would you like for me to walk you to your door?"

Her heart did a double beat. "Yes, I think so. Would you mind?"

"Not at all." He threaded her hand through his arm again, and they returned to Ventura Tower. At the entrance to the stairwell he held out his hand for the flashlight. "May I?"

"Thank you," Johnnie said politely, handing it to him. He went first, and they made their way through the passages and two stairways to the third floor.

The silence was remarkable and seemed to roar in Johnnie's ears much more insistently than the echoes she had heard before.

Esteban said nothing, though he cast one anxious look at her as he opened the last door to the hallway leading to Johnnie's room.

It was quiet, so quiet. The only sounds were their breathing and their footsteps. Johnnie noticed rather dully that Isabella made no sound; she neither panted nor made padding sounds when she walked.

When they reached Johnnie's door, Esteban opened it and without hesitation went inside to shine the light meticulously all around the room, for Johnnie's sake, she suspected. Then he threw the flashlight on the bed and lit the six candles in the candelabra on the night table.

Suddenly the candles hissed, and the flames faltered. "What's that?" Esteban muttered.

A low, insistent tone sounded in the hallway.

He hurried to the door, pushing Johnnie behind him, but she stepped out into the hallway after him.

Isabella stood six feet down the hall from Johnnie's door. The hackles on her back were stiff and spiky. Her head hung low in a threatening stance. She was growling, a low, continuous gravel in her throat that was unmistakably a warning.

Esteban and Johnnie looked past her, down the passageway.

It was empty. Isabella still growled and took one low-slung, stalking step down the hallway.

Esteban and Johnnie were motionless, listening, their eyes straining to see anything that might be discernible to a human eye, their ears straining to hear what only Isabella could hear.

Suddenly Isabella's head came up alertly, and her ears cocked forward. After several long moments the hackles on her back smoothed down, and unconcernedly she turned around and trotted back to Esteban, taking her usual stance a few feet behind him and to his right.

Esteban and Johnnie looked at each other.

"Perhaps it was nothing," she whispered.

"Perhaps it was something," he muttered.

They stared at each other in the silence.

Then Esteban lunged forward, threw his arms around Johnnie, and pulled her breathlessly close in a hug. His face was buried in her hair, and his warm hands pressed against her back. Johnnie held him desperately, conscious of his great strength, of the heat emanating from his powerful body.

"Johnnie," he whispered hoarsely, then put his hand under her chin and lifted her face to his. He kissed her, hard, possessively, passionately, and Johnnie's head began to swim. It seemed that the kiss lasted for days, eons, or maybe only seconds. . . .

Abruptly he dropped his hands and stepped back. Johnnie could see the dark glitter of his eyes even in the shadows. "I have to go now," he said brusquely.

"Yes," she murmured, trying to calm the beat of her heart. "Yes, you'd . . . better . . . go now."

He stepped toward her, reaching for her, but with a jerk pulled away. "I've . . . I'm going now," he repeated with obvious frustration. "Good night, Johnnie."

"Good night, Esteban," she sighed.

He turned to walk away, but Johnnie couldn't keep herself from watching him. He looked like a mythical beast of the underworld, his shadow enormous and black.

He turned around and said, "Don't be afraid anymore, Johnnie. I won't let anything happen to you."

Her eyes softened, and she barely restrained herself from reaching out to him. "I know."

"I'll . . . watch over you."

"I know," she said again helplessly.

He stood, studying her, reluctant to leave. She pressed her fingers to her lips, then lifted them to him. He drew a sharp breath, then turned and was swallowed up by the darkness.

Sixteen

A knock sounded lightly on Johnnie's door. "Señorita James?" came Mrs. Rosado's cheerful voice. Through her sleepy haze, Johnnie heard her knock twice, a little louder this time.

Scrambling out of bed, Johnnie threw open the door. Mrs. Rosado was obviously trying not to stare, but she did look quite surprised. Johnnie looked at Mrs. Rosado, then down at herself and demanded, "What time is it?"

"Seven o'clock, Señorita James," Mrs. Rosado answered politely. "Time for el desayuno," she added, as if Johnnie couldn't figure out if it was seven o'clock in the morning or seven o'clock in the evening. Though Mrs. Rosado didn't say so, Johnnie guessed she looked a little disoriented. She was still wearing a V-neck pullover sweater and jeans. A tennis shoe was tumbled on top of the bedcovers.

Johnnie wheeled and almost ran to the bathroom, muttering to herself, "Goodness sakes! I haven't overslept since I was a teenager!" Almost skidding to a stop, she looked back at the housekeeper and grinned. "I feel like a teenager!"

"You look like a teenager," Mrs. Rosado sighed. "I should know, I have two of them. They sleep in very strange clothing, too." Hastily she added, "*Perdóneme*, Señorita James. I did not mean—"

"No! It's all right!" Johnnie cried from the bathroom over the sound of water rushing into the bathtub. "It is very strange of me!"

Shaking her head and *tch-tch*ing softly, Mrs. Rosado carefully arranged Johnnie's breakfast tray, picked up the tennis shoe from the bed, ruffled through the crumpled bedclothes and found the other one, then lined them up neatly just underneath. "Just like a teenager," she muttered with a smile, then left.

Johnnie James had never been so desperately hurried to get to work, and she'd never had such difficulty getting ready to go to work. First she chose a gray suit, then a black suit, then, squinting at the bright sun already glaring through the windows, chose a white suit with silver buttons. The high-necked blouse she normally wore under it was nowhere to be found. She decided to wear just the jacket buttoned up and felt deliciously daring, though the neckline was not cut low at all. Then she could only find one white shoe, and the first pair of pantyhose she put on had a run. The watch she chose had interchangeable leather straps. In the watch case she found the brown strap, the black one, the red one, but no white one. She decided to wear her silver watch, which she found in her jewelry box, entangled with the white leather strap of her other watch, so she yanked them apart and wore the one with the white strap.

Johnnie was in entirely too much of a hurry to French-braid her hair, and for some reason her hair simply refused to go into the usual quick French twist. Johnnie brushed it feverishly, willing herself to hurry. As she stared at the mirror, she suddenly really saw herself.

Her cheeks were flushed, her tawny-colored eyes sparkled, and she was half smiling. Even her hair looked more alive.

Johnnie frowned, then stuck out her tongue at the excited lady in the mirror. "You'll see him. Just calm down. Slow down. You'll see him," she told herself in her best accountant's advisory voice.

Taking her own good advice, Johnnie gathered up her things in a more collected manner and started to leave. Then, turning back around, she hurried to her closet and brought out a slim white leather clutch, dumped her lipstick, compact, and loose money in it, and went to work.

She'd been in the office about an hour when the door opened and Esteban came in. Her heart started beating just a little faster, and she dropped the pencil she was using. She hoped he didn't notice.

"Good morning, Johnnie."

"Good morning, Esteban," she said uncertainly. He sounded . . . funny.

"May I sit down?" he asked.

"Of course," she said, smiling and gesturing to the antique chair his grandfather had built.

Esteban didn't smile back. He looked just as he always did, his eyes full of impersonal warmth, his voice kind, his manner courtly. Johnnie's stomach began to hurt.

"Did you sleep?" he asked.

"A little. And you?"

"Yes, thank you. So nothing else happened last night?"

Everything happened last night! her mind furiously shouted, but Johnnie James was a disciplined woman. Mirroring Esteban's calm detachment, she replied, "No, nothing at all."

"Good. That's good," he said, showing the first microscopic hint of discomfort. His eyes roamed the room and finally came to rest on Johnnie's face.

She couldn't quite meet his eyes. She was afraid he would see everything she felt—the bewilderment, the desire, the memory of his kiss . . . the hurt. Clearing her throat, she asked, "Was there something you wished to discuss with me? Work, I mean?"

"Hmm? Work? Oh. No, no, I just wanted to make sure that you are all right this morning," Esteban responded with a little confusion. Then he seemed to recall that he was her boss because his expression became a little more focused and his voice a little more natural. "You do know that you are in no way obligated to keep any certain hours. Would you like to take the morning off? The day off?"

Now Johnnie was able to meet his eyes; she was fully in control. How long it would last she didn't know, but she would make sure that it lasted longer than Esteban's visit. "Thank you, but no, I'm fine. I prefer to keep regular business hours. And since you mention it, I want to let you know that I believe I'll be finished here by the end of the week."

His eyes flickered. Johnnie didn't have the faintest idea why—if it was pain or pleasure or merely a trick of the light. She told herself she didn't care.

"Will you?" he asked casually. "So soon?"

Johnnie gave a careless half shrug. "That all depends upon you, Esteban." She watched his startled look with perverse pleasure. "If you only want your accounting software up and running, that can be done in two more days. If you want me to train Diego on the software, that will take until Thursday. If you want training for anyone else, say, on the inventory module, that will take another day. It simply depends upon the scope of the services you desire."

Johnnie couldn't help herself. She sounded supercilious. She sounded snobbish. She wished she could take back every word, every inflection, every millisecond of the speech. But she couldn't and she knew it, so she pushed the regrets out of her mind.

Esteban rose a little quickly and walked to the door. "Thank you, I understand," he said with unfailing kindness. "Can we discuss this later, with Diego?"

"Of course," Johnnie said hastily. "Anytime. At your convenience."

"Thank you," he said again.

"You're welcome. Of course," Johnnie said again.

And that was that.

For two days they spoke to each other as if they were two strangers who had accidentally rammed into each other on the street. At night Johnnie cried pitifully. During the day she was professional, polite, efficient. Esteban came to the office twice each day, but Diego only came once, on Tuesday morning, to reclaim his old habit of sticking his head in the door and giving her a charming greeting that was both hello and good-bye.

On Wednesday night Johnnie was lying huddled in bed, willing herself not to think so much so she could go to sleep. It was difficult. Her head ached from weeping, and it seemed that she couldn't get warm.

A small rustle sounded at the door, as if someone were rubbing their hand across it.

Johnnie jumped out of bed and threw the door open. "Esteban?" she breathed.

But it was only Ferdinand. He stood in front of her door, watching her gravely, his tail barely waving. "Oh, hello, Ferdinand," she said sadly. "I guess I'm glad to see you anyway. Would you like to come in?"

Ferdinand wagged his tail a little more positively, but he refused to come into Johnnie's room. Since she couldn't bear the thought of leaving the door open, with a sigh she closed it and went back to bed. She heard the same rustling noise and realized that Ferdinand was lying down in front of the door, brushing up against it as he did.

"At least he sends Ferdinand to watch over me," Johnnie whispered weakly, only to have the tears begin again.

But slowly a thought pushed itself into her tortured mind. *Wait a minute . . . I can understand a guard dog being up wandering around the grounds all night . . . but I never asked Esteban what he was doing!*

Why was Esteban up walking around, fully clothed at three-thirty in the morning?

In fact, why was Esteban right in front of the Ventura Tower door at exactly the same moment she came bursting out?

Could it have been because . . . all the time . . . he was some-

where close . . . close to my room . . . close to me. . . ?

Suddenly the fully formed, terrible thought made Johnnie tremble, and her chest drew tight with dread.

Could it have been Esteban all the time, on the stairs, watching me, following me?

Why?

When Mrs. Rosado brought breakfast the next morning, Johnnie was already up and ready for work. She invited Mrs. Rosado in, anxious to have her café con leche. She felt disheveled, her mind was dull, her eyes felt as if they had fine grit in them, and her stomach was gnawing. Johnnie realized she had hardly eaten anything for two days.

Mrs. Rosado gave her a disapproving look. Johnnie was immaculately groomed, as usual, but it was obvious that she had slept very little, if any. "I bring you a breakfast tortilla this morning, Señorita James," she said firmly. "Please try to eat some of it. It is rich, but I think you will like it." It was a soft flour tortilla filled with scrambled eggs, chicken, ham, and cheese.

"Thank you so much, Mrs. Rosado," Johnnie said, obediently taking a bite. It really was good. She looked at the woman curiously for a moment. "Mrs. Rosado, would you tell me something?"

"Perhaps," she answered honestly, fussing with Johnnie's second cup of coffee.

"Tell me about the legend of Taíno Castle."

Straightening up and folding her hands primly in front of her apron, Mrs. Rosado raised her eyebrows. "No one has told you of this yet?"

"No."

"It is not a legend. It is a true story, and it is terrible."

"I would like to hear it," Johnnie insisted. "Won't you sit down?"

Mrs. Rosado shrugged, then perched on the edge of one of

the bench seats, her hands clasped tightly in her lap. "Roberto Diego Ventura enslaved the six hundred Taíno Indians who lived on this island. He forced the men to work, to build the castle. He forced the old women to be servants. He forced the young women to become prostitutes. He was a terrible man."

"Yes, it seems that he was," Johnnie agreed.

"He was a cruel and bloody man," Mrs. Rosado emphasized, "but never could he conquer the Arawak *cacique*—the chief, the king of the tribe. Roberto Ventura took the cacique prisoner, but he could never make him bend his knee to him or do any work. Roberto tortured him, but the cacique never gave in to him. Finally Roberto Ventura lost patience and decided to have him executed."

Mrs. Rosado drew a deep, shuddering breath. "But instead of killing him cleanly, Roberto ordered him taken down into one of the caves and then had the cacique's own tribesmen seal the entrance. The cacique never spoke a word while they were doing this. He only lay on the floor—he could no longer stand from the beatings—and watched them in silence."

"How awful!" Johnnie murmured.

"It is worse," Mrs. Rosado asserted. "Later that night everyone in the keep and both of the sea towers could hear long, moaning cries and terrible wailing, the groans and sounds of grief. The cacique, you see, knew that the caves would carry the sounds up into the castle because it was built right on top of the caves. He knew that Roberto Ventura even had tunnels going down into the caves, so he could hide his treasure there. So the king had his revenge: For four days and four nights he groaned and cursed and wailed and wept . . . and Roberto Diego Ventura had to listen to every last breath he took, until the very last one.

"Because, you see, after the tribesmen sealed up the cave with rocks, they refused to show Roberto the entrance. None of the pirates knew; to them all the cliffs looked alike, and they had been stupidly drunk the night Roberto had the cacique sealed in. Roberto killed eighteen tribesmen in four days, trying to make them tell him where the cacique was. But they never did, and they died, and *el pirata* almost went mad. And then the cacique died. About a month later, Roberto Diego Ventura went back to Spain and never returned."

"That is one of the most horrible things I've ever heard," Johnnie said grimly.

"No, señorita, it is not," Mrs. Rosado retorted as she rose and went to the door. "You have never heard the cacique wailing at night." She left, closing the door firmly behind her.

"Oh, but I have," Johnnie said softly.

The morning passed in the usual way. Johnnie worked, said hello to Diego at eight-thirty and good-bye at eight-thirty-two, exchanged chilly pleasantries with Esteban at nine-thirty, and returned to her work.

At exactly noon she stopped, picked up her briefcase, and walked to Ventura Tower. For the last two days she had been taking a break at lunchtime, even though she only drank juice or water. She had been spending the hour on her balcony.

The day was as bright as a diamond. She was surprised, when she first looked up at the sky, to see a few wispy clouds scudding along. They were the first clouds she'd seen since arriving at Taíno Island. She watched them idly and thought of a cotton candy machine she'd seen once at the fair. A shiny steel drum, turning fast, with fragile threads of spun sugar magically appearing, mysteriously growing, becoming more substantial, until it was actually real, something to touch and taste, instead of the airy almost-nothing it started out to be. . . .

Idly, dreamily, Johnnie looked down the sheer drop to the rocks below. She had found that the faraway playful geysers and spouts of the breakers against the reefs usually had a cheering effect on her.

To her surprise, a short way out from the foot of the cliffs was a small boat. Actually, it was an inflatable rubber dinghy, bright red, with fat sides, and Johnnie reflected that it seemed perilously close to the surf crashing against the jagged boulders lining the cliffs. In it were four people: a man, a woman, and two children. The man and woman and older girl were waving frantically. The man held a large white piece of cloth that he waved methodically over his head. The small child was either lying down or sitting huddled in the bottom of the boat.

Johnnie snapped to attention and tried to make sense of the scene. She could make out the people and could tell that they were calling, but there was no way for Johnnie to hear what they were saying.

As if she'd been burned, Johnnie jumped. *Stupid! White flag—distress signal!*

Straightening and pressing herself close to the railing, Johnnie waved her hands over her head slowly once, twice, three times. With hugely exaggerated gestures she pointed to herself, then down to them, shouting, "I'm coming! I'm coming down!" Of course they couldn't hear her, and Johnnie thought that her amateurish semaphores were probably just nonsense gestures to the people. But she saw that the woman and young girl stopped waving, their faces turned hopefully upward. The man made a triumphant thumbs-up sign.

Johnnie whispered, "Oh, thank you, Lord," and took off running.

Even before she reached the stairwell she'd kicked off her shoes. Her mind disdainfully clamored that she was probably overreacting, and there was really no need for such dramatics. But Johnnie remembered the tiny form huddled in the bottom of that boat and pictured the woman's and the girl's faces, turned up toward her as if in prayer.

She ran faster.

She burst into the front door of the keep. Rita and Consuela were sitting at one of the dining room tables, polishing silverware.

"Where is Esteban?" Johnnie demanded.

The young girls exchanged looks, their eyes wide, then Consuela managed to say, "He's with Señorita Torres."

"Go get him. Right now!" Johnnie ordered, breathing heavily, her eyes flashing like a tiger's.

Rita dropped a silver spoon but seemed to be frozen into immobility by Johnnie's manner and appearance. Consuela swallowed hard and stared at Johnnie.

Johnnie looked from the older girl to the younger and decided that Consuela was probably her best bet. "Consuela! Come with me. I'll speak to Mr. Ventura, but I need you to show me to Miss Torres' rooms."

"Sí, señorita," Consuela said with resignation, rising and gliding toward the back of the room.

"We must hurry," Johnnie said as calmly as she could.

Consuela's dark eyebrows flew upward, but she replied, "Sí, señorita," and quickened her pace.

As the elevator majestically rose to the fourth floor, Johnnie took a deep breath and smoothed her hair back. At least her French twist was still in place. Looking down at her clothing, she was grateful now that she'd worn the beige suit. The skirt was long, almost to her ankles, and had hundreds of tiny pleats. It wasn't the type of clothing to take a jog in, but it was certainly better than some of her skirts. Johnnie smoothed her hair again nervously. She knew she looked harried—perhaps even a little deranged—and the fact that she was running around like Chicken Little, barefoot, didn't make her feel any better.

She felt a moment's hesitation. What if Esteban despised her for interrupting him while he was . . . doing whatever he was doing with Nuria? What if he thought she was making a totally irrational scene over a fishing boat? What if he simply didn't believe her?

But even before these doubts could take hold in Johnnie's mind, her heart simply took over.

No matter what Esteban felt, or didn't feel, for her, whatever his opinion of her behavior, no matter how suspicious his actions seemed to her, no matter how much she was mistaken about this situation, Esteban Ventura would help her. With a certainty and a trust she'd never before had about anyone, Johnnie suddenly knew this. There was no deception in Esteban Ventura. This surety was as real to her as the sights and sounds surrounding her. Esteban was an honorable man, a kind man, and he would never turn away from her if she needed his help.

This jarring revelation brought scalding tears to her eyes.

"Oh, fine!" she snarled, brushing them away fiercely. She'd forgotten about Consuela, who was standing quietly by her side, her eyes riveted on the changing numbers above their heads. *Oh, well,* Johnnie thought with savage amusement, *she might as well think I'm a raving lunatic, too. . . .*

They reached the fourth floor, and Johnnie was out the doors nearly before they were opened. She was in a long, anonymous hallway, with eight doors stretching down the hall to her left and eight doors to her right. "Hurry, Consuela!" she snapped.

Consuela jumped as if Johnnie had slapped her, then started running down the left-hand hallway. She stopped at the third door and pointed to it dramatically, then stepped back for Johnnie to knock on the door. She didn't go far, though. No doubt she'd decided not to miss this scene with the crazy Senorita James for anything in the world.

Johnnie smoothed her skirt, swallowed convulsively, and knocked loudly on the door. "Esteban? It's Johnnie. I need to speak to you! It's an emergency!"

Both Johnnie and Consuela could hear an indignant outburst from Nuria, but only seconds later the door was wrenched open.

Esteban stared at her, his face creased with worry. "Yes, Johnnie? What is it?"

Behind him Johnnie could see into the suite. Nuria was reclining on a red velvet couch, dressed in yellow silk lounging pajamas. In front of the couch was a table holding a backgammon board with a half-played game and a chair on the other side of the table. The chair was overturned, lying on its side on the carpet. Nuria was screeching, "What? Johnnie? Johnnie James? How dare you, how dare you—"

Without turning around, Esteban said loudly enough to be heard, but in an even tone, "Be quiet, Nuria."

The shrieking stopped as if someone had suddenly clapped his hand over Nuria's mouth. She looked as if she'd been struck.

"What is it, Johnnie?" Esteban asked again, stepping out into the hallway.

Johnnie was so grateful, and so relieved to be able to trust his great strength, that she felt physically weak. "There's a boat at the foot of the cliffs below my balcony. I think they're in trouble."

Esteban drew in a sharp breath, looked down at Johnnie's bare feet, and wasted no time asking questions. "Diego's not here. Will you come with me?"

"Yes, I need to. There's a woman and two children on the boat."

Esteban wheeled and ran to the elevator, which was still on the fourth floor. He was at the elevator before Johnnie had even started; she was staring after him in astonishment at his speed.

"Come, Johnnie," he called. "Hurry!"

As she ran, Johnnie heard Nuria begin a tirade. "Esteban? Esteban! You are leaving me? Wait! Wait! Who's that? Consuela? You come here, you stupid girl! Someone come back here right now and tell me what's happening! Consuela!"

Consuela ran fast enough to join them on the elevator. Esteban eyed her, and she looked fearful for a minute. Then Esteban winked. Consuela blushed furiously and bowed her head, her thick mane of hair hiding her face.

Esteban turned to Johnnie. "The boat is below your balcony? Is it a big boat?"

Johnnie shook her head. "It's a rubber raft, an inflatable."

"With a motor?" Esteban demanded, his eyes narrowing.

Johnnie thought, then shook her head again.

"Not good," Esteban gritted. "Johnnie, how far out was the boat? How far out from the rocks?"

Johnnie met his eyes squarely. "I'm sorry, Esteban. I can't judge distances. I don't know."

"It's all right," he said absently. "Don't worry, you've done well, Johnnie. Very well."

Johnnie felt as proud and grateful as if she had won the Nobel Peace Prize. "Thank you," she whispered.

Esteban was deep in thought for a moment, then he gave a resigned half shrug. "I rode Cacique up here. We'll both have to ride down to the landing."

This was not nearly as unwelcome an idea to Johnnie as Esteban thought. "Fine," she managed to say.

The elevator finally reached the first floor, and Johnnie and Esteban ran out the front doors of the keep. As he burst outside he gave a piercing whistle, and Cacique came galloping right up to the steps. Esteban jumped on him, then reached down one strong hand for Johnnie. She clasped it, and effortlessly Esteban lifted her up and gently maneuvered her behind him. Instead of letting go of her hand, he pulled her arm tight around his waist. Turning his head, he instructed her, "Hold on tight. Both hands, Johnnie. We have to hurry."

Johnnie was only too glad to obey.

Seventeen

"*C*acique! *Dése prisa!*"

The vigorous horse leaped forward at Esteban's sharp command. After only two or three strides he was at a full Paso largo. The long, straight hind legs propelled the horse, with his forelegs arched and his hindquarters low. The graceful gait made an unbelievably smooth ride for Esteban and Johnnie, and Cacique never faltered, never slowed. He could, if he must, maintain the Paso largo over any rough terrain for hours.

For Johnnie, it seemed much like a sweet dream. She felt dazed, yet her senses were so sharpened that she wondered if she were suffering from some kind of shock. If she was, it was certainly pleasurable.

Clasping Esteban tightly around the waist, she marveled at the strength of his body. It was like embracing a stone pillar, a live statue that lived and breathed and radiated warmth. Her face was turned, her cheek resting against his back, and his rough denim shirt smelled of clean cotton and the sun. She could feel the deep crevice down the middle of his back, formed by the hard layers of muscle on each side. She closed her eyes and sighed.

The ride seemed to be not at all like a horse galloping. With her eyes closed, Johnnie imagined that Cacique was running in slow motion, in utter silence through a soft world of mist and clouds spun as finely and as sweetly as cotton candy, his hooves never actually touching solid ground. . . .

Esteban's shoulders tensed, and Johnnie could feel the sinews in his back straining. He was reining in Cacique, murmuring softly, "*Muy bueno*, Cacique, bueno. . . ."

The horse slowed down, straining to come to a stop. Before he did, Esteban slid off, neatly bringing Johnnie with him. Even when her feet touched the ground, she wasn't sure how he'd done it.

He was already hurrying into the boathouse, so Johnnie ran after him. He leaped into the yacht and turned to her. "Untie—"

But Johnnie was already untying the stern moorings.

"Good," he muttered, then disappeared into the pilot-house. The smooth engines started immediately. Johnnie finished untying her, and *Flamenco* backed easily out of the boat-house. As soon as Esteban was in clear water he opened up the motor, and she roared straight out to the open sea. Johnnie shaded her eyes to look anxiously ahead; they were going due north, not curving around to the east where the dinghy was floundering.

Tapping noises sounded. Above her, Esteban was knocking on the window, motioning her to come up. She scampered up the little ladder into the wheelhouse. Esteban looked somber as he explained patiently to Johnnie, "You know we have to get out to sea in this channel, and in this boat we must stay at least a mile out from the island because of the coral reefs."

"Oh no," Johnnie groaned. "I . . . I'm not sure, but I don't think they were a mile out. It was . . . they were—"

"I told you, don't worry, Johnnie. You've already been much smarter and done much better than anyone could." He was tending the wheel carefully because they were going so fast, but he reached out to take her hand and squeezed it reassuringly. Johnnie clasped it hard with both her own, then released it so he could manage the steering.

As soon as Esteban judged they were far enough out, he took

a hard right, and they raced along the northeastern end of the island. As they rounded the eastern promontory, they could immediately see the red dinghy and two people waving their arms. They had drifted closer to the breakers and the dangerous shoals. *Flamenco* seemed far away from the small boat.

"Mmm," Esteban growled, frowning darkly. "If I go in there, we'll scuttle. That won't help those people."

"Are you sure?" Johnnie pleaded, unable to take her eyes off the boat and the figures waving frantically to them.

"Yes, I've scuba-dived those reefs. Not right here, but it's not charted in detail, and I don't know of any lane."

"What about the *Flamenco*'s lifeboat?" Johnnie asked desperately.

With frustration Esteban replied, "Two sturdy dinghies just like that one. With no motors. We'd end up in the same situation, caught in the surf and barely able to keep a distance from the rocks, much less row away from them."

Now Johnnie could see that the man was sitting in the back of the little boat, paddling hard. It was true. He never gained anything, although he was keeping the dinghy from piling up brutally on the rocks. But how long could he keep up such strenuous work?

Johnnie looked around the main deck of the yacht helplessly, her eyes and mind frantically searching for something, anything that they could use, something to do, some way—*Dear Lord Jesus, please help us! Please save those people! Show me how, help me think. . . .*

Johnnie grabbed Esteban's arm. "Esteban! Isn't that a winch?" She pointed to the stern of the boat.

"Yes, for deep-sea fishing," he answered, puzzled.

"Is there some way to attach it to the dinghy, and then—"

"Row out to them and winch both dinghies back in!" Esteban finished the thought, his voice raised with hope. He bit his bottom lip, looked at the winch, and then looked at Johnnie. "Do you know how to work a winch?"

"No. I know nothing about them. But I have to try!"

He hesitated only a second. Then his jaw squared, and his eyes turned hard. "All right. It's going to be difficult, Johnnie, but I know you can do it." He wheeled the boat around so that the stern faced the little red dinghy struggling so far away from them. Then he flipped a toggle switch; Johnnie heard a smooth hum and a rhythmic clanking sound and knew he was dropping anchor. "Come on," he ordered.

He hurried down the ladder first, and in spite of the gravity of the situation he courteously helped Johnnie down. Then he went to the stern of the boat.

"Here is the power switch," he told Johnnie, then flipped it. "This winch has an 8,000-pound pulling power, which means it's really powerful, Johnnie."

"Okay," she said calmly, looking over the mechanism carefully.

"When I row out, you're going to have to reel the cable out slowly so there is slack in the line," he continued, his voice soothingly confident. "Here is how you feed the line. It has three speeds: slow, medium, and fast."

"So far, so good," Johnnie muttered.

"Not really," Esteban said, his voice tight, "because I have no idea which speed to use when I'm rowing out. You'll just have to watch and judge for yourself and make adjustments."

"I have good judgment," she said coolly. "I just disguise it skillfully."

A tense smile flitted across his strong features. "I agree. Now, this is how you reverse the power and pull in the line. Slow, medium, fast."

"I understand."

"Good." Esteban popped up a locker hidden in a bench seat along the side of the deck. Pulling out a thick, folded yellow square, he pulled on an attached line and tossed it over the side of the yacht. Magically, a yellow dinghy inflated, the rounded sides instantaneously thickening. The small, flexible craft skimmed the water below, taking on the shapes of the waves that rocked it. Johnnie looked doubtfully at the thin rubber bottom.

"If . . . if you should hit a reef, wouldn't it just tear that thing to pieces?"

Esteban shrugged. He was feeding out the winch cable to attach to the mooring rope of the dinghy.

"This cable hook won't work. Would you get me a double snap swivel out of that locker, please?"

Johnnie had no idea what a double snap swivel was, but she looked in the locker and recognized it when she saw it because she could picture in her mind what Esteban needed to do. She handed it to him.

Without looking up he nimbly threaded the cable through one of the locking rings and fed out a length of the end of the cable to twist around itself and attach the ring. "Would you hand me—"

Johnnie slipped a heavy-duty wrench into his hand.

"You're smart."

"Not really."

"Yes, really." With the wrench he tightened the thick steel cable, then quickly threaded the dinghy's nylon rope through the other locking ring and began tying a complex knot. "Would you get me another rope, please?" he asked politely. Johnnie hurried to the sail locker and pulled out a neatly coiled length of nylon mooring rope.

"Will this do?"

"Yes, thank you. I'm going to tie their dinghy to this one, Johnnie," he explained carefully, "and put the two children in with me to distribute the weight. When I'm ready, I'll stand up and give you a signal. You're going to have to pull us in slowly so we won't tear the rubber mooring ring out of the dinghy. Understand?"

"Yes."

He finished the knot and tossed the line over the side. "Are you ready?"

"Yes, I'm ready," Johnnie said sturdily.

"You can do this," he said and kissed her lightly on the lips. Then he bounded down the ladder, and Johnnie handed him down a paddle. He raised it to her in a quick salute, and then sat down and began rowing.

Johnnie went to the winch, swallowed hard, and fed out the line at a slow speed. It was too fast; it fell into the sea.

"Now what?" she moaned. "He forgot to tell me what to do if 'slow' is still too fast!"

Watch, judge, make adjustments.

Steadying herself, she studied Esteban's progress—it was fast—and realized that he was taking up the slack quickly. She kept her hand right on the control but never looked at the winch. Focusing on the yellow dinghy, she watched the winch cable like it was made of threaded gold. When she began to see the line at the end of the dinghy show some tension, she fed out some more cable. After only a few moments—though to Johnnie it seemed much, much longer—she realized that if she quit thinking about it, quit trying to measure it with her eyes, and just watched both the dinghy and the cable, she could actually sense when she needed to let out some more line.

Within minutes Esteban reached the red dinghy. Leaning far over the side of his boat, he locked a massive arm around the side of the red one, then tossed one end of the yellow rope to the other dinghy. The man began tying off, first to Esteban's boat, and then to his own, while Esteban held the two dinghies together in the wild surf.

Quickly, Esteban's arms reached out, and the woman handed him the smaller child. The young girl stepped into the boat, and Esteban handed her the child. He stood up, turned to Johnnie, and pumped his arm high twice.

Johnnie took a deep breath and reversed the winch. The slack tightened, and Johnnie tensed as she watched it pull on the little red dinghy. For a long moment nothing happened; both of the boats tossed and fretted in the waves. Then it did appear to Johnnie that they were moving toward her, though it was hard to know since she had no fixed landmark by which to judge.

Yes, they were definitely moving closer. Esteban had picked

up the paddle, but Johnnie saw him drop it and lunge toward the front of the dinghy. He grabbed the steel cable about two feet above the moorings, then stood up, feeding the line through his hands. Propping one foot on the tightly inflated side, he strained backward.

For one frightening moment Johnnie thought he was signaling her to stop the winch, and her fingers touched the control, but she yanked them back as though they'd burned her. "No, it's yanking out the mooring—he's just trying to relieve some of the pressure—I hope," she added.

The man in the dinghy behind was still frantically paddling, trying to help the two boats get out of the deadly riptide.

Johnnie felt frozen, barely breathing, her eyes riveted on Esteban's straining figure. She could see by his stance that he was pulling hard on the cable, leaning backward at an impossible angle. The winch was, in effect, pulling Esteban, and by the great strength throughout his body he was pulling the two dinghies along.

Finally, as if coming out of a trance, Johnnie saw that the boats were clear of the line of frothy white breakers close to the cliffs. The winch hummed steadily. Esteban relaxed and began rowing, more to keep the boats from drifting to one side or the other than to help the forward motion.

They covered the open sea quickly. Johnnie realized she was leaning far over the stern, straining, her fingers numb and cramped on the "slow" switch.

The dinghies slid up to rock gently alongside the *Flamenco*.

Esteban climbed the ladder first, holding what Johnnie could see now was a little boy in the crook of one arm. The boy was about five years old, she judged, with fine brown hair plastered to his head, and wide, vacant blue eyes. "He's exhausted, wet, and in shock," Esteban told her as he brushed by her to take the boy below.

Johnnie leaned over the side to help the young girl aboard. About sixteen years old, Johnnie thought she might have been pretty if she weren't so horribly sunburned. She was sobbing hysterically. The wife came next, a slender blonde of about forty. Without saying a word to Johnnie, she grabbed her daughter and hustled her below.

"Howdy," the man gasped as he crawled weakly up the ladder. "I'm John Wayne Cunningham from Fort Worth, Texas." Johnnie helped him up as best she could. When he stood on the deck of the yacht, he threw two meaty arms around her and gave her a hug that would have choked a grizzly. "And, ma'am, I'm here to tell you that it's a pleasure to meet you!"

Johnnie's nose was squashed against his chest. "Thag you. Dice to beet you, too, Bister Cuddighab."

He released her, stepped back, and threw himself down on a bench seat at the side of the boat. For a long time he took great lungfuls of air, then seemed to recover some strength. He looked Johnnie up and down. "Why, you're just a little bit of a thing! And you saved our lives!"

"No, no, I didn't. Mr. Ventura did," Johnnie protested. "Anyway, I'm Johnnie James. I'm glad I could help."

"Help! You saved us, little girl!" he boomed, jumping up to shake her hand so vigorously that Johnnie was almost yanked off her feet. "Little bitty girl saved us from murderin' cutthroat pirates!"

"What?" Johnnie cried, horrified. "Pirates! But where—" Abruptly Johnnie realized that this robust man, though he seemed to feel all right, was probably in shock. She noticed for the first time that his hands were wrapped in rags, and thin, watery blood had soaked through the one on his right hand. It dripped steadily onto the polished oak deck of the *Flamenco*.

"Mr. Cunningham, you better go below now and wrap yourself in a blanket," she ordered. "I'll find a medical kit and come down to attend to your hands."

"Naw, thank you, ma'am," he drawled, lifting his hands to turn them back and forth in front of his eyes. "This here hurts like a prairie fire, but I've seen worse the days I was stringing barbed wire fencin'. I'm gonna talk to that fella first—figger out what we need to do."

Esteban came up the stairs from below and started toward Cunningham, his hand outstretched. "Mr.—"

Cunningham was lean and tough looking, and he covered the ground in two strides. He threw his arms around Esteban unselfconsciously and hugged him tightly. Esteban looked surprised but clasped the man in his arms the same way he embraced Diego.

"God was with us today, my friend," Esteban told him.

Cunningham nodded, tightened his hold on Esteban for a moment, then released him. "I reckon He was. I never paid much attention to Him in my life, but you can bet your best bull I been bendin' His ear the last two days." He eyed Esteban with bright blue eyes. "What's your name?"

"I'm Esteban Ventura, and I'm glad to meet you, sir."

"Son," John Wayne Cunningham rumbled, "you and Miss James here saved me and my family. I can't think of anything to say right now but thank you. Thank you kindly."

Esteban flashed a brilliant smile at Johnnie as he replied, "You're kindly welcome, Mr. Cunningham."

Eighteen

*M*urderin' cutthroat pirates!"

Johnnie walked into the dining room of the keep just as John Wayne Cunningham crashed a rawboned hand down on the table. The coffee cups shuddered in their saucers.

Cunningham and Esteban both hastened to their feet as Johnnie approached the table. They were sitting in the arbor, Cunningham drinking great quantities of water and also gulping down steaming café con leche. His hands were bandaged with clean gauze. He had changed into a pair of jeans—Diego's, Johnnie suspected, because Cunningham was tall and lean—and someone's denim shirt. He was also wearing a pair of stingray-skin cowboy boots, and Johnnie wondered where Esteban had scrounged those up.

"Please, sit down," Johnnie said hastily, gesturing dismissively to the two men. "I just wanted to tell you, Mr. Cunningham, that your wife and children are all asleep. We found some suitable clothing for them, and Mrs. Rosado and her two daughters are staying in the connecting suite should they wake up and need anything."

"Thank you again—and again, ma'am," Cunningham murmured.

"You're welcome, Mr. Cunningham."

"We've called the police and the Coast Guard, Johnnie, and

I told them to bring a doctor. They should be here soon," Esteban told her.

"That's good. No one seems to have sustained any serious injuries, Mr. Cunningham, but a doctor can probably give your wife and daughter something better for that sunburn, and as for Rebel—it would just be better for a doctor to have a look at him. So unless there is something else you'd like for me to do, Esteban, I'm going back to my room."

He frowned. "Won't you stay? Mr. Cunningham is explaining what happened to him and his family, and I thought you'd like to know."

"Well . . ." Johnnie glanced down at herself in embarrassment. She was still barefooted. The bottom of her long skirt was wet and smudged. Although she couldn't remember looking at herself in the mirror since the morning, she was certain that her face was dirty and her hair was wild. The sea wind had pulled loose the hairpins anchoring her French twist, and it seemed to hang dankly about her face. "I just look so . . . bedraggled," she muttered.

"And you're usually so neat," Esteban declared, his eyes sparkling.

Johnnie's head whipped up, and then she gamely smiled. "Yes, I am, aren't I? Mr. Cunningham, if you promise to overlook my appearance, I would like to hear your story."

"Ma'am, to me you look like an angel and always will," he rasped, then yanked out a chair for her. "I'd be honored if you'd sit down here at the table with me."

They settled themselves, and Esteban prepared a cup of coffee for her. Johnnie saw with curiosity that he fixed it exactly how she liked it—pouring the cream in first, then the coffee, then two spoonfuls of sugar. She wondered how he knew—and why he had cared to find out.

"Miss James, I was just tellin' Mr. Ventura here about them murderin' cutthroat pirates," Cunningham growled. "We'd been down around the Windward Islands and had moseyed on up to Nevis. Drue Ann decided she had to see the Turks and

Caicos for some reason I ain't never understood—to me all these little bitty islands are just alike. Anyways, we set out for the Mona Passage. We were putterin' along, mindin' our own business, a week out from Charlestown. I'd just throw out the anchor at night, you see, and whenever we got up we'd sail on."

His lean jaw tightened, and suddenly John Wayne Cunningham didn't look or sound so much like a big, dumb cowpoke anymore. "Those punks boarded us in the middle of the night. Just came right on my boat while me and my family were asleep. Never said a word. Just waved guns at us and motioned us to get dressed. One of them had thrown out the lifeboat and tossed in a lifesaving kit, with life jackets and blankets and food and water." He shook his head. "And an electronic distress and homing signal. But it didn't work. Just flat refused to work. Dead as a rock. Ain't that something?"

"So you've been at sea for three nights and two days?" Esteban asked incredulously. "And you had to row?"

"Yep," he replied carelessly. "And I'll tell you something, too, Mr. Ventura. I was praising God for the clear skies so I could steer due north. Knew I'd hit Puerto Rico. It was a miracle because in the Windwards and Leewards there's been a low, gray soup in the sky all week long. Day and night. Never have enjoyed a clear and clean sunrise so much in my life."

Just then the heavy doors to the keep swung open silently, and several men entered. They were speaking in Spanish, in low tones. One of them, evidently the doctor, hurried straight to the elevators. Around the great wall of greenery in the arbor came Diego, the Coast Guard Lieutenant Gregory Dyess, and Ponce Police Lieutenant Ray Leone. As Esteban and Diego were making introductions, Antonio Serralles trailed the three men into the arbor and slipped into a seat by Johnnie. He had been in San Juan for the past three days attending to business.

"I hear you've had an exciting day," Serralles murmured to Johnnie. "And I hear you're a heroine. But this didn't surprise me. I already knew it."

Johnnie took his hand and squeezed it. "I'm so glad to see

you, Mr. Serralles. I've missed you."

He looked completely surprised, and then pleased. "Have you, Miss James? Perhaps something has happened that you wish to talk to your old friend about, hmm?"

"Perhaps," Johnnie said wearily. "Maybe we can talk later?"

"Maybe," Serralles rasped, "if Lieutenant Little-Brain over there doesn't throw me in the hokey for piracy on the high seas."

"What? You can't mean Lieutenant Leone suspects you? And it's 'pokey,' " Johnnie meticulously corrected him.

"Pah! He suspects he can see past the end of his pencil nose, and he is wrong. I wish he did suspect me so he would leave Esteban and Diego alone! Maybe I'll act guilty to throw him off the smell!"

"Scent," she giggled.

Esteban was frowning at them as if they were two school-children, so they both rather guiltily sobered up. John Wayne Cunningham had told his abbreviated story to them, and Lieutenant Dyess was beginning to question him. Lieutenant Leone took out a stubby yellow pencil, licked the end of it, and began to write in a grubby notebook.

"You have a crew, Mr. Cunningham?" Lieutenant Dyess asked.

"Nope, sure didn't. I pilot the *Angelina* myself. My wife can pilot her, too."

"How many men were there?" Lieutenant Dyess asked him.

"Three. And I know you're gonna want descriptions, and I can't hardly oblige you. They wore ski masks, Lieutenant. Just plain ol' black ski masks. They were all three dressed in worn jeans, white T-shirts, and tennis shoes. Black leather gloves. One was about five-ten, the other two were shorter, about five-eight, maybe. All three average build."

"Could you see anything else? Tattoos, scars?"

Cunningham shook his head. "Nothing. Brown-skinned, but I dunno if it was because they were Hispanic or if they were just tanned. It was dark. Couldn't tell the color of their eyes."

"The guns?" Lieutenant Dyess said succinctly.

"Steyr Aug automatic assault rifles, .485 millimeter rounds, fourteen-inch suppressed barrels. Not new, but clean and kept up."

Lieutenant Leone and Lieutenant Dyess glanced uncertainly at each other.

"You can tell this in the dark?" Lieutenant Leone asked suspiciously.

Cunningham's shrewd blue eyes rested on him for several moments before he answered. "Yep. I collect guns. I have a Steyr Aug."

"Would you spell that, please?"

Cunningham patiently did so while Leone resumed writing in his little notebook.

"How did they get on your boat? Did you see another boat near?" Lieutenant Dyess asked.

"Nope. Didn't hear anything, didn't see anything. Just woke up, and they were there. I figger another boat eased up alongside, and they boarded. Then they musta waited for a little bit, until their boat took off. Maybe so we wouldn't see it—be able to identify it. Anyway, there wasn't any other boat around when we got into the lifeboat."

Dyess frowned darkly. "Did they assault you or your family in any way, Mr. Cunningham?"

"Funny thing," he murmured. "They didn't ever touch us, not one of us. Didn't even really point those rifles at us. Just motioned with them. Guess they knew there was no way I was gonna try something. Not with my wife and kids standin' right there at short range." His blustery voice deepened with grief.

"It would have been a foolish thing to do, Mr. Cunningham," Lieutenant Dyess said firmly. "And you don't strike me as a fool. I guess the thieves knew that, too, and it probably saved your life and your family's."

"Figgered that myself," Cunningham muttered, "but it don't ease my temper much."

"Your boat, she was insured, yes?" Lieutenant Leone asked brightly.

"Sure," Cunningham shrugged.

"For how much?" Leone demanded.

Cunningham stared at him for a long time before answering. Finally he answered quietly, "For what she cost me. Two million dollars."

Loud gasps sounded from everyone in the room except Esteban and John Wayne Cunningham.

"Two million dollars!" Lieutenant Leone muttered. "She is a big boat, eh?"

"Yes," John Wayne Cunningham said dryly, "she is a big boat. And I'm awful glad I have her insured to the hilt. You know why, Lieutenant?"

"I would imagine you would like to have your two million dollars back," Lieutenant Leone answered superciliously.

Cunningham's eyes narrowed to slits. "Wrong, pardner. See, Lloyd's of London is gonna have about fifty people working on this, so they won't have to give me my two million dollars back. And that's just fine with me. I'd rather they'd find the *Angelina*, and I don't care if they find her broken down in two thousand pieces. 'Cause if they find my boat, then they're gonna find the men that stole her from me. And that, Lieutenant, is worth more to me than my money."

"Of course," Leone said smoothly. "And I assure you, Mr. Cunningham, that the Ponce police will be working on this, too. We believe that these pirates have struck in these waters before." His flinty black eyes turned to Esteban. "You, Señor Ventura, acted very quickly today to save these people's lives. You are to be commended."

"No. Miss James is to be commended. She saw them. And if it hadn't been for her help, there is no way I could have brought them in."

All eyes turned to Johnnie. "The Lord was taking care of the Cunninghams, and He just put me there to help," she murmured. Johnnie was a little surprised at herself; normally she wasn't so bold in speaking of her firm belief in the Lord's protection. Esteban looked pleased, she saw, and John Wayne Cunningham smiled warmly at her.

"I'm glad He picked somebody with some good sense," Cunningham declared. "'Stead of some dummy who'd just smile and wave at the fools out fishin' in the little boat."

"Yes, it is true," Lieutenant Leone agreed with a hint of impatience. "Señorita James is to be commended, too. Now I want to do my job well, which is to find out who put you in this position in the first place, Mr. Cunningham." Relentlessly he turned back to Esteban. "Mr. Ventura, where were you Monday night?"

Esteban opened his mouth to answer, but a loud blast from John Wayne Cunningham stopped him.

"Whoa! Wait just a Texas minute! You confused, Lieutenant Leone? This here's Mr. Esteban Ventura! You remember? The same Esteban Ventura you was commendin' a while ago! He's the one who came and got the dinghy we was fixin' to get killed in!" he roared indignantly. "Don't you kinda think I woulda noticed if this big bull was one of the murderin' cutthroat pirates that stole my *Angelina*?"

But Lieutenant Leone wasn't the least bit fazed by this withering outburst. "I just would like to know what Mr. Ventura was doing Monday night."

Esteban glanced at Johnnie, whose face had drained, leaving her eyes wide and distressed. She hadn't realized until this moment what Esteban had been doing on *Monday* night.

He had been with her on Monday night. At least on Tuesday morning. At three-thirty A.M.

Johnnie felt a burning in her throat and swallowed hard. Just today, just a few hours ago, she had come to discern in her spirit that Esteban Ventura was an honorable man. He was innocent, even of hurting her; Johnnie didn't know why he had been so cool to her since that night, but she knew in her heart that there was no cruelty, no spite, no maliciousness in him. And neither was he guilty of any sort of dishonesty.

And if she told Lieutenant Leone about Monday night, she would implicate him in this piracy. At least, in Lieutenant Leone's eyes she would.

She and Esteban were still staring at each other, Johnnie with distress, Esteban with an intensity that was hard to decipher.

"—that Mr. Ventura was not one of the men who boarded your boat," Lieutenant Leone was saying to John Wayne Cunningham. "But tell me, Mr. Cunningham, from your description of these men—their dress, their refusal to speak—don't you think that they are probably working for someone? Someone very smart; someone who has connections in the island ports; someone who has access to travel plans filed with the harbor masters?"

"Yep, sure do," Cunningham growled, "and it ain't him." He jabbed a work-thickened forefinger at Esteban.

"It's all right, Mr. Cunningham," Esteban shrugged. "I suppose Lieutenant Leone is just doing his job as he sees fit. I'll answer the question, and then perhaps he will feel better able to move on in his investigation." He turned to Leone. "I was alone Monday night, after about six o'clock, which is when I finished dinner with my brother and Nuria Torres. I went to my room and went to bed. But I couldn't sleep, so I got up and walked around the castle grounds."

"Yes?" Leone said sharply. "Did you see anyone else?"

"Yes, I did," Esteban replied calmly. "Miss James. She, too, was unable to sleep and came down to go for a walk."

Again all eyes turned toward Johnnie, who sighed deeply. Suddenly, she was very tired.

"It's all right, Johnnie," Esteban said softly. "Just tell him the truth."

Johnnie's eyes widened. "But . . . do you believe me, Esteban?"

"Yes, I do," he answered quickly, while all eyes at the table went back and forth between them. "I can't understand how it happened, but I do believe you."

"Thank you," she whispered, then faced Lieutenant Leone's sharp eyes. "I heard noises Monday night. It woke me up. I went out of my room and decided to go downstairs. That's when I saw Mr. Ventura."

Leone leaned forward. "Yes? Noises? Where is your room?"

"It's in the Ventura Tower. Third floor."

"The sea tower, yes? On the cliffs?" Leone pointed, and Johnnie nodded. "Noises? What noises?" he asked eagerly.

"It . . . it sounded first like voices, echoing through the passages, I thought . . . but by the time I got dressed and went out in the hallway, I decided it must have been the sound of the sea, the waves," Johnnie answered uneasily.

"That's not possible," Diego declared. "You can't hear the sea in the passages of the sea towers. They are all sealed—all interior passageways. Miss James, are you certain that you heard something? People have thought, have imagined, in this castle—"

"I'll ask the questions," Leone interrupted him sharply. "Did you say voices, at first? Could you hear voices, Señorita James?"

Johnnie shook her head. "Not really. Not any voice I could identify, or make out words, or hear the . . . the . . . tone and timbre," she said with frustration.

Leone sat back in his chair and stared at her intently. "Since you have been here, have you ever heard anything like this before, Señorita James?"

Johnnie shifted uncomfortably in her chair and dropped her eyes. "Yes," she said in a small voice.

"When?" Leone asked like a shotgun.

"One week ago. Last Thursday night." Johnnie looked back up, but her gaze rested sadly on Esteban Ventura. "The night before you were here the last time."

Leone shot out of his chair and said to Lieutenant Dyess, "I'm going to get a search warrant."

Dyess rose more slowly and said cautiously, "I don't think

that Miss James hearing the surf in her room constitutes prob-able cause, Lieutenant Leone."

"I want to search this castle," Leone insisted.

Esteban rose, too, and faced the two lieutenants. "You don't need a search warrant, Lieutenant. I give you permission to search the castle. The entire island, if you want."

"Esteban!" Diego protested. "Don't let this *peon* scare you!"

Esteban turned to his brother and smiled. "Diego, I'm not scared. That's exactly why I'm giving him permission to search. You know we have nothing to hide. Certainly not Mr. Cun-ningham's yacht."

"Guess not," Cunningham muttered, giving Lieutenant Ray Leone a look that would have broiled a T-bone.

Lieutenant Dyess said steadily, "Ray, you know I'll support you if I can. But the next couple of days are liable to be pretty busy for us, and for your department, too." He gestured ex-pansively, a wide wave of one arm. "This place looks like it'd need a whole team and a whole day to search. I know I don't have the manpower to spare right now, and we may not have a day. In fact, I need to get back to base right now and check on the progress. I'm thinking Damien is really going to show up here."

"Who's Damien?" Cunningham demanded.

Lieutenant Dyess turned to him and replied quietly, "I for-got you've been out of communication for two days, Mr. Cun-ningham. As it turns out, you don't know how lucky you are to have gotten off the open sea. That pea soup you were talking about in the Leeward and Windward Islands? That's a low-pressure system. Behind it, pushing it along, was a tropical storm that formed off Cape Verde a few days ago and barrelled across the Atlantic. This morning it swung north, sped up, and turned into a huge, tightly formed high-pressure system."

"Oh no," Johnnie murmured, and the rest of them looked grim.

" 'Fraid so," Dyess said somberly. "They named it Hurricane Damien. And if it stays at its present course and speed, it'll hit Puerto Rico in two days."

Nineteen

O ver the mid-Atlantic near the equator, two summer winds coming from opposite directions often meet and begin a dangerous dance. First they circle each other warily, and then they sometimes speed up, twirling in a counterclockwise motion that the earth itself accentuates by its rotation.

The ocean contributes hot, moist air, and the twining winds draw it up between them. As the sea's breath rises and cools, it turns into water and adds energy to the dance, acting as a sort of steam engine, making the winds rise higher and spin faster. Condensation quickens to create thunderclouds around the core of the towering ring-shaped storm. And the steam engine becomes the eye of the hurricane.

As Coast Guard Lieutenant Gregory Dyess was speaking of it, Hurricane Damien was dawdling along at about twelve miles per hour, drawing breath from a great empty expanse of the Atlantic Ocean known only by the designation 55° longitude, 17° latitude.

This rather sterile title did not describe the turmoil that the area was in at the moment, for Hurricane Damien was strengthening each moment; its winds were now up to ninety-two miles per hour. Each step of the furious dance was drawing it closer to the Caribbean's necklace, the long chain of isles known as the Windward and the Leeward Islands. Beyond these fragile barrier islands, nestled inside the warm, sweet waters of this most tropical of seas, was the arc of tiny islands of the Lesser Antilles and the larger islands known as the Greater Antilles: Cuba, Hispaniola, Jamaica, and Puerto Rico.

ᏭᎻᎬᎾ

Regardless of the fact that a hurricane was steamrolling toward them, Johnnie James was tired. Immediately after Lieutenant Dyess and Lieutenant Leone left, she excused herself and went to her room. After her bath she slept through the remains of the evening and the night.

At five o'clock her alarm sounded, and Johnnie awoke easily. John Wayne Cunningham had asked her to attend a sunrise service in the chapel to give thanks with his family. John Wayne's daughter, Angelina, had moaned and groaned at the idea of getting up before dawn, but Johnnie understood and approved of the idea. It was a small sacrifice, a special gesture of thankfulness to the Lord. Johnnie always attended Christmas Eve Midnight Mass with a friend who was a Roman Catholic. This service, to her, was one of the most special times of her year, and she knew that a sunrise service in the small chapel of Taíno Castle would be a lifetime memory.

First Johnnie chose a lovely sky-blue linen sheath with a short matching jacket, but then recalled that the Cunninghams had only jeans and sweaters to wear. As soon as Esteban had gotten them settled in, he'd managed to get sizes from the distraught Mrs. Cunningham and then had dispatched Nuria to Ponce to buy them all two pairs of jeans, some denim work shirts, two sweaters, socks, nightclothes, and underclothes. To Johnnie's surprise Nuria had seemed eager to go and had stoutly maintained that her ankle was fine, though it was still slightly swollen.

Though Johnnie hated to admit it, Nuria had actually willingly volunteered to help the Cunninghams. She had told Mrs. Rosado, Rita, and Consuela to stop waiting on her and had gathered up all kinds of cosmetics and toiletries to give to Drue Ann and Angelina. She had also sat with five-year-old John Wayne Cunningham III, whom everyone called "Rebel." He was still listless and refused to speak, staying curled up in a little ball, sucking his thumb. But his eyes tracked people and brightened somewhat when his mother came into the room. Nuria had sat with him for an hour while his mother showered and ate.

Since the Cunninghams would be unable to dress for the service, Johnnie decided to wear jeans, a rather mannish plain white blouse, and western boots. Hurrying downstairs, she stepped outside and was struck by the change in the weather.

The nights and early mornings on Taíno were generally cool, sometimes even chilly when the crisp Caribbean breeze skipped over the tiny island. This morning the air was heavy with heat. The sky was a deep blue-black, and the brilliant stars had faded to irregular points of gray. No sign of dawn lightened the eastern horizon. Johnnie gave a small shrug and hurried to the chapel. There was always something moody and dark, a sense of brooding, when a hurricane approached. Damien must be coming nearer.

The lovely stained-glass window of the chapel glowed softly. Esteban and John Wayne Cunningham were outside, waiting for her.

"Thank you for coming, Miss James," Cunningham murmured, clasping her hands warmly in both of his. "I especially wanted you and Mr. Ventura here with me and my family."

Esteban took Johnnie's arm and held it close, to Johnnie's surprise and pleasure. "Johnnie and I are thankful that you and your family are safe, Mr. Cunningham, and honored that the Lord has given us all a refuge here."

"Y-yes, we are," Johnnie added, stammering a little at Esteban's easy entwining of their names and feelings. But she liked it very much and pressed closer to him. "And since we all seem to have been drawn together for a purpose, it seems to me we should be on a first-name basis. Please call me Johnnie."

"As you've prob'ly noticed," Cunningham drawled, "I

really like everyone to call me by my given name. 'Specially good friends."

The three entered the chapel. Drue Ann Cunningham held Rebel on her lap and had her arm around Angelina. Mrs. Rosado, Rita, and Consuela sat behind them. In the family gallery on the upper story Diego and Nuria sat close together, and Don Serralles sat behind them. The radiant light came from hundreds of votive candles that covered the chancel from the pulpit, on the two steps leading up to it, and all along the altar.

John Wayne Cunningham led the way and sat down close to his wife, speaking quietly to her. Esteban and Johnnie seated themselves on the bench just on the other side of Angelina, whose pretty brown eyes were filled with wonder at the solemn beauty of the chapel. She smiled sweetly at Johnnie, who reached over and squeezed her hand.

Drue Ann Cunningham was attractive and assertive and came to stand in front of Johnnie. "Miss James—Johnnie—would you hold Rebel for me?" she asked quietly. "He still hasn't said anything, but he watches you. He likes you."

"Why . . . why, of course," Johnnie replied, holding her arms up for the little boy. "I'd love to." Rebel nestled close to her, sighed, and stuck his thumb in his mouth. Esteban put his arm around Johnnie and caressed her lightly. Johnnie smiled at him and saw that his dark eyes glowed much like the candles in his chapel.

John Wayne and Drue Ann stood up in front of the altar. John Wayne hesitated for a few moments, searching the faces in front of him, then slid his arm around his wife and pulled her close. "Me and Drue Ann aren't Christians," he said bluntly. "I don't guess I ever said a prayer in my life until three days ago. Drue Ann's told me she's never given it much thought, either.

"Well, when you face death, you face God." He shook his head sadly. "That's when I started prayin', and I'm here to tell you that most of it was bargaining. It was hard for me, too, 'cause I ain't never been in a position where I didn't have anything to bargain with. But that's all I knew to do, and I spent the best part of two days offering God everything I could think of—including my life—if He'd just save my family.

"And He did." John Wayne Cunningham's burnt-leather face creased into an angelic smile. "And now I got a question for you, Johnnie, and you, Esteban. Seems like I owe God something, and I always pay my bills. So what do I do now?"

Esteban and Johnnie smiled at each other with delight. "May I?" Esteban asked her.

"Of course," Johnnie said, rocking Rebel back and forth a little. "I probably need to hear it again, just so I'll remember and be thankful, too."

Esteban jumped up and hurried to the Cunninghams, then took John Wayne's and Drue Ann's hands in his. Shaking his head, he told them quietly, "You don't owe God a thing. You know why? Because His Son, Jesus, already paid your bills. He died to pay for your sins, my sins, everyone's sins. So all you need to do is know this in your heart and ask Him to forgive you for your trespasses. He is already your Savior. Ask Him to come into your heart and be your Lord."

John Wayne and Drue Ann glanced at each other and nodded. Drue Ann's blue eyes filled with tears, and she asked shakily, "We kinda knew that, but we had to ask, to know. John Wayne's a methodical man. You're sure that's all we need to do?"

Esteban smiled. "I'm positive. And after we pray, you'll know it in your heart, too. Would you like for me to pray with you?"

"Sure would," Cunningham said firmly. "Seems like once again you're the man who knows what to do."

"Not I," Esteban responded, "but Jesus. He always knows what to do"—he cast a warm glance over his shoulder at Johnnie as he finished—"even when we don't quite trust Him and think we know better ourselves." He turned back to the couple and led them to the glowing altar. "I'll pray with you, and God is faithful and just to answer our prayers and lead us into righteousness."

Drue Ann dropped to her knees, crying steadily.

"Best thing I ever couldn't buy in my life," John Wayne said as he knelt beside her.

The three knelt at the altar, and Mrs. Rosado and her two daughters joined them. After a few moments Angelina burst into tears, jumped up, and ran to throw herself on her knees between her parents. Rebel sat up in Johnnie's lap and watched his family with interest. Johnnie whispered to him, "Your mother and father and sister are praying to Jesus. Do you know who Jesus is?"

He turned dull blue eyes to her face, his thumb still stuck in his mouth. Then he nodded solemnly.

"Would you like for me to pray with you right now and thank Jesus for bringing you and your mom and dad and sister here?"

Rebel considered her for a few moments, his eyes resting on her mouth. Popping his thumb out of his mouth, he reached up with a stubby forefinger and laid it lightly on Johnnie's lips. "I can say thank you to Jesus, too," he said firmly. "I already know Him. He's been talking to me."

Johnnie smiled brilliantly. "I'll bet He has, Rebel. I'll bet He's told you that He's going to keep you safe, and that He'll always watch over you and take care of you."

Rebel nodded, and his eyes were suddenly sharpened with knowledge beyond his years. "That's right. And He said He'll watch you, too, My-Johnnie." With that he tapped on Johnnie's chest, then bowed his head.

Johnnie drew in a sharp breath, then bowed her head. But it was a long moment before she could speak, and then all she could do was whisper, "Thank you, Lord Jesus."

⟨∞⟩

After about an hour of prayer, Esteban read a psalm, and the service came to an end. Diego, Nuria, and Serralles slipped out, while everyone else gathered in a loose group around Johnnie, who was still seated, holding Rebel. He seemed content to stay in her lap, but now he was alert and responding to the conversations, looking back and forth from one speaker to the other. Rita and Consuela took candle snuffers and began putting out the numerous flames.

"John Wayne, I can arrange for a limousine for you and your family from the docks to the airport," Esteban told him. "And if you'll let me know whether you plan to fly commercial or charter a plane—"

"Just one minute there, friend," Cunningham protested, raising one hand. "You runnin' us off your island?"

"Of course not," Esteban countered, crossing his massive arms in front of his chest. "You and your family honor my house and will always be welcome here. But I just assumed that since this hurricane is coming, you'd want to go back to the mainland."

John Wayne put his arm around Drue Ann's shoulders and looked down at her. She smiled and nodded. "Me and Drue Ann talked about it, and if you'll have us for a few more days, we'd like to stay. I got a lot of business to take care of here, with the *Angelina* bein' stolen and all, and us here without identification or passports or anything. But that's not the only reason. I told you, I always pay my dues." His shrewd blue eyes went up to the stained-glass window. A sultry dawn backlit it now. "Looks to me like you're going to need some help nailin' this place down."

"But I can't expect you to help me with that!" Esteban protested. "You are my guests, and I couldn't allow it."

Drue Ann Cunningham laughed. "Esteban, we already think of you as a close friend, but you don't know my husband very well. He's the most stubborn man in Texas, and there's some awful stubborn cowboys there." Her voice softened to a velvety lilt. "And besides, this place has been a blessed haven for us. I want to stay, and more than anything I'd love to be able to do something to help you."

"That's right," Cunningham rumbled. "Drue Ann's right. And I'll tell you something else. I could have about sixty cowboys choppered in here today and batten this whole island down tighter'n a storm cellar. But somehow, I'd just rather do it myself. With my own hands." He looked down at his raw and work-worn hands and turned them over. "If you think we can get it done, Esteban, that's what I want to do," he finished in a low voice.

Esteban nodded slightly. "Again, you honor me and my house. I thank you, and I accept your offer of help." He glanced down at Johnnie and Rebel, who were listening with interest. "And you, Johnnie? Would you like to fly out today and come back next week?"

"Are you kidding?" Johnnie countered. "I've gotten two weeks' worth of work on those computers! I'm going to do double backups and download everything to Atlanta. Then I'm going to break down the equipment, wrap everything in plastic, and store it in the basement of the keep. Mrs. Rosado has already promised me some shelves in the buttery."

Esteban's eyes were alight, but he said soberly, "You sound like you know what you're doing, Johnnie. I wasn't aware they have hurricanes in Atlanta."

"They don't. But my mother lives in Fort Lauderdale, and she refuses to believe in hurricanes—until they come close. Then she always calls me in a panic. I'm the only person on earth who flies *into* Miami when a hurricane's coming!"

Esteban, John Wayne, and Drue Ann chuckled. Esteban said gratefully, "I am glad you'll stay, Johnnie. And though I can't take responsibility for making this decision for any of you, I am glad you're all staying. Taíno Castle has withstood countless hurricanes over the centuries, and it's never lost one stone." He smiled at Drue Ann. "It is, thanks be to our God, a refuge and a shelter from the storm."

"I'm staying, too," Rebel piped up. "I'm not scared anymore!"

Drue Ann and John Wayne looked at him in surprise, then his father swooped down to lift Rebel high in the air. "Where you been, boy? We were worried about you!"

"I was lost," he declared, giggling a little. "But she found me." He pointed to Johnnie.

Johnnie blushed with pleasure, and John Wayne Cunningham roared with laughter. "You're right, Reb! I tell you, we were all lost, but now we're found! Thank God!"

"Oh, thank God," Drue Ann Cunningham echoed, tears filling her eyes once again.

⟪⟫

Mrs. Rosado prepared a breakfast buffet for everyone at the keep, and Johnnie realized that she hadn't eaten anything but a few bites of breakfast yesterday and took care to eat heartily. She knew she was going to need her strength. This day would be a long day of hard work.

They were all seated at the long table in the arbor, and after everyone finished, Esteban rose to address them. Johnnie was seated next to him, and during the meal they had discussed everything that needed to be done. He had asked her help in delineating tasks, and Johnnie thought with satisfaction that they had thought of everything. *We make a wonderful team*, she thought happily.

As Esteban began speaking, Johnnie felt a tap on her shoulder. She turned, surprised to see Rebel standing behind her chair. "Hello, Reb. What's up?"

"I want to sit with you," he declared. Without waiting for her to comment, he climbed up into her lap. Johnnie looked down at Drue Ann, who was seated down at the other end of the table.

"Do you mind?" she called to Johnnie.

"Not if Reb doesn't," Johnnie replied. "And if you don't."

"Mind?" Drue Ann responded. "Not hardly. I thank God for you, Johnnie."

Esteban looked down at her and murmured very quietly, "So do I." Then he looked up and said clearly, "I thank God for each and every one of you. I'm not ashamed to admit that it wouldn't be possible for Diego and me to get ready for a hurricane by ourselves. But once again, I would like to tell you that if you should change your mind, I'll be glad to take you to Ponce, and no one here would blame you at all."

Each person looked questioningly around the table. Johnnie scrutinized all of them, and not one person looked fearful or doubtful, not even Rebel.

"We're staying," John Wayne Cunningham boomed.

Everyone at the table nodded in agreement.

"All right. Thank you, my friends," Esteban said. "If I felt we were in danger, I would evacuate. But I believe that Taíno Castle is strong and safe."

"I agree," Mr. Serralles said quietly. "I was here right after Hurricane Hugo. The grounds were a mess, but not one stone of the castle was moved. Some of the things in the rooms where the arrow ports were still opened were wet and blown around, but the structure of the castle will withstand anything."

"That brings me to the first task," Esteban said. "I've installed storm shutters on every glass window. You might not have noticed them—they're corrugated tin, and they fold back into a vertical line on each side of the window. Don Serralles, would you be responsible for shuttering each window of each room in the castle?"

"Of course," he agreed.

"Good. Now for the biggest problem: the water. We have two wells inside the castle grounds and two pumps. We have to assume that we'll lose the electricity. I have backup generators for the pumps, but if even one of them should go out, we'll have problems with the water. Either tonight or in the morning everyone should fill up the bathtubs. In the kitchen are plenty of clean containers. Take four to your rooms and fill them up."

Mr. Serralles nodded. "I can help with that, too, Esteban. And I will also issue flashlights to everyone, with spare batteries, and when I'm shuttering the windows I'll check every room for candles and matches."

"Thank you, Don Serralles," Esteban said gratefully. "Now,

we have a refrigerator and freezer on a generator, as well as a gas stove, but cooking by candlelight is no fun. So Mrs. Rosado is going to be cooking enough food for the next two days. Nuria, would you be kind enough to help her?"

"Of course, Esteban, I'll do anything you say," Nuria said in a low, intimate tone.

"Thank you," he said easily. "The other things that need to be done will be hard manual labor. All of the outside furniture must be moved indoors. Rita and Consuela have offered to do this, but—"

"I can do it," Diego chimed in. "Unless you have something else for me, Esteban. What about the horses?"

"Horses?" John Wayne Cunningham repeated, his eyes brightening to laser blue. "I figgered you had horses, with all them nice boots you got, Mr. Ventura, and I thought some of 'em had been rode in! I'd be awful pleased to volunteer to take care of the horses."

"Oh, me too!" Angelina cried.

"You said the magic word," Drue Ann sighed. "Horses. They'll probably be in our rooms tonight."

"You'd be leadin' 'em in there right behind me," John Wayne said, playfully elbowing his wife in the ribs.

"True," she agreed with equanimity. "John Wayne and Angelina and I will be glad to take care of your horses, Mr. Ventura. Just tell us what to do."

Esteban frowned. "I'm worried about the stables. They have stone foundations, but wooden sides and roof. I was going to try to move the horses up to the castle, into the old stables."

"No tryin' to it," John Wayne declared. "We'll do it. What's the problem? Gotta put down straw and bring up some hay and feed?"

"I'm afraid it's not going to be that easy," Esteban maintained. "I haven't repaired the stalls in the old stables here in the castle because I was going to convert them to guest rooms, you see. They're going to have to be checked, and probably some minor repairs done."

"Just hammer and nail work?" John Wayne asked.

"I think so," Esteban ventured, "but your hands—"

"No problem," Cunningham interrupted hastily. "Don't worry yourself about that, and don't worry about your horses, Mr. Ventura. Me and Drue Ann and Angelina will take real good care of them."

Esteban sighed. "That would be a great help to me, Mr. Cunningham. I worry about my horses, probably too much, and the two boys who assist me are going to need to stay with their family in Ponce. And there's another important task that I must take care of—"

"What's that?" John Wayne asked. "Anything I can do?"

Esteban shook his head. "No, if you'll take care of my horses, I can handle this by myself. It's the stained-glass window in the chapel. I had to special order storm shutters to fit it, and they're not here yet. That window is two hundred years old, and I'm going to make sure that it's boarded up and insulated inside and outside."

"I can help you with that, Esteban," Diego volunteered.

"Thank you, brother," Esteban said. "Now, I think that's everything. If you need to know where anything is, Mrs. Rosado will know. If you have a problem, come ask me or Diego."

"I have a problem," Nuria commented sharply. "I don't quite understand one thing."

"What's that, gatito?" Esteban asked good-naturedly.

"What's *she* going to be doing?" Nuria snapped, motioning impatiently to Johnnie.

Esteban's eyes narrowed. "*She* has work to do in the offices. Is that all?"

Nuria was not intimidated by Esteban's stern tone. She smiled impudently up at him. "Yes, Esteban, that will be all. For now."

Twenty

*E*veryone at the table stood up and started toward the door, talking among themselves in low voices. Johnnie, still seated with Rebel in her lap, looked up at Esteban. "What about Isabella and the puppies?" she asked.

"They'll be fine right where they are," he assured her. "Just before it hits I'll go down and secure the door that goes out to the gate."

"What about water and food?" Johnnie inquired. "And does the straw need changing?"

"Yes, I haven't had time to get to them today," Esteban admitted, then smiled down at her. "Why don't you and Rebel take care of that before you start on the offices? You have time, you know. And as soon as Rita and Consuela finish with the outdoor things, I'll send them to help you move the computers."

Johnnie looked at Rebel, who was paying close attention to the conversation. "Would you like to help me take care of Isabella and her puppies?"

"Sure," he said stoutly. "I like dogs, and they like me."

"I'll bet they do!" Johnnie agreed. "Okay, let's go ask your mom and dad."

John Wayne and Drue Ann were grateful for Johnnie's offer to take care of Rebel. "He's a good boy," Drue Ann said, smiling and smoothing Rebel's fine brown hair. "And he certainly has taken a liking to you. I'm not sure if he calls you My-Johnnie because he's trying to say 'Miss Johnnie'—or if he really thinks you're *his* Johnnie. Anyway, if you don't mind taking care of him, I think it's good for him to be with you right now."

"I . . . I don't mind," Johnnie said, a bit flustered. "It's just that I haven't been around children much. If you think I'll be all right with Rebel, then I'd love to have him with me."

"All right with him?" Drue Ann smiled. "You saved his life. To us you're better than a guardian angel."

"Oh no, no," Johnnie protested. "But I do like him. And I think he likes me. So I guess we'll try not to get into too much trouble."

"We're going to go save the puppies now, Mama," Rebel said, pulling on Johnnie's hand. "Bye."

"As you can see, we're on an important mission and in a hurry," Johnnie laughed as she allowed Rebel to pull her out the door. "We'll catch up with you later."

As she left she noticed two things: Esteban was smiling at them, and at his side Nuria was watching them, frowning darkly.

But Johnnie didn't care.

The sun had well risen, though it looked as if it were an alien star from a far planet. Instead of the cheerful yellow disc that usually shone on Taíno Island, it seemed bloated, the edges indistinct, its color a peculiar orange. The sky was a nondescript tint somewhere between blue and gray. The effect of the light was that the landscape was visible, but the brilliant hues were lackluster, as if matte black had been added to the color mix. Thin tendrils of mist floated and curled along the ground and wound around the flowers and shrubs.

As she and Rebel walked through the gardens, Johnnie was suddenly struck by the sounds. The birds' calls were muffled, as if they were singing with cotton in their mouths. Their footsteps on the adoquines seemed loud and jarring. No breath of fresh air whispered through the leaves of the trees.

Johnnie stopped on the path, and Rebel, holding her hand, looked up at her questioningly. "The coquí . . ." she murmured half to herself. Rebel slipped his hand out of hers and wandered over to a tree. Johnnie stared around, listening hard. The coquí were calling busily, as they did day and night, but they sounded . . . different.

"A frog," Rebel announced. He pointed to the tree trunk and leaned close.

"Yes, there are lots of frogs in the gardens," Johnnie said, rousing herself. "No, Reb, don't—"

He'd made a grab for the tiny frog, but it had scampered up the tree trunk. "Can I have one?" he asked in disappointment, turning back to Johnnie.

"You'll have to ask Mr. Ventura about that," she answered, motioning him to come back on the path. "They're his frogs, and he's probably the only person who could catch one."

Rebel came obediently back to the path and skipped a little ahead of Johnnie, but he never went far. "They sing loud, don't they?"

"Yes, they do."

"They sound sad," Rebel said, ahead of her.

A half smile curled Johnnie's lips. "Yes, Rebel," she whispered, "I believe they do."

They made their way through the gardens and straight across the bailey. Rebel asked where they were going, and Johnnie pointed to the gatehouse. "There's where—"

But Rebel turned around and took off running across the green swath of grass. He started whooping and calling out, mocking the call of the coquí, "Coooo-eeee, Coooo-eeee," over and over.

Johnnie laughed. She had truly witnessed a miraculous recovery in him. Many children who suffered such trauma often stayed catatonic for days or even weeks. Now he seemed perfectly normal and looked energetic, his eyes bright, his skin flushed. The only remnant of his shock were slight delicate blue smudges under his eyes.

"This way, Reb!" she called, pointing to the door on the

south side of the gatehouse. "And wait for me so I can introduce you to Isabella!"

Obediently Rebel went to the door and waited for her.

When she reached him, she knelt down to his eye level. "Now, Isabella is a nice dog, and she'll love you, Reb. But don't whoop and yell, or you might scare the puppies, and Isabella wouldn't like that. Okay?"

"Okay," he said solemnly. "I'll be good."

"I know you will." Johnnie rose and opened the door. "Isabella," she called softly. "It's Johnnie. I've brought someone to meet you." She went into the semidarkness of the gatehouse. "This is Rebel, Isabella. Reb, this is Isabella, and these are her babies. Aren't they darling?"

He nodded. "Darling," he repeated in his little-boy lisp.

"C'mon." She took his hand and led him to where Isabella lay on her pallet. Isabella watched unconcernedly as Johnnie and Rebel knelt down beside her. When Johnnie stroked her lightly, her tail thumped a few times. "Here, you want to pet her? See, like this."

Reb stroked her head, and Isabella's dark eyes seemed to soften as she watched him. Her tail thumped harder.

"She does like you, I can tell," Johnnie said.

"Would she let me pet her puppies?" he asked.

"Of course she will. She knows you'll be very gentle."

To Johnnie's amusement, Rebel went to squat in front of the puppies, who were lined up along Isabella's stomach. But they weren't nursing; they were sound asleep. Rebel reached out to touch each one and stroked all six of them with a slightly grimy little hand.

Then he picked up one of them, and Johnnie watched Isabella carefully to make sure she didn't object. But she had laid her massive head back down, and though she watched Rebel, her tail was still thumping very slightly.

"This one's mine," Rebel announced. "His name is John."

"Well . . . Rebel, you'll have to ask Mr. Ventura—and your parents—about that," Johnnie stammered.

"Mama and Daddy won't care," he said staunchly. "And why do I have to ask Mr. Ventura? They're Isabella's puppies, aren't they?"

"Hmm. Yes, but—"

"She wants me to have John," Rebel said firmly. He held the tiny ball of white fuzz close against his chest, supporting the puppy just right and rubbing his thumb over the little round head. The puppy never even woke up.

"Well . . . we'll see," Johnnie temporized. "The babies will have to stay with Isabella for a few more weeks anyway."

"John is mine," Rebel said stubbornly.

Smiling, she commented, "You named him 'John' after your father? That's nice."

But Reb was shaking his head violently. "No. Not just daddy. It's my name, too. And yours."

"Oh!" Johnnie exclaimed. "I . . . I hadn't really thought of that! We do all have the same name, don't we?"

Nodding vigorously, Reb declared, "And now it's his name, too."

Rising and dusting off her jeans, Johnnie chuckled. "Okay, Reb, you win. Hello, John. Now why don't you just sit and play quietly with the puppies and pet Isabella while I clean up their house and fix them some food and water."

"Okay." He bent his head and pressed his face against the puppy named John. "You doing all this 'cause that hurricane's comin'?"

Johnnie stopped and looked at him closely, but he kept his head bent, his hand stroking the puppy over and over. "No, we take very good care of Isabella all the time," she answered slowly. "You aren't scared, are you, Reb? Of the hurricane?"

"No," he replied quietly. " 'Cause He told me this is a real good hiding place."

" 'He'? Who is 'he'?"

"Jesus."

By five o'clock it appeared that the sky had lowered to only a few hundred feet above the ground. It was a monotonous, monochrome gray, and the hazy orange ball of the sun barely seemed able to burn through it. The mists in the garden had thickened and seemed to move of their own volition from here to there, appearing as a wall of fog in one place, only to melt and rise up from the ground somewhere else. The atmosphere felt like a tangible substance made of equal parts heat and water with only a dash of air thrown in.

A storm surge had begun. As the hurricane moved north, the gathering winds forced a great tide to precede the storm itself. Naturally, it posed no danger to Taíno Castle, but the waves were crashing far above the normal high-tide mark on the beach. The sound of the sea was much louder than usual; the thunder of the surf was audible everywhere on the island except inside the castle itself. It was disorienting, unsettling, to hear and see such an angry, thunderous surf while the air was so deadened.

Soon after five o'clock everyone on the island started trickling back into the keep for dinner. They all looked tousled and harried and smudged. The adults were milling around restlessly, thirstily drinking bottled water, while Angelina and Rebel were already munching on almonds and chunks of coconut and swigging down fresh lemonade.

Esteban raised his voice slightly to get the attention of the room. "It sounds to me like we've done it," he said wearily. "I can't thank you enough, my friends."

The room was filled with murmurs of relief and satisfaction.

"We have an update on Damien," Esteban went on, and the room grew very quiet. "It hit Antigua just before noon, and they lost all power and communications at twelve-ten. It's moving in a straight line at about twelve miles per hour, and the winds are up to 114 miles per hour." He checked his watch. "It hit St. Kitts and Nevis just a few minutes ago, and they're both out of power and communications, too. It's heading straight for St. Croix—and us."

No one said a word.

Esteban's voice dropped to an even, calm tone. "It looks like St. Croix will get hit at about four o'clock in the morning. If it keeps on this path and at this speed, it will be here around noon tomorrow."

For long moments no one spoke. Then John Wayne Cunningham barked, "We're ready. This whole place is tight as a cinched saddle. And as for me and my family, we're gonna eat some of Mrs. Rosado's good fixin's and then get us a good night's sleep."

"Sounds like a wonderful idea to me," Johnnie agreed, stretching like a cat in the sunshine. A chorus of assent sounded.

"Good," Esteban said with satisfaction. "And just so you'll rest easier, I want you to know that Diego and I will take turns monitoring the radio all night. Hurricanes don't always stay on schedule."

"That's true," Johnnie agreed, stifling a yawn, "and it's so annoying. I just despise hurricanes that sneak up on you. Especially early in the morning."

Everyone laughed—except Nuria. "I don't think you're very funny," she bristled. "I guess you haven't ever seen the god Huracán when he's angry, Miss James."

"Oh, I've been through several hurricanes," Johnnie said mildly. "And I don't mean to make light of them. It's just that I have a pretty good idea of what we're in for, and I feel very secure here."

"Do you?" Nuria shot back. "I think that is what they said about the *Titanic*, hmm?"

Angelina sat up straight in her chair, her brown eyes round and frightened. Rebel looked at her, puzzled. She asked in a small voice, "Mama? Are we . . . is this—"

Drue Ann walked over to her daughter and laid her hand on her shoulder. "It's all right, Angie. We're under God's protection, exactly where we're supposed to be." She looked up at Nuria, her eyes now flashing ominously. "Miss Torres, you don't have to be afraid. You're safe here," she said in a deceptively soft voice.

"I'm not afraid," she retorted sulkily. "But perhaps you should be."

Esteban, moving like The Lynx, soundlessly catwalked across the room and appeared directly in front of Nuria. "That's enough," he said quietly, but the room was so heavy with silence that the words seemed to burst through the air. "Enough, Nuria. Perhaps you should go to your room and rest."

Jerking straight upright, her shoulders stiff and squared, Nuria's dark eyes glinted like mica. "You are sending me to my room, Esteban?" she challenged him. "You want to come with me?"

Esteban turned his back on her and took two deliberately slow steps away from her. "Now, Nuria!" he said, his jaw clenching tightly. "Leave now."

She left, but she was laughing as she did, and the ugly sound of it echoed mockingly through the great hall of the keep.

Twenty-one

A light knock sounded on her door, and Johnnie jerked awake, startled. The room was inky black, the air close. Sounds seemed deadened in the still air. Disoriented, she wondered where she was.

"Johnnie?" Esteban called and tapped on the door again. "Johnnie, wake up. It's Esteban."

"Oh, horrors," Johnnie muttered when she came to her senses. She couldn't see a thing. Now she remembered that the storm shutters were closed tightly, and the door to her balcony was shut. The air was as heavy as a velvet mantle in summertime. Her rose-colored satin pajamas felt slightly damp, though Johnnie wasn't warm. "I'm coming, Esteban! Just a minute!" she called.

Feeling the nightstand by her bed, she grabbed the matches and lit the six fresh candles in the candelabra. Then she threw on her matching satin robe and hurried to open the door. "Good morning, Esteban. Hello there, Ferdinand," she murmured, nervously trying to arrange her mussed hair with one hand.

In a quick movement, Esteban reached out and lightly clasped her wrist. "Don't," he said quietly. "You look lovely."

Johnnie gulped. "I . . . I couldn't—"

"It's true," he said in a low tone. His dark eyes flamed, and

he brought her hand up, then bent over it. To Johnnie's surprise—and exquisite pleasure—he turned her hand over and
pressed his lips to her palm. Passionately, his mouth warm, he
kissed her hand for a long moment, then brushed a light kiss
against her wrist. Johnnie couldn't breathe.

With an obvious effort he let go of her hand and took a small
step back into the hallway. "I came to tell you that Damien hit
St. Croix at four o'clock this morning, just as predicted. But as
soon as it cleared the island it sped up to about twenty miles per
hour. It's still heading straight for us, and it's going to hit in
two or three hours."

"What time is it?" Johnnie asked, desperately trying to clear
her muddled mind—and quit swooning over Esteban's touch.

"It's about six. I'm going to wake everyone, then go lock
up the dogs and the horses. How much do you have left to do
here? Can you go to the keep right now?"

"In my pajamas?"

Esteban appeared to seriously consider the joke. "They are
very nicy pyjamas. Like a wedding trouser."

"Wh-what?" Johnnie stammered, blushing furiously.

"So, no, I don't think you should wear them to the keep,"
he went on in a thoughtful tone, but his dark eyes were glinting.
"You should save them. For your wedding trouser."

"My . . .my . . . wedding—But I don't have a wedding trouser!" Johnnie said weakly.

"Perhaps you should."

"I should? But—You mean—" With a groan Johnnie shook
the thoughts out of her head, then gave him a playful push. He
moved to grab her hands, but she backed away into her doorway
and teased, "And it's 'trousseau.' If you're going to talk about
it, sir, you'd better get it right."

"Mmm," he grunted. "Who has had time to say it right in
the last few days? But I will, Johnnie, I promise, as soon as I
can."

"Wh-what?" Johnnie stuttered. "What do you—oh, never
mind, Esteban! Go away! You're . . . upsetting me!"

"Sorry," he said unrepentantly and flashed a wide, mischievous grin over his shoulder as he and Ferdinand headed down the hallway toward the stairway. "I'm leaving, but you have to promise to come to the keep in—" he turned and shone his flashlight on his watch—"half an hour."

"An hour."

"All right, an hour. But if you are not there by then I'm coming back to get you."

"Mmm, sounds promising," Johnnie half whispered in a low tone. Esteban stopped dead and whirled around, his eyes wide. He took a step back toward Johnnie, but laughing, she darted inside her room and slammed the door.

"My, you certainly are cheerful for someone in the path of a hurricane," Johnnie told herself after a few moments, still leaning against the door and trying to make herself breathe properly again. *Esteban . . . Esteban, you take my breath away. . . .*

"Get dressed!" she ordered herself sternly. Squinting in the near darkness, she decided to open the balcony door to let some light into the room and into the bathroom. The door was heavy; although it was new, Esteban designed it to fit with the sixteenth-century aura of the castle. Made of oak four inches thick, it was expertly hung, the iron fittings well oiled, and it swung open easily and silently.

Johnnie slipped out onto the balcony to face a menacing world.

A thick black predawn sky was paling slowly at the edges to a sickly ash blue. Close overhead it was glumly overcast, like the rain-sogged roof of a rotting gray tent. The air, even though sunup was still an hour away, was fevered. On the southwest horizon the sky briefly gleamed now and then with the ominous, soundless slash of heat lightning. Far below the beleaguered Caribbean was an odd dun color, and the whitecaps were like dirty rags flung into the air by an angry beggar. Against the barrier rocks, the raging surf was stifled and dull, a peculiar monotonous thumping that made Johnnie swallow hard to make sure her ears weren't stopped up.

As she surveyed the foreboding scene, she suddenly noticed the luxuriant plants surrounding her. "Oh, dear, the hibiscus," she muttered, bending down to look under the long branches of thick greenery. "Six big pots . . . I have to bring them in." She grasped one, then stopped and stood up, dusting her hands off.

Get dressed first, you ninny. You'd better save these great pyjamas for your wedding 'trouser'! Because maybe someday Esteban . . .

"Johnnie! Get a grip!" With that cry she hurried into her room.

She took a quick shower, then filled up the tub. Hurrying, she put on a minimum of makeup and searched through her closet to find something to wear. She'd only brought two pairs of jeans, and they were both filthy. She decided to wear her denim skirt, a long skirt that was tightly fitted through the waist but was gored to an attractive fullness that swirled around her ankles. Pulling on a white T-shirt and her Western boots, she was satisfied with her appearance, although she thought disapprovingly that her hair looked rather tousled. It was naturally wavy and full, and one half of it fell over her eye when it was parted on the side. She checked her watch and decided she didn't have time to put it up. All joking aside, Esteban was busy and didn't need to be coming back up here to check on her every few minutes while she dawdled around.

After making sure there were no loose articles lying out in the bedroom or the bathroom, she hurried back out to the balcony and started bringing in the pots of hibiscus. They were big and heavy, but Johnnie could lift them, and she lined them up against the interior wall. She didn't think the storm shutters would give, but with a hurricane she couldn't be sure. The treacherous winds could invade a room and blast everything as if there had been an explosion, and then blow gallons of water in through the smallest opening. At least the plants would have a chance in here; they were certain to be shattered to bits out on the balcony.

As she was lifting the last pot, she heard a strange sound.

In the thick silence any sound was strange, she realized, and she thought for a moment that she only heard it inside her head.

But it was real. It was a dog barking, loudly and urgently. And it was coming from below her balcony.

The plant crashed to the deck, and Johnnie lunged to the railing and looked straight down.

Directly below her, on the small ledge of ground that anchored the castle on this side, was Isabella. She was standing at the edge of the cliffs, looking down and barking repeatedly. Another movement in her peripheral vision caught Johnnie's eye.

Walking unconcernedly along the cliff toward Isabella was a small figure wearing a yellow rain slicker.

Rebel was following the dog.

Johnnie gasped and leaned out perilously far over the waist-high balcony railing. "Rebel! Rebel, no!" she screamed.

Rebel looked around as if he'd heard something, but he never looked up. Johnnie was about fifty feet above him, and the sound of the surf must have been much louder down on the cliff's edge.

Isabella, however, heard her and looked up. Then the dog caught sight of Rebel behind her and ran to him, barking. Rebel petted her happily with one hand, the other clutched close to his chest. Johnnie could now see a smudge of white against the bright yellow rain slicker. Rebel was carrying his puppy.

Johnnie froze with terror. She thought that Isabella would surely attack the child and take back her puppy. But Isabella merely nudged Rebel, and he kept on petting her enthusiastically. The dog barked urgently, then went behind Rebel and took the back of his rain slicker in her teeth, pulling on it gently. Rebel looked behind him, and Johnnie could clearly see him laughing. Impatiently the dog looked back up at Johnnie, barked once, then ran back to where she'd been looking over the cliff, barking sharply.

"Rebel!" Johnnie screamed again but finally realized that the child couldn't hear her, and even if he could, she doubted

that he'd just turn around and toddle back into the castle. She'd
have to go get him.

Running as fast as she could, she quickly considered whether
to go get help. But there was no telling where she could find
Esteban, and if she went all the way to the keep to look for the
others she'd be wasting precious time. Without wavering, she
headed straight for the door at the back of the south quarters
that led outside the castle grounds.

Breathing hard both with fear and exertion, she covered the
narrow strip of land behind the castle at a furious pace, her heavy
skirt flapping around her legs. A sudden shock of thunder
crashed as loud as heaven's timpani, but Johnnie didn't even
start. She was concentrating fiercely on heading straight to
where she'd seen Rebel standing.

As she rounded the gentle curve of Ventura Tower, she dug
in her heels and slid to a stop.

Rebel was nowhere in sight, and neither was Isabella.

Thunder jarred the earth again, and as suddenly as if the sky
had overturned bowls of water, a hard rain fell.

"Oh, Lord Jesus," Johnnie cried out in anguish. "Help me,
help me . . . where is he?" Panicked, Johnnie ran to the cliff and
almost skidded over the precipice. Already the thick green grass
was sodden and slippery. Falling to her knees, Johnnie peered
over the side of the cliff.

There was a path, much like the one she and Esteban and
Diego and Nuria had followed last Sunday. Imbedded in the
cliff, a series of plateaus connected by narrow ridges wandered
in a jagged pattern down to the sea. Johnnie saw Rebel's rain
slicker about twenty feet below her and to her left. "Rebel!" she
cried frantically. But the rain was a relentless cacophony, and
from here the surf was indeed deafening.

Johnnie scrambled down onto the tiny pathway threaded between the protective outcroppings of rocks that formed the
cliffs. In several places the right-hand side was a sheer drop
straight down.

Johnnie took a deep breath and began moving as quickly as

she could. The thunder was almost continuous now, roaring and growling like a child's nightmare monster. The cloud bank above the southern horizon had taken on a sickly yellowish tint. It was an eerie light for seven o'clock in the morning. Johnnie knew that this was not Hurricane Damien; it was one of the fierce squalls that often precede a hurricane. Desperately she hoped that it would pass and there would be a lull before the hurricane reached Taíno so she could get Rebel back to safety.

Johnnie slipped and slid and stumbled toward the little yellow slicker, never taking her eyes off it. Rebel seemed to be as relaxed as if he were taking a walk to the playground, but Johnnie was having a harder time of it. Once, she fell against the boulders, cutting and bruising the palm of her hand, but she never slowed down.

Finally she reached him. Putting out her hands she grabbed the little boy's shoulders and whirled him around. "John Wayne Cunningham the Third!" she hollered over the clamor of water cascading down. "What do you think you're doing?"

Suddenly his eyes became round and scared. He opened his mouth and said something, but Johnnie couldn't hear. The wind picked up abruptly, now whipping her wet skirt so hard it hurt her bare legs. Rebel staggered a little to the side from the force of it.

Johnnie threw herself to her knees and screamed, "Reb, we've got to get back to the castle! You've got to come with me right now!"

He shook his head and pointed ahead of them, down the path. "Isabella," he mouthed. He tried to say something else, but Johnnie could hardly even hear her own thoughts, the din was so pervasive.

Ruthlessly she picked him up, puppy and all, and turned around. But the wind shrieked as if in outrage and fought her, whipping her hair so savagely that it stung her face and blinded her completely. She managed to take one step, then it seemed as if the winds shoved her against the side of the cliff. Her hold on Rebel fumbled, and he tried to wiggle out of her grip. Frantically she held him close to her and tried to look around. It was hopeless; there was no place to hide and no way she could carry the child up the cliff, and in this storm he couldn't climb up by himself. Hurricane Damien was close, and his dance would dash them to pieces if they didn't find shelter.

Around the path Isabella came bounding. Without slowing she ran straight to Johnnie and barked twice, staring hard, straight into Johnnie's eyes.

"Help us, Isabella, help us!" Johnnie shrieked.

The dog took Johnnie's skirt in her sharp teeth and yanked twice on it, very deliberately. Then she backed a few feet down the path and watched Johnnie expectantly.

"All right," Johnnie whispered desperately, then put her mouth close to Rebel's ear. "Get over here, close to the cliff! Hand me the puppy, Reb!"

He pulled away from her in alarm, and Johnnie yelled, "I promise I'll hold him tight! And you can hold on with both hands. Okay?"

After a second he nodded and handed Johnnie the sodden little bundle. She stood up, shifted the puppy to her right hand, and put out her left to steady herself along the cliff face. Reb was in front of her, and Johnnie could only pray helplessly that he would hug the cliff as closely as he could.

But Isabella came to stand close enough to Rebel so that she was actually touching him, positioning herself between him and the sheer drop to the rocks below. Rebel laid one hand, pinched and white with the cold and wet, on her strong back. Isabella took a step, then patiently waited to make sure that Rebel walked with her. The dog even glanced back to see if Johnnie was following.

"Oh, thank you, God," Johnnie almost sobbed. "I think you've really sent us an angel. A big, furry, strong, beautiful angel!"

Johnnie never had any clear idea how long the descent took them. They moved very slowly and carefully. Without fail, when they passed a place where the right-hand side of the walkway was empty air, Isabella pressed against Rebel, crowding him securely against the cliff face.

They went farther and farther down, and Johnnie began to doubt and fear. What in the world would they do? All she could see below were jagged boulders and a violent surf pounding them. Anxiously she looked back up at the castle looming above, and wondered, almost hysterically, if she could just snatch Rebel up and run straight back to that haven. . . .

In the midst of the earthly tumult, Johnnie's mind suddenly heard Esteban's deep voice, echoing strong in the chapel, *"Thou art my hiding place and my shield: I hope in thy word."*

Johnnie's brow cleared, and even her vision seemed sharper. Though she knew that the dog couldn't hear her, she whispered calmly, "Lead on, Isabella."

They were almost at sea level now. Every so often the last grasping fingers of a great wave slopped up onto their feet. Mostly now they walked on the slippery ledges of rocks that lined the bottom of the cliffs.

Only one step ahead of her, the dog and Rebel seemed to disappear. Johnnie's heart lunged, but then she saw they had turned a sharp corner to the left—but into what?

The wind still tearing at her and screeching with outrage, Johnnie edged around the corner.

It was a cave. An enormous entrance to a great cavern loomed inside the cliffs. It was, in fact, more like a tunnel—a water tunnel, for the sea flowed steadily into it, though it was set far back from the breakers. Great escarpments thirty feet high stood as mighty sentinels on each side of the opening. It would be very difficult, almost impossible, to see the cave opening unless you were at sea and directly opposite the entrance.

Johnnie hesitated, still standing outside in the wildness. But inside the cave Rebel and Isabella stood, watching her impatiently. Rebel motioned to her. Johnnie edged closer and saw narrow ledges on either side of the rush of water flowing into the depths of the cave. Still hanging on to the cliff face, she stumbled into the opening.

The wind continued to howl, but by a trick of aerodynamics it didn't actually blow into the cave entrance. It was as if there were a sheet of glass shielding the opening. As soon as Johnnie stepped inside the cave, Isabella trotted farther back into the tunnel.

Rebel grabbed Johnnie's hand and pointed toward Isabella. Johnnie nodded, and they followed the dog. With each step the terrible din lessened, but the light grew dimmer.

They followed Isabella for a while, but Johnnie's steps began to drag. She had brought no flashlight, no candles, no matches. There was no way she was going to allow Rebel to stumble around in the dark in here. The rush of water flowing past them wasn't at all violent, but it was steady and fast.

Abruptly Johnnie realized that her ears were ringing bass notes, but she could hear a sound. A tiny little sound, high-pitched. It was the puppy she held, whimpering a little.

"J-just a minute, Rebel," she said tentatively, shocked at how loud her voice sounded and how quiet it actually was in the cave. Light still filtered in from the entrance behind them, but just ahead the way curved, probably into darkness. Isabella stood in front of them, waiting patiently, her tail wagging almost imperceptibly.

The little boy looked up at Johnnie, searching her face with the grown-up eyes she'd seen in Rebel before. "You aren't scared, are you, My-Johnnie?" he asked innocently.

"Yes, I am," she muttered, "and you should be, too."

He looked crestfallen. "Well, I am, a little," he admitted. But Johnnie realized that this precocious child was just humoring her, and a tense smile flitted across her face.

"John Wayne Cunningham the Third," she sighed, "when we get through this, I'm going to lock you in the tower."

He eyed her, his blue eyes sparking as devilishly as his father's. "Oh no you won't. You wouldn't do that."

"No, I wouldn't," Johnnie agreed.

"You love me," Reb said with a child's rock-steady certainty.

"Yes, I do," Johnnie said softly and took his hand.

"Can I hold John now?" he asked. "I think he wants me."

Johnnie was pretty certain that John, like his namesake—or one of them, at least—just wanted to go home. But since that wasn't possible at the moment, she handed the little puppy to Rebel. "I think he does want you, Reb. Here, now tell him that everything is going to be all right."

"Okay. It's all right, John," he said in an adult's tone of reason. "Your mama is here, and My-Johnnie is here. We'll be all right."

"Hmm," Johnnie murmured, half to herself. "So what is John's mama doing now?"

Isabella was watching them with obvious impatience. Once, she nipped out a sharp little bark and turned to look ahead, then back to Johnnie. Her movements and intentions were so clear and so deliberate that Johnnie almost laughed. Isabella truly was painfully patient with the stupid humans who couldn't understand a simple command bark and could barely see or hear for themselves.

"It's true," Johnnie muttered. "She can see and hear much better than I . . . maybe we should follow her, go farther back in the cave. Maybe it leads back up and comes out somewhere close to the castle."

As suddenly as it had begun, the wind and rain stopped. An immediate lessening of the darkness outside continued for a few minutes, until the light from the entrance to the cave crept a little farther inside. But it was a deadly jaundice shade, a ghastly warning that worse darkness was coming.

Johnnie knew that it might be only minutes before the hurricane hit. She couldn't risk trying to go up the cliff again. If the tremendous storm rushed in on them, winds over one hundred miles per hour could pick them up as if they were just little bits of paper and fling them easily into the maelstrom.

Wavering, she considered whether to sit right here and wait out the storm. But immediately she knew that would be a stupid thing to do. The cave entrance was fully a hundred feet away from them, but all it would take would be the thrust of a single gust of wind, crashing into the cave. Either the water would swamp them, or they would simply be blown—somewhere. Probably not somewhere good.

"All right," Johnnie said with resignation. "Let's go, Isabella."

"Good," Rebel whispered under his breath.

Johnnie ruffled his hair and said as calmly as she could, "Now, Reb, it might be dark up there. Really, really dark. We'll have to walk slow and be careful. Okay?"

He shrugged. "Isabella shines. Like an angel."

"Yes, well . . ." Johnnie really couldn't think of any answer to this. It did seem that the dog's white fur was visible even in the inky blackness. They had rounded the corner, and though ambient yellow light was still at their back, it was very dark ahead. Isabella, like a benevolent ghost, shimmered white, floating soundlessly just ahead of them.

They walked slowly, Johnnie with hesitant, sliding steps, Rebel with confident but short steps. The cave steadily curved around, and the air grew moist and cool. The inlet's flow sounded louder but not as fast. Johnnie could hear droplets hitting the water, a cool, echoing sound that reminded her of the sleepy afternoon rains in Atlanta.

They walked and walked, and soon the light behind them completely dissipated. Johnnie was amazed when she realized they could still see. She couldn't figure out if their eyes had simply adjusted, or if there was some sort of phosphorescence in the water and in the rocks of the caves. Her vision was vague and dim, but she could see the way and the water plunging along beside them. Johnnie could even make out the ledge on the other side of the cave, fully thirty feet on the other side of the underground river.

"Look up there," Rebel clamored. "It's light. See?"

Johnnie narrowed her eyes, but she couldn't be quite sure. It looked like a glow ahead, but if it was, it wasn't a light that was straight ahead of them.

They walked farther, and the light did grow brighter. But it was around a long, gentle curve, so they bore constantly to their left.

When they finally stepped into the lit chamber, she, Rebel, and Isabella froze as if they were photographs from another time.

The chamber was immense; the ceiling disappeared above them, and the water below the cliff they were standing on formed a great pool. In the pool was an enormous yacht, three stories high.

Beside the yacht, in the lurid spotlight of two gas lamps, stood Diego Ventura and Nuria Torres. They were shouting, arguing fiercely. Johnnie realized in a vaguely disinterested way that because they had come up through the path that curved so steeply away from the chamber, sound didn't carry that way. It carried the opposite way, past Diego and Nuria, into the tunnel that lay beyond them, which sloped gently upward. When the three had stepped into the chamber, it was like the sudden blast of a radio.

"Listen to me, Diego!" Nuria snapped. "I heard the girl! She was telling Rita and Consuela that her father had hidden ten one-thousand-dollar bills in the other lifeboat! I know those stupid peons would have already taken their wallets and jewels, but—"

"Nuria, you listen to me," he interrupted angrily. "We can get it later! That hurricane is coming, and Esteban will be wondering—"

"Diego, you fool! This boat might be swamped later! It would be stupid to feed ten thousand dollars to the fish!"

Rebel was standing stock-still, his eyes huge, clutching the puppy close. Suddenly he turned to Johnnie and said in a small voice, "That's my daddy's boat."

The argument stopped as if a butcher knife had cut them out of the air. Diego and Nuria turned.

Twenty-two

*D*iego and Nuria looked at the sodden little company in disbelief. After several tense moments Johnnie laid her hand on Rebel's shoulder, and they began walking toward where the couple stood. Isabella stayed close to Rebel and didn't move to greet Diego and Nuria. Instead, the dog merely watched them rather cautiously, as if she weren't quite sure she recognized them. As they passed the stern of the luxurious yacht, Johnnie saw the name: *Angelina*.

"What are you doing here?" Nuria finally asked with an odd detachment.

Johnnie's mind clicked along at computer speed. She decided to bluff. Pushing Rebel gently in front of her, she said carelessly, "It's a long story. This child is cold and soaked through. Does this passage lead back up into the castle?"

Nuria, by a very subtle movement, slid to stand in front of Johnnie and Rebel as they approached. Since it was quite a graceful maneuver it did not carry an overt threat, but she effectively blocked their way. Johnnie and Rebel stopped, and so did Isabella—though Johnnie thought that the dog was now watching Nuria with a hint of hostility.

Johnnie looked past the girl as if she were of no consequence. "Diego, I need to get this little boy back to the castle and get him warm and into some dry clothes. Please tell me if that passage goes back up into the castle."

To Johnnie's dismay—and dawning horror—Diego refused to meet her eyes. Instead, he watched Nuria helplessly.

With her dark eyes now flashing ominously, Nuria very slowly, very carefully, kept her burning gaze trained on Johnnie's face and backed up three steps to stand at Diego's side. They began to speak in Spanish but didn't bother to lower their voices, as they knew that Johnnie wouldn't be able to understand their words.

But what Nuria and Diego did not know was that Johnnie could *understand* some Spanish. It was true, she didn't practice speaking the language, and she could read it better than piece together the spoken word. But she did have a sizable vocabulary stored in her head, and each day she came to comprehend the speech better.

Diego asked uncertainly, *"Ahora, ¿qué vamos a hacer?"*

The Spanish translator inside Johnnie's head whispered, *What are we going to do now?*

Nuria gave Johnnie a look that would have felled a fighting bull. *"Diego, ¡ellos saben! ¡Oyeme! ¡Ella salió en este huracán sola!"*

Tremulously, Johnnie realized that Nuria was telling Diego that she had come out in the hurricane by herself. Diego was looking at Johnnie doubtfully, and he cast a puzzled glance at Nuria.

She laid her hand lightly on his arm. Johnnie stared at Nuria's hand and noticed that it was beautiful, slender, with perfect long nails polished a light peach color.

"El risco, Diego," Nuria said softly, seductively. *"El risco."*

The cliffs, Johnnie thought hazily.

Diego stiffened and grabbed Nuria's wrist. *"Qué*! No! No, Nuria! ¿Qué vas a hacer, matar al niño, también?"*

El niño . . . little boy . . but what is 'matar'?

Her brain was suddenly branded with the word: *Matar* means kill!

With surprising speed and strength, Johnnie picked Rebel

up, dashed to the rocky ledge, jumped the three feet over the water onto the side of the boat, then down onto the main deck. Setting him down, she gave him a firm shove. "Get below now, Rebel!" she ordered. "Now! Lock the door, and don't open it for anyone! Now!"

Rebel jerked backward, then ran to the door at the bulkhead. But he was pale and shocked, and he hesitated, looking back at Johnnie. Furiously, Johnnie turned back around to see Nuria walking toward the yacht, her face, in the uncertain light, appearing shadowed by malevolence. Johnnie looked around her desperately; at the stern of the boat two crossed oars were displayed. With desperate quickness she ran and grabbed one, then went back to stand at the side of the deck. Raising the paddle like a baseball bat, she growled fiercely, "Don't do it, Nuria! If you set one foot on this boat, I'll bash your brains in! I will!"

"Señorita James," Nuria said with calm amusement, "I just want to take the little boy back to the castle. You're scaring him. Come here, boy. I won't hurt you." She did, however, stop a foot from the ledge.

"No, Rebel. I told you, get below now!" Johnnie's gaze never wavered from the slender woman in front of her. Behind Nuria, Diego watched with horror, but he seemed to be frozen, powerless to either help or hurt. Johnnie didn't hear a sound behind her and knew that Rebel couldn't move, either.

Nuria's eyes narrowed to black slits. "You stupid cow! Get out of my way! And put that down!" She took a step toward the yacht and positioned herself to jump.

Johnnie tightened her sweaty grip on the oar and gritted her teeth.

Suddenly, as if she'd been propelled from a catapult, Isabella threw herself into the air, square onto Nuria's back. Nuria went straight down to the cave's path. She landed face first, arms outspread, and lay still.

Isabella got a mouthful of Nuria's shirt from the back of her neck, then hunkered down by her slender form, growling ominously. The deep, menacing sound echoed throughout the strangely majestic chamber.

Slowly, Johnnie lowered the oar, but she still kept a firm grasp on it as she stared at Diego. He looked stricken, his face drawn, his eyes vacant as he stared down at Nuria and the great white dog growling fiercely beside her. Taking a half step toward them, he whispered faintly, "Nuria, oh no—Isabella . . . no—"

The dog looked up at him, the ferocity in her expression clear. Again she growled, a dire warning for Diego to keep his distance.

"Oh no, no," Diego murmured in a broken voice. Johnnie thought she could see tears shimmering in his eyes.

A loud, rhythmic thumping sound started, and then was crazily repeated over and over again, bouncing around the great cave. Diego didn't seem to notice as he appeared mesmerized and paralyzed by the sight of Nuria's still form. But Johnnie heard it clearly, and it grew louder and louder and faster and faster. Finally she realized it was footsteps, hard steps, a man's steps, running fast. Someone was coming down the chamber behind where Diego and Nuria had been standing.

Johnnie was terrifed, thinking that some of the men, the pirates, were coming. Her hands now trembling, her shoulders fiery from tension, she got a better grip on the oar and glanced over her shoulder to see Rebel standing helplessly, staring at Nuria and Isabella with round, dark eyes, automatically stroking the puppy over and over again.

Oh, Lord Jesus, please help me, Johnnie prayed with anguish. *Please help me. . . .*

Like a clap of thunder, Esteban burst into the chamber, with Ferdinand close behind him. They stopped together, between one step and the next.

Esteban looked first at Diego, then at Nuria lying on the floor of the cave, and finally at Isabella who was still clamped down furiously on Nuria's shirt. Esteban's dark, unfathomable eyes went to the yacht, to the unseen ceiling of the great chamber. His eyes found Johnnie, and he studied her, then looked at

Rebel, a small, pale ghost standing behind her.

There seemed to be no passage of time, no sound, no air to breathe in the cave. For a split second Johnnie actually thought she was in the midst of a horrible nightmare.

Then Esteban stepped forward, followed closely by Ferdinand, and shoved Diego roughly aside. He knelt down by Nuria. Meekly Isabella loosed her clothing and sat down by Esteban. "Good girl," Esteban whispered sadly.

At that moment Johnnie felt as if she woke up. Dropping the paddle with a great crash, she ran back to Rebel. Falling to her knees, she threw her arms around him and whispered over and over again, "It's all right, Reb. Don't be scared. It's all over now. We're all right. . . ."

Behind her she heard Esteban say in a staccato voice, "Isabella! Ferdinand! *Vigilar por trabajo!*" The two dogs stood guard over Nuria and Diego, who now knelt beside each other.

Weakly Diego muttered, "Esteban, you don't have to do that."

"Don't I?" he retorted harshly, then jumped onto the yacht.

Johnnie felt his strong arms go around her and Rebel, and for the first time that horrible day, she relaxed.

Twenty-three

*T*he silence within the walls of the keep was as tomblike as the silence outside. Except for the occasional scream of a frightened bird, the world around them seemed to have died. Everyone stood at the windows, their eyes roaming over the unnatural landscape. The grass glistened brittlely under a yellow-green sky. Not a single leaf of any tree moved. The mellow gray brick of the castle looked flat black. The quiet was unsettling, but the stillness was frightening. In the space of a few minutes, the world looked like a hard acrylic painting done by a feverish artist.

Johnnie stood by Drue Ann Cunningham as she held Rebel. Beside them was Angelina, and close behind them was John Wayne Cunningham. Standing by Angelina was Consuela and Rita, and Antonio Serralles hovered close behind them. They were in front of one of the panoramic 8×8 windows that Esteban had had installed in the dining room, watching the coming of Hurricane Damien.

Johnnie felt a warmth and a weight on her shoulders and knew Esteban had soundlessly slipped up to stand behind her. She put her right hand up to join with his.

"It has a certain beauty, doesn't it?" Esteban murmured.

"Dangerous beauty," Johnnie agreed.

The company stood in silence for a long time, mutely watching the earth and heavens. Suddenly the sky turned a sullen copper color.

"He is here," Esteban said softly. "I'm going to close the shutters."

Wordlessly he and John Wayne went outside and pulled the aluminum folding shutters over the window. The keep was cast into a muddy gray dimness.

"We will use the electric lights for now," Mrs. Rosado said calmly. "Though we're almost certain to lose them. There are candles and flashlights on the big table in the arbor, everyone. And I think we should go ahead and light the torches, too."

At that moment the wind began. It sounded like the low moaning of a man in pain.

The great double doors flew open as if they had been struck by a giant's hand and crashed back against the walls. Esteban and John Wayne struggled to close them, and Esteban had to push against them with all his strength as John Wayne threw the great iron bolt.

Everyone went over to the long table in the arbor. Mrs. Rosado had set up a table next to it with coffee, hot tea, cold drinks, water, and light snacks and fruit. After helping themselves to the food, they all settled down comfortably at the big table. But no one spoke, and they all looked at Esteban and Mrs. Rosado expectantly.

"How is she?" Esteban asked her.

Mrs. Rosado, seated on one side of him, shrugged lightly and took a sip of hot coffee. "She woke up and was in much pain. So I gave her two of your pills, Don Serralles, and now she sleeps. She has a . . . mm—" she made a motion, clapping her palm to her eye—"what do you call it—black eye? Swollen, already turning blue. I think her nose is broken. And her head—" She grimaced. "I don't know. She hit hard. It might be . . . *la conmoción?*" She glanced at Esteban for confirmation.

"A concussion," he said quietly. "She really should be taken to the hospital, but—" He made an expressive gesture toward the outside.

"I should go back and sit with her," Mrs. Rosado sighed.

"No, she'll sleep soundly for a long time," Serralles said firmly. "We can do nothing more for her. We must check on her periodically, but for now you should be here with us."

Mrs. Rosado looked slightly ashamed, but relieved.

Outside, the continuous baritone of the wind changed to a higher, more pervasive bass note. Clattering sounded against the shutters. The rain had begun.

"I will tell you what Diego has told me," Esteban began with resignation. "Nuria introduced him to a man named Luis de Badajoz, who lives in Cartagena, Colombia. She had met him here last year when she was performing at the Wyndham in Old San Juan. He made Diego a business offer. Diego and Nuria were to store yachts here, in the cavern. For this Badajoz would pay them a good sum of money." Esteban frowned darkly and clenched his jaw with tightly controlled anger. "Diego said it sounded so simple, so easy."

"Found out there was a little more to it than that, huh?" John Wayne grunted. "First rule of business: If it sounds simple and easy and it's good pay—it ain't."

"No, it wasn't, of course," Esteban agreed dryly. "Because first Diego had to chart the reefs on that end of the island. Then he had to chauffeur the men—the pirates—back and forth through the channel. So he had to deal with them extensively, and they don't sound like a pleasant lot with whom to deal."

"They aren't," John Wayne growled. "Murderin' cutthroat pirates."

"Did I hear them?" Johnnie asked softly.

Esteban looked at her, his face filled with wrenching regret. "Yes, Johnnie, that's who you kept hearing. You see, Diego knew, of course, of the outside entrances that I had sealed up. One of them was a door in the passages between Ventura Tower and the keep. I never explored any of them; there were five, and I knew they all led down into caves in the cliffs. I just had them rocked up. Diego and Nuria had one of them broken down. There were four sizable rocks in the masonry, and they could remove them and slip through into the passage down to the sea. But they couldn't replace the rocks, you see, from the other side. So there was an airway through to the passages, and the sounds of the sea and voices carry clearly up through the passage and into Ventura Tower. That's how I found the tunnel, you know. I came to the tower to get you, and the noise of the wind and waves was loud throughout the tower. I went to find its source, and as I got closer I could even hear voices, though I could only catch a few words."

"I did, the first time," Johnnie told him. "I heard Diego's voice, and I thought I heard arguing."

"You probably did," Esteban sighed. "That was when they stole that yacht in Ponce. Diego had tried to tell them not to bring any yachts while you were here because he knew you'd be able to hear everything. But they came anyway."

A long silence fell in the room. No one—except Johnnie—could quite meet Esteban's gaze. She smiled at him, and his eyes softened.

He took a deep breath. "I must offer each of you my deepest apologies for my brother's wrongs. I am so terribly sorry, especially to you, John Wayne and Drue Ann, and to your children, for your terrible experience. I am so sorry, Johnnie, for your hardships. Don Serralles, I know you love Diego, and I know this has hurt you deeply, and you, too, Mrs. Rosado and Consuela and Rita. This has—" his voice broke slightly, becoming low and guttural—"shamed me and grieved me deeply. Please . . . forgive me, and I ask that you pray for Diego and for Nuria."

"I do not hold you responsible, Esteban," Johnnie said clearly and loudly. "And though I don't believe you have done anything wrong, if you had I would forgive you instantly. Diego I will pray for. Nuria"—she assumed a pained look—"I will have to pray about first."

Esteban looked slightly amused, while Drue Ann grinned engagingly. "Me too," she agreed loftily. "I can forgive Diego. How can a man that beautiful be virtuous? You know those gor-

geous ones are always up to something! But that Miss Torres—
now, I'm going to have to ask the Lord to forgive me first before
I can talk to Him nice about her!''

Muted laughter sounded around the table. John Wayne
drawled, ''Why, darlin', I think you're jealous of her!''

''That's right,'' Drue Ann countered shamelessly. ''She's
young, she's beautiful, she's graceful, and she hasn't had to go
through two face-lifts, three liposuctions, and a tummy tuck like
I have!''

''Mama!'' Angelina exclaimed, embarrassed as only teen-
agers can be.

''Never you mind,'' Drue Ann told her with mock sternness.
''You'll find out sooner or later.''

''She's not to be envied now, Drue Ann,'' Esteban ventured.
''She's had an . . . unhappy life. I'm not excusing her, because
she was one of the lucky ones who could have done better, had
a good life . . . but she's ruined it. She'll probably spend a long,
long time in prison.''

''I know,'' Drue Ann said, suddenly tender and soft. ''And
though I can't quite feel sorry for her yet, I will. And I do feel
sorry for you right now, Esteban. Please don't grieve over her
sins and your brother's. They made their own decisions. It's obvious to anyone with eyes and a heart that you're not like them
at all.''

''Shoot,'' John Wayne declared, bearlike, ''I hadda uncle
that died in Leavenworth. Stabbed an officer. He was executed.'' He shrugged. ''I liked him, even loved him, I guess.
Hurt me like a brandin' when he died. But I always knew I
wasn't like him, and that I couldn't have helped him or changed
him.''

''And you know about my nephew,'' Don Serralles said sor-
rowfully to Esteban, then turned to address everyone. ''He's in
prison in New York. He went to the mainland to work, and he
seemed like a good boy . . . but the fool got dead drunk one
night and went for a joyride. He . . . he hit a car with a woman
and her twelve-year-old son—it killed both of them.''

A sad silence fell on the group as they all looked inward at sorrows and regrets and doubts. The wind was rising, furious now, shaking the shutters as if demanding to be let in. The rain sounded like leather thongs whipping against the thin metal sheets.

"Well, I've got the worst criminal of all in my family," Johnnie finally said dryly as everyone began to come out of their reveries. "A lawyer."

John Wayne Cunningham grinned mischievously. "You poor li'l girl," he sympathized.

"Thank you, but nothing really helps," Johnnie said with a tragic air. "Anyway, I can get Diego a great lawyer, Esteban. My father. By the time Robert Landry James gets through, the jury will be apologizing to Diego for bothering him."

"Especially the women," Drue Ann offered helpfully, her blue eyes sparkling.

"Your father is R.L. James?" John Wayne exclaimed, his eyes lighting with sudden recognition. "Of Atlanta? The lawyer who—"

"Yes, the famous—or infamous—lawyer who got a verdict of 'Not Guilty on All Nine Thousand Charges' for Joseph Carranza," Johnnie said derisively. She turned to Esteban and continued in a tone of careless irony, but her expression showed her pain. "They called Carranza *El Garrote*—supposedly because he had a stranglehold on the cocaine traffic coming into the southern United States from Central America. At least I think that's why they called him that—I really didn't want to know. Two key witnesses against him completely disappeared. Just"—Johnnie snapped her fingers angrily—"disappeared. They still haven't found them. And my father was chief counsel for the defense, and he is a very precise and studious man. He found hundreds of obscure technicalities that ruled out much of the physical evidence. So El Garrote is a free man."

"But . . . but I thought your father was an accountant with Andrews, Smith & Wesley," Esteban said in bewilderment. "Didn't you tell me that, Don Serralles?"

"Yes, I did, and it's true," Serralles said with a grandly dismissive gesture. "I didn't know Diego was a murderin' cutthroat pirate, or I would have given you the good news that Johnnie's father is also a smack criminal lawyer."

"Thank you so much," Esteban told him dryly.

"And it's 'crack' criminal lawyer, Don Serralles. He is an excellent accountant and a prestigious lawyer," Johnnie went on recklessly, determined to tell the whole story to Esteban. "He was a meek and mild and quiet little head of the legal department for ten years. Then he sort of . . . changed, around when he reached fifty. He divorced my mother, opened a subsidiary criminal law practice, and started taking on these high-profile criminal cases. With El Garrote, he just blossomed," Johnnie said sarcastically. "I'm on my second stepmother now. She's two years younger than me."

"Than I," Esteban gravely corrected her, his expression amused but also filled with sympathy.

"No, she's six years younger than you," Johnnie retorted, her color high. "And by the way, my mother drinks. A lot."

"Mmm. Is that all?" Esteban asked.

"Yes. Isn't that enough?"

He reached over to take her hand. "It seems that we all have sorrows and grief in our lives, doesn't it? But I have come to know one thing, being here with all of you. . . ."

"What's that?" John Wayne asked curiously.

Esteban smiled with warmth and gratitude. " 'There is a friend,' " he quoted, " 'that sticketh closer than a brother.' "

The gusts of wind were violent now, and the electricity faltered, then died. They began to hear thuds here and there, and once, a loud crash against the shutters startled everyone. But the shutters held, even though the storm was likely tearing shrubs and small trees up and flinging them through the air. Though they were in the midst of violent tumult, it seemed remote and distant, because all of them felt as if they were in an undefeatable fortress. Which, in a manner of speaking, they were. They were surrounded by walls ten feet thick that had withstood centuries of nature's wrath, and trusting in God. Together they talked and laughed and ate and drank.

The noises rose to their wildest rage, the winds screamed first on one side of the house, then on the other. The scraping and crashing of debris sounded as though the storm were clawing at the walls.

Then, as if a giant cleaver had descended from the sky and cut off all sound, the wind stopped and the rain was stanched. Calm came so suddenly that everyone was visibly startled.

But the air was heavier than ever and there was a choked feeling to it, making it hard to breathe.

"It's the eye," Esteban said quietly, his voice sounding sharp and harsh in the deafening silence.

They waited for the wind.

It took twenty minutes for Damien's eye to pass over the small island. To Johnnie it seemed both like forever and only moments.

The first half of the hurricane had come from the east; now from the west the whips and lashes of air resumed, and the deluge of rain began as suddenly as it had stopped.

About an hour later, when it seemed as if the earth and sky must be exhausted, the wind gave a long, shuddering groan and abruptly ceased. The rain continued to fall, but it sounded listless and lifeless against the metal screens.

Johnnie was sitting on the floor playing with Rebel when she looked up, then scrambled to her feet. Diego stood in the dining room, his hair disheveled, his face pale, his eyes dull.

"She's gone," he said in a choked voice. "Nuria's gone!"

Armed in bright gloves,
I stood at dirty dishes.
My son was at toys in our kitchen's corner.
Over the dryer my wife and his mother
Told of the bulldog's taunting
the Weimaraner.

—From *Haunting the Winerunner*
by John Wink

Twenty-four

*T*he night came, eerily soundless.

The electricity stayed off, and the phones were dead. Everyone was exhausted as they returned to their rooms to sleep.

With the morning, the sky, cloudless and innocent blue, gleamed brighter than Johnnie had ever seen it. It was as if the storm had polished it to the jeweled intensity of a precious aquamarine stone.

Early in the morning she stood in the kitchen, washing up some odd dishes that she and the Cunninghams had used for breakfast. No one else had come into the dining room at such an early hour, so Johnnie and Drue Ann had managed to scrape together something for the four of them—Angelina was still asleep—to eat. Afterward, John Wayne and Drue Ann had decided to find Esteban to see what they could do to help. Taíno Castle was untouched, and the horses and Ferdinand and Isabella and the puppies were fine. But the gardens were a depressing wreck. Johnnie had offered to watch Rebel while she cleaned up the kitchen.

He sat on a high stool at a cooking island in the center of the kitchen, completely absorbed in playing with his "men." Since Rebel didn't have a single toy with him, and none could be found on the island, Esteban had given him pieces from his chess set, made of finely carved ivory over a hundred years old. Drue Ann had been doubtful of giving such valuable things to a five-year-old, but Esteban had insisted. Rebel did play roughly with them, but he hadn't chipped one piece, and he counted them each time he got them out to make sure he hadn't lost any. And he hadn't.

Standing at the sink, Johnnie looked over her shoulder at him, amused. He had lined up several of the chess pieces in a straight line, and they seemed to be the spectators. Six other pieces appeared to be performing a play with profuse and descriptive sound effects. Johnnie idly wondered how all little boys learned to make the same clever explosion and fighting sounds.

Esteban came in, looking deathly tired and depressed. "We went to Ponce at first light," he told Johnnie without preamble, sinking onto another high stool by Rebel. "Diego turned himself in. Since all of Puerto Rico is a disaster, Lieutenant Leone was kind enough to release Diego to my custody for now, and they're going to come out to pick him up, probably tomorrow. The Coast Guard is out looking for Nuria. But—I don't know—it would be a miracle if she made it through."

"Could she . . . handle the *Angelina*?" Johnnie asked hesitantly, looking down at Rebel. None of them knew exactly how much of the frightful drama of yesterday Rebel had understood. He seemed to be suffering no ill effects from the horrible scene down in the cavern, but he had been unnaturally quiet during the storm. He'd insisted on staying either in his mother's or "My-Johnnie's" lap, but he hadn't reverted to sucking his thumb. Today he seemed to be untroubled and energetic.

Esteban frowned. "Diego says she's a good pilot. I didn't think she knew the bow of a boat from the stern—but then again I didn't know her very well, did I?"

"Murderin' cutthroat pirates!" Rebel snarled. The white knight seemed to be engaged in a fight to the death with two black pawns.

Esteban smiled, watching him, and went on, "She wasn't a navigator, though. The best she could have hoped for was to wait out the hurricane just out from the coast, and then head straight south. She would eventually hit Venezuela. But . . . it doesn't look good, Johnnie. We found the *Angelina*'s other life-boat in the cavern, cut to shreds."

"She went out in that storm without even a lifeboat?" John-nie gasped.

"I know," he said quietly. "We can do nothing but pray."

Rebel growled, "You can't have him!" Evidently the two black pawns were trying to capture the white king, but the white knight was fighting them valiantly. Esteban sat up straighter and watched Rebel's play more closely.

"I can pray for her now," Johnnie said firmly, half to herself. "I will pray for her." Stripping off her sticky yellow rubber gloves, she poured herself and Esteban a cup of café con leche. "How's Diego?"

"Sick at heart over Nuria, and he seems truly repentant. He said he's going to testify against Badajoz."

"He has to," Johnnie sighed. "And I think that's a good sign. It seems to me, Esteban, that he never had 'malice afore-thought.' He was just weak, because it's obvious he's so in love with Nuria. And he was jealous of you, wasn't he?"

"He was, and that makes this all the more painful," Esteban said in a low voice. "I loved him so much . . . I still do." He slid his arm around Johnnie's waist, and she moved closer to him.

"Of course you do," she murmured, "and you always will. We . . . we'll do anything we can to help him, always."

He looked up at her, his eyes heavy lidded, his expression intent. "I pray you mean that."

"I . . . I do."

"I hope to hear you say that soon, in a different context," Esteban said, lifting one eyebrow.

"Oh, Esteban," Johnnie stammered, blushing. "I . . . I—"

"Johnnie," he said gently, taking both of her hands in his, "I . . . need to explain to you why I was so cold after the night in the tower. When I was younger, I"—his face wrinkled into a rueful smile—"fell in love all the time. With many women. Do you understand what I'm saying?"

"Yes, of course, Esteban. I haven't been an angel, either."

"No? I thought you were," he said, his dark eyes sparkling. "Anyway, after I became a Christian, that all stopped. It was hard, but I've been . . . alone now for eight years. And then you came—"

"And the first word I said to you was 'No!'" Johnnie murmured regretfully. "But, Esteban, it's because I . . . I was so attracted to you from the first minute I saw you . . . and I was . . . I was afraid."

"Funny you should say that. I told you once that I didn't fear anything but my God. So it does seem that I was a liar after all, because I was afraid of something else. I was afraid of falling in love with you," Esteban said bluntly. "I'm sorry if I hurt you. I just . . . have been alone so long, I thought—" He frowned, then muttered, "I don't know what I thought. But I know what I think now." He raised Johnnie's hand to his lips and brushed a quick kiss against her palm.

"Take that, you murderin' cutthroat pirate!" Rebel roared. One of the black pawns lay fallen, and the white knight stood over it. "My Johnnie bashed your brains in!"

"Oh, Rebel! For goodness' sake, I didn't—"

But Rebel was deeply engrossed in his high drama. "Confound it, you!" The black knight came galloping in and yelled to the other black pawn, "C'mere, you big dogs!" Two white rooks bopped over at the black knight's command. "*Vigilar* for treasure!" the black knight yelled lustily. "*Vigilar* for treasure! *Vigilar* for treasure!"

Esteban roared with laughter. It took Johnnie a few moments, but then she recalled Esteban's "guard" command to Ferdinand and Isabella: *"¡Vigilar por trabajo!"*

Giggling, she said, "It appears we'd better watch out for treasure, Esteban!"

Still chuckling, he declared, "Sounds like imminent treasure!"

"Flying!" Rebel announced, and Johnnie and Esteban assumed that the watched-for treasure was airborne, for Rebel took the black knight and the white knight and held them high above his head, then made two circles of the cooking island, with appropriate loud propeller sounds. Then he headed out into the dining room, where they could clearly hear the flying treasure buzzing around.

Esteban turned around on the stool and pulled Johnnie close to him. He kissed her slowly and gently, which made her feel weak, then pulled back and made a pedantic pronouncement. "Life," he said grandly, "is a circle."

"That's . . . nonsense," Johnnie breathed rather unevenly. She was tracing the strong line of his jaw to his chin with one fingertip.

"No," he ordered, "just think." Grinning, he quoted, " 'Armed in bright gloves, I stood at dirty dishes—' "

" 'My son was at toys in our kitchen's corner.' " Johnnie's tawny brown eyes searched his face, a smile tugging at the corners of her mouth.

" 'Over the dryer my wife and his mother—' " Esteban reached up to smooth her hair ever so gently.

" 'Told of the bulldog's taunting the Weimaraner. . . .' " Johnnie finished in wonder. " 'Taunting the Weimaraner!' 'Haunting the Winerunner!' I finally see! The whole thing was a misunderstanding!"

"Just as we were," Esteban murmured, then rose to his feet and crushed her to him, murmuring against her hair and then her lips, " 'Poetry has always started here . . .' "

The rest was left unsaid.

BOOKS BY LYNN MORRIS

The Balcony

CHENEY DUVALL, M.D.*

1. *The Stars for a Light*
2. *Shadow of the Mountains*
3. *A City Not Forsaken*
4. *Toward the Sunrising*
5. *Secret Place of Thunder*
6. *In the Twilight, in the Evening*

*with Gilbert Morris